ALSO BY MIA COUTO

THE
SWORD
AND THE
SPEAR

THE SWORD AND THE SPEAR

SANDS OF THE EMPEROR: A MOZAMBICAN TRILOGY

Book Two

MIA COUTO

*Translated from
the Portuguese by David Brookshaw*

Farrar, Straus and Giroux   New York

Farrar, Straus and Giroux
120 Broadway, New York 10271

Library of Congress Cataloging-in-Publication Data
Names: Couto, Mia, 1955– author. | Brookshaw, David, translator.
Title: The sword and the spear / Mia Couto ; translated from the Portuguese by David
  Brookshaw.
Other titles: Espada e azagaia. English
Description: First edition. | New York : Farrar, Straus and Giroux, 2020. | Series:
  Sands of the emperor : a Mozambican trilogy ; book 2 | "Originally published
  in Portuguese in 2016 by Editorial Caminho, Portugal, as A espada e
  azagaia"—Title page verso.
Identifiers: LCCN 2020012323 | ISBN 9780374256890 (hardcover)
Subjects: LCSH: Mozambique—Fiction.
Classification: LCC PQ9939.C68 E8713 2020 | DDC 869.3/42—dc23
LC record available at https://lccn.loc.gov/2020012323

Designed by Abby Kagan

Our books may be purchased in bulk for promotional, educational, or business use.
Please contact your local bookseller or the Macmillan Corporate and
Premium Sales Department at 1-800-221-7945, extension 5442, or by e-mail at
MacmillanSpecialMarkets@macmillan.com.

www.fsgbooks.com
www.twitter.com/fsgbooks • www.facebook.com/fsgbooks

1 3 5 7 9 10 8 6 4 2

I shall not say
Silence stifles and muzzles me apace

Silent I am, silent I shall remain
For the language I speak is of another race

—JOSÉ SARAMAGO, "POEM WITH MOUTH SHUT"

CONTENTS

CONTENTS

INTRODUCTORY NOTE

Summary of the First Volume, *Woman of the Ashes*

Most of the southern part of the Portuguese colony of Mozambique was, at the end of the nineteenth century, occupied by the State of Gaza. In 1895, the Portuguese colonial government embarked on a military offensive in order to affirm its absolute dominion over the colony, which, at the time, was disputed by other European nations. The king of the State of Gaza at the time was Ngungunyane (whom the Portuguese knew as Gungunhane).

In this context of war, the young Portuguese sergeant Germano de Melo is sent to occupy a military post in a village called Nkokolani, located in the territory of the VaChopi ethnic group (known to the Portuguese as Chope). The VaChopi are a people who have been occupied and massacred by the powerful VaNguni, and for this reason have established a military alliance with the Portuguese authorities.

At Nkokolani, Germano falls in love with Imani, a VaChopi girl educated by the Portuguese at a Catholic mission run by Rudolfo Fernandes, a priest originally from Goa.

The war brings about a series of dramatic events in the life of Imani's family—within a few months, her brother Dubula is killed, and her mother hangs herself from a sacred tree in the back garden. Her father, Katini Nsambe, who is a musician, survives, along with her younger brother, Mwanatu, a mentally handicapped boy, to whom Germano, out of pity, gives a job as a guard at the military post.

To alleviate his loneliness, Sergeant Germano de Melo writes a sequence of letters to the counselor José d'Almeida and to Lieutenant Ayres de Ornelas. A friend of the sergeant's, an Italian woman called Bianca Vanzini Marini, comes to visit Nkokolani. Some days afterward, Germano is shot in the hands while defending himself from a crowd marching on the military post, at the head of which is Mwanatu, Imani's helpless brother. In an act of desperation, Imani uses a gun to defend her brother. She, along with her father, Katini, and Bianca and Mwanatu, urgently transport the injured sergeant up the River Inharrime in the direction of the only hospital in the region, where his life may be saved.

THE SWORD AND THE SPEAR

THE EMPEROR

They took him away beyond the sea
There where bodies are the same as coral
And so the burden of his bones
Was forgotten.

He did not tread on the beach
When he left.

A wave would return him, they said
Some trembled, abandoned.
Others sighed, relieved.

They cast salt on his name
So that we should spit on his memory.

But our spittle
Was stuck in our throats.

Through his exile
We distanced ourselves
From who we were.

That dead man
Was us.

And without him
We would be born
Less alone.

1

MURKY WATERS

Everything always begins with a farewell. This story begins with an ending: the end of my adolescence. At the age of fifteen, traveling in a little boat, I left my village and my past behind. However, something told me that farther ahead I would reencounter the rancors of old. The dugout was taking me away from Nkokolani but bringing my dead nearer to me.

We had been heading upstream from Nkokolani for two days in the direction of Mandhlakazi, the place the Portuguese call Manjacaze. We were traveling with my brother Mwanatu in the bow, and my old father at the stern. Along with us were Sergeant Germano de Melo and his Italian friend Bianca Vanzini.

Our oars struck the water without respite. And they did so because of an urgent need: We were taking Germano de Melo to the only hospital in the whole of Gaza. The sergeant had seen his hands smashed to pieces in an accident for which I was responsible. I had fired at him to save Mwanatu, who was at the head of a mob preparing to attack the military outpost defended by the solitary Germano.

It was vital that we should reach Mandhlakazi, where there was the only doctor working in our whole nation, the missionary Georges Liengme. The Swiss Protestants had been careful in their choice of location for a hospital: next to the emperor Ngungunyane's court and far from the Portuguese authorities.

Remorse weighed heavily upon me for the entire journey. The shot had smashed the Portuguese man's hands and rendered them largely useless, the same hands that I had helped resuscitate so many times from the fits of delirium that had beset him. Those masculine fingers that I had dreamt of so often had all but disappeared.

For the whole journey, I sat with my feet submerged in the bloodstained water of the dugout's bilge. It is said we can die from loss of blood. It is the opposite. We die by drowning in it.

Our craft advanced slowly and silently, sluggish as a crocodile. The waters of the Inharrime were so still that for a moment it seemed as if the river itself were floating, rather than the boat. The silvery wake our progress left behind meandered like a ribbon of water amid the lands of the VaChopi. I leaned over to glimpse the restless reflections above the sandy riverbed, tireless butterflies of light.

They are the water's shadows, my father commented, resting the oar on his shoulders.

He rested his arms on this improvised beam. My brother Mwanatu plunged his hands into the water and, rolling his tongue around, he produced an odd mixture of sounds that I translated as follows:

My brother says this river is called the Nyadhimi. It was the Portuguese who changed its name.

My father, Katini Nsambe, smiled condescendingly. He had a different explanation. The Portuguese were, according to him, civilizing our language. And apart from this, one could not expect purity from those who baptized the waters with a name. For even we, the VaChopi, change our names during the course of our lives. It had happened with me when I changed from Layeluane to Imani. Not to

4

mention my brother Mwanatu, over whom the sacred waters had been poured in order to cleanse him of his three previous names. He had been baptized three times: at birth, with his "bone name" linking him to his ancestors; with his "circumcision name," when he had been subjected to the rites of initiation; and with his "white name," conferred upon him when he went to school.

Then my father returned to the matter in hand: When it came to a stretch of flowing water, why did we find it so hard to accept the will of the Portuguese? As far as the River Inharrime was concerned, they had invented two names for it because two currents flowed together in one riverbed. They relieve each other in turn, depending on the light: It is one river during daytime and another at night. And they never flow together.

That's how it has always been, each one in turn. Only now, because of the war, have the waters mingled.

At the spot where the Inharrime and Nhamuende meet, there is a small island covered with trees and rocks. We paused here. My father ordered us to get out of the boat. I didn't wait for the dugout to reach the shore. I plunged into the tepid waters and let the river embrace me, its current carrying me forward. The words of my late mother, Chikazi Makwakwa, came back to me:

When I'm in the water, I'm a bird.

That is what they say of the dead when they are buried. But no one ever buries their voice. My mother's words remained alive, even though, but a few months before, she had cast herself from a tree, using only her weight to kill herself. She hung swaying from a rope like some persistent nocturnal heart.

The island where we stopped was not only a resting place but also a refuge. All around us, the war was setting the world alight.

Leaning on Bianca, his Italian friend, the Portuguese asked to be put in the shade. He was gently told that the sun had long set. He took a few steps forward and fell to his knees.

She's the one who killed me, he screamed, pointing at me. *It was her, that bitch.*

He was advised to save his strength. The Italian woman gave him something to drink, and, cupping her hand with water, she cooled his face. To my surprise, Bianca came to my defense. She was adamant in her argument: the ill-fated bullet had not been fired by me, but by the blacks who attacked the garrison. The Portuguese remained unshaken in his accusation: I was the author of the crime, he was right in front of me. But Bianca answered unequivocally: It was true that I had fired the shot, but he was not the intended target. And she added: If it hadn't been for that shot, the sergeant would no longer be in the land of the living, for he would have been brutally killed by the furious mob.

Imani saved you. You should thank her.

It would have been better if she had fired a second shot and hit the target properly.

At that point, his speech became muddled as the fever gripped his soul. Bianca helped him to lie down. She then signaled to me to take her place. I hesitated. I heard Germano's almost lifeless plea:

Come here, Imani. Come here.

I complied, apprehensive, while Bianca moved away. The Portuguese man's hoarse breathing silenced the noise of the river. From my bag I took out an old notebook, which I placed on the ground by way of a cushion. It had been a long time since the sergeant last used a proper pillow. It might have been his tatty old Bible, or sheets of paper torn from the notebook he used for writing. The truth was that he could only get to sleep with his head resting on paper.

On this occasion, however, he rejected the improvised cushion.

He looked at me strangely, complaining that he did not want me near him. When I made to move away, he thumped his feet violently, as children do when they cannot get their way. *Stay with me*, he pleaded. Once again, I obeyed. And the man rested his head on my legs.

Motionless, almost without breathing, I let him contemplate me. I could sense his feverish eyes surveying my breasts, my neck, my lips. Until he stammered some words that were barely intelligible:

Kiss me, Imani. Kiss me, for I want to die. To die inside your mouth.

For years, it had been like that: At the height of the drought, my grandfather planted seeds, three at a time, in the parched, lifeless soil. Grandmother would try to make him see reason, as if reason had any place in an existence that was more arid than the desert. And her husband would reply:

It's the rain I'm sowing.

As a skilled marimba player, my father never took to agricultural work. Now, on that tiny island where we were resting, his fingers did what they had always done: They tinkled the sand as if he saw a tuneful keyboard in everything. But it was a music that consisted solely of silence, some desperate message for anyone on the riverbank who might know how to listen to the ground.

But no one was listening to the earth anymore: Throughout the area, Portuguese soldiers and Ngungunyane's troops were getting ready for the final confrontation. It was not the victory itself that motivated them, but what would follow. The magical disappearance of those who had once been enemies, and the righting of an error in the divine plan. My grandfather planted futile seeds. And with his fingers, my father lulled the slumber of those sleeping in the earth.

This was the sad irony of our time: While we desperately sought to save a white soldier, a slaughterhouse for thousands of human beings had been established only a few kilometers away. Caught in the middle of such senseless, bitter exchanges, we VaChopi were at our most vulnerable. Ngungunyane had vowed to exterminate our race as if we were animals that God regretted creating. We depended on the protection of the Portuguese, but their support was subject to temporary agreements drawn up between Portugal and the VaNguni.

Sergeant Germano de Melo was one of those creatures who had come from the other side of the world to protect me. As a little girl, I believed that the angels were white and blue-eyed. Their watery complexion was a sign that they were blind. As a recent arrival in Africa, Father Rudolfo was circumspect when answering my questions about heavenly creatures.

I'm not familiar with the angels around here. People assure me they have wings, but only those who have never seen them say that sort of thing . . .

Of one thing I was sure: My angel would be white and have blue eyes. Like this sergeant who, years later, would be propped on my lap. The cloth bandages around his arms were his torn wings. This was a messenger of the night. Only in the dark did he remember the message he was bearing. This divine missive now slept between his lips. I accepted his entreaty, and leaned over his mouth.

Now more awake and less peevish, Germano emerged from his drowsiness in order to whisper in my ear:

Tear out the pages of the notebook and scatter them around us. Let's make a bed.

I slowly detached a few pages, and as I was preparing to scatter them on the ground, I hesitated and paused in what I was doing:

But where are you going to write your letters to your superiors?

I have no superiors. I'm the last soldier in an army that never existed.

It was all an invention, starting with the garrison at Nkokolani. Even my brother Mwanatu, with his fake uniform and dummy rifle, was a more genuine soldier than he.

I think they forgot about you, I suggested tentatively in order to comfort him.

I received orders to return to Lourenço Marques a long time ago.

So why didn't you go?

I'm not in Africa because they forgot about me, Germano said. *I'm here because I forgot about them.*

I don't understand.

I'm here because of you.

I was aware of footsteps in the grass. They were looking for me. Then I heard my father dispersing the others:

Imani is taking care of the Portuguese. Let's leave them alone.

Their voices and laughter drew farther away, fading into the darkness.

Eventually we returned to the boat, where they were waiting for us. Bianca's long noisy sigh was my reprimand. And we set off in the direction of Sana Benene. Situated on the banks of the Inharrime, this was not exactly a village. With the advent of war, dozens of refugees had set up camp around the church built by the Portuguese there a long time before.

As we reached the first bend in the river, we got a huge fright that almost wrecked our journey. Coming in the opposite direction, gliding along with the current, loomed a vast, shining monster. This colossal creature cut through the waters, silent and glowing like a chunk of the sun. It gradually drew closer like some metal crocodile, invading first our eyes and then our souls.

It's the nwamulambu*!* our father whispered, terrified. *Don't say a word, don't look straight at it.*

This mythical creature of the waters could not be confronted without running the risk of our eyes running dry and our brains shriveling. My brother crossed himself, my father rowed with the utmost caution, as silently as possible. This god of the rivers who summoned earth tremors and brought rain could not be disturbed. And I thought: The rivers were once our brothers, spinning a liquid web to protect us. Now they are allied to our enemies. They have become water serpents, tortuous thoroughfares down which traveled angels and demons.

That terrifying encounter was brief. But it left me with a deadly, lingering premonition. Fortunately, no one noticed our presence: Our dugout passed by unseen. The sergeant was lying in the bottom of the boat, and the white woman, Bianca, was sleeping under a *capulana*. Only we three blacks were visible. I calmed down: For all intents and purposes we were local fishermen in a dugout. Nothing about us could arouse suspicion, nothing could trouble the spirits of the river.

When I opened my eyes again, the *nwamulambu* had disappeared in the mist and we could breathe again. Bianca awoke still in time to catch a glimpse of it in the distance. She took a good hard look at it to see if she could catch sight of the charismatic Mouzinho de Albuquerque standing at the strange river creature's rail. But the craft was drifting around the bend in the river and the Italian woman burst out laughing:

A monster? That thing? That's a blockhouse.

Bianca explained that what had given us such a fright was nothing more than one of those fortified rafts used by the Portuguese to navigate the rivers in the south. The superstructure emitted such a glow because it was made of zinc panels fixed to a wooden frame. The white soldiers sought protection inside it, thus avoiding surprise forays by black rebels. Hidden in the vegetation along the river-banks, African warriors would target launches. The thick forest was impenetrable territory for the Portuguese. Only local folk were familiar with the paths through the mud and the huge roots emerging from the trunks of trees like edifices turned on their heads. These tracks opened out at the will of the gods and closed again after every ambush.

More than cutting through the surface of the water, our boat was cleaving a dense silence. All that could be heard around the sergeant were the flies, whining like banshees.

Suddenly, we caught sight of a man waving at us from the bank. Father was wary about stopping. It might be a trap; given the times, no one could be trusted. The intruder continued, waving an envelope at us while calling out the sergeant's name. As we approached him, he identified himself: He was a messenger from the military post at Chicomo. He had a letter to deliver to Germano de Melo.

2

FIRST LETTER FROM LIEUTENANT AYRES DE ORNELAS

Standing with a triggerless weapon over one's shoulder on the walls of a ruined fortress, with a customs house and a palace where slothful, poorly paid employees, arms folded, watch the trade being done by strangers that we ourselves cannot do; waiting every day for blacks to attack, and at every hour having to listen to the scorn and disdain with which those traveling in Africa speak of us, none of this, in all honesty, is worth it.

—OLIVEIRA MARTINS, "BRAZIL AND THE PORTUGUESE COLONIES," 1880

Chicomo Garrison, July 9, 1895

Dear Sergeant Germano de Melo,

Do not be surprised, my dear sergeant: This letter is being penned by Lieutenant Ayres de Ornelas, thus fulfilling the duty, albeit without the same diligence, of replying to your frequent missives. I was told you had been gravely injured during an attack on the military post at Nkokolani. I have also been informed of your evacuation to the church at Sana Benene, from where I assume you will be transferred to the hospital run by the Swiss doctor Georges Liengme. You should be aware that this man Liengme, who is more of a doctor than a missionary, is someone we view with the utmost antipathy. This doctor, who will supposedly treat your wounds, has incited the natives to revolt and should have been expelled from Portuguese Africa long ago.

Do not forget, Sergeant: At Sana Benene you are in the hands of kaffirs who appear to be our friends. But you are a Portuguese soldier. You should have been evacuated to the garrison at Chicomo, where we have a doctor and an infirmary. Any other superior would have had you punished. I shall close my eyes, but only for the time being. You, Sergeant, will doubtless know which course of action you need to take once you are in possession of all your faculties. I have instructed the bearer of this letter to take the opposite route to the one you are following, that is, that he should travel downstream towards the mouth of the Inharrime. In this way, I am sure the message will be delivered to you in person and without delay.

More than anything, I wish to make you a promise in these brief lines: I am going to arrange for you, dear sergeant, to return to the fatherland with all possible haste! You deserve this favor—just as I deserve to achieve the highest ranks in the military hierarchy. I am destined for such positions and I have only been barred from my vocation for leadership by an unfortunate conspiracy. Others, such as Paiva Couceiro and Freire de Andrade, have been promoted on the pretext that they are veterans of Africa. As far as António Enes is concerned, I have no experience in waging this war. Portugal is suffering the humiliating effects of the Ultimatum, our government is in the midst of an ocean of political and financial scandals, and our people are crushed by the oppression of everyday existence. What does all this mean? It means that Portugal needs heroes. I cannot understand why someone who has demonstrated such talent in his short but intense military career is not being given such a chance.

As I told you, as soon as I am promoted, I shall make sure you are transferred to Portugal. However, I must give you the following warning: You will have to travel alone. That black woman whom you praise so much in your letters will have to stay in Mozambique. I have asked myself countless times what attributes you see in this kaffir woman, Sergeant. But that is beside the point, an outburst of no consequence. You can rest assured that we shall not abandon the woman: With the knowledge she has of our language, she may prove very useful to us. Once the campaigns of pacification are over, we shall give her shelter in our military post at Nkokolani. The girl will no doubt pine less for you there. For the building— half shop and half garrison—bears some resemblance to what we all are: hybrids, somewhere between ducks and peacocks. But the structure is also like those stone pillars that the navigators of old erected wherever they stepped ashore along the African coast: a proof of civilization on a continent where darkness ruled.

Finally, I wish to state how happy I am to exchange correspondence with you, my dear sergeant. This propitious encounter is the result of an irony of fate: Your letters were initially addressed to Counselor José d'Almeida. Now, our counselor friend has an intense dislike of letters and telegrams. From his full height of two meters, Almeida shrugs his shoulders, narrows his clear eyes, which contrast with his black beard, and proclaims: *I won't read a word!* He justifies this attitude as follows: *I am surprised by no one. From Lourenço Marques, all I get are reprimands; from the interior, all I get is botheration.*

This was why I was charged with the responsibility of replying to letters addressed to him, including all correspondence with the Royal Commissioner, who, even now, believes it is Counselor Almeida who is replying to his solicitations. And this was how, quite by chance, I came into contact with your letters, so full of sensitive thoughts and observations that, forgive the bluntness of my comments, one could hardly credit that they had been written by a sergeant from the provinces. Little by little, I began to discern in you someone with whom I could share my unease at being so far from home and from my dear mother. Our correspondence is not a product of deceit. It is a predestined meeting of twin souls. And it was also how I became acquainted with the companions you encountered on your journey: your beloved Imani, whose soul is so Portuguese; the girl's father, Katini

Nsambe, a musician who is so loyal to our flag; Imani's brother, so handicapped by nature but nevertheless devoted to the Portuguese presence; and finally, that strange Italian woman, Bianca Vanzini, so removed from Catholic moral values and customs, but who has provided our soldiers with such delectable services. All these people are now my companions in these arid African backlands.

It is true that profound differences separate us. I am twenty-nine and a convinced monarchist. You are some six years younger and were deported to Mozambique because of your republican beliefs. A curious divergence of opinion: In Africa, we occupy the same trench; in Portugal, we are behind opposing barricades. I confess, my dear sergeant: If the Republic triumphs, I shall resign from the army and leave Portugal. You were exiled by the monarchy. I shall be the monarchy in exile.

I have, however, learned that politics cannot be the instrument for building and destroying friendships. In my party's ranks, there are people of whom I am deeply ashamed. And among my adversaries, there are folk who have enabled me to grow. The barriers between human beings are of another order. The truth is that we two, at the cost of great misunderstandings and petty untruths, have broken through these barriers. Our correspondence is a celebration of how these differences can be overcome. In a land crossed by great rivers, each letter is a dugout crossing distances. If I were a poet, I would put it like this: A word crosses a margin and becomes a mirage. Sadly, all these little reflections have a ring of pretentiousness about them and make me appear ridiculous.

P.S. I await you here at Chicomo as soon as possible. Do not waste any opportunity that may present itself to return to your natural path, your destiny. I sense it in the air that something conclusive is going to happen soon, and it would be good to have you here with me. You will certainly be in better company than with that perfidious Swiss.

3

ONE CHURCH UNDER ANOTHER CHURCH

Do not travel: for you will never return. Only those who were once happy return.
—A PROVERB FROM SANA BENENE

Rivers do not just traverse lands and soil. This river up which we were traveling crossed territories of fire, riven by hunger and blood. But our dugout managed to put a distance between us and all that: As we navigated through dense forests, the war seemed far-off and remote.

Eventually, we reached a backwater where the current was less strong. We had arrived at Sana Benene. Next to the shore there was an old church, the walls of which looked as if they were made of water in the noon light. Wading heavily through the water, Mwa-natu pushed the craft toward a little wooden landing stage.

Along the riverbank there were rows of stakes, from the tops of which hung fishing nets. The boat finally came to a stop, its hull creaking as it rubbed against the rotting planks of the landing stage. My father grinned: It wasn't a noise, but the start of a tune. He ca-ressed one of the planks where we moored, in that dreamy way he used to stroke the keys of his marimba.

Can you hear the boards groaning, Imani? It's the tree calling for its offspring.

Leaning on his Italian friend, Sergeant Germano de Melo hurried to get out of the boat. He staggered about on dry land in a daze: The river had invaded his eyes. He gazed dispiritedly at the path leading to the cluster of dwellings. In the embrace of roots and trunks, the church seemed to have been born before the river itself.

Is the hospital here? the Portuguese asked in a faint voice.

We were still a long way from Georges Liengme's hospital at Mandhlakazi. We would spend the night on church premises before setting off for our final destination at first light.

The weakened sergeant staggered up the footpath with Mwanatu supporting him from behind. Halfway up the slope lay the scattered remains of the church steps. Rain and time had dislodged the steps leading to the building. The slabs of paving seemed to be returning to the ground from which they had been torn.

At the entrance to the church, we clapped our hands to show our respect. We do not knock on doors as the whites do. The door is inside the home, the house begins when you cross the threshold of the front yard.

Father Rudolfo Fernandes soon emerged from the shadow. It was years since I had last seen him. I spent my entire childhood with him at the church in Makomani. It was with the priest that I learned to speak and write the language of the Portuguese. Let us say that it was through him that I learned to stop being a young black girl of the VaChopi people. Rudolfo Fernandes had aged; his beard was white and his hair long, disheveled and graying. He came over wiping his hands on his dirty, frayed cassock. When he realized who I was, he raised his eyes to the heavens and gave me a heartfelt embrace:

God be praised, Imani, my little Imani! Just look at you! What a beautiful woman you've turned into!

After we had entered the church, I introduced my traveling companions. The priest shook each one warmly by the hand, except for my brother Mwanatu, to whom he gave a welcoming hug. The sergeant was the last person to be greeted. Germano de Melo was a white man and a soldier. He was worthy of special treatment. Rudolfo stretched out his hand decisively, and only then noticed that his gesture could not be reciprocated. Germano waved his stumps clumsily and muttered:

I lost them, my hands I mean.

Outside, in the open air, his words would have been inaudible. But within the four walls of the church, the sergeant's feeble voice gained the resonance of an echo: *I lost them, my hands I mean.* The priest contrived some brief consoling words:

Injured whites and blacks come here. This looks like a house of worship. But it's a hospital.

The church smelled musty, its walls damp and sticky.

In the last flood, the water came up to there, the priest said, pointing to a mildew stain on a wooden beam. And he chuckled, as if detecting some disapproval in our silence:

I like it as it is, a church washed by the river.

The altar displayed religious figures, carved from aged wood. Crushing the flakes of paint shed by these statues in his fingers, the priest declared:

It never dies, wood is always alive.

And my father was in complete agreement. Mwanatu got all muddled when he crossed himself, his entangled fingers and hands all over his body. And he hailed God, addressing him as "Your Excellency." Doves fluttered among the joists in the ceiling, their agile wings lashing the air like whips, when Rudolfo called in the direction of the side door:

Bibliana, come and see! Come and see who is here!

We heard heavy, plodding footsteps in the atrium: Whoever was coming wasn't barefoot. Suddenly, the priest opened the doors and proclaimed enthusiastically:

This is my Bibliana! Come here, girl.

A tall, thin black woman appeared in silhouette against the light, wearing a red silk dress. A pair of military boots gave the figure an even more imposing air.

Bibliana works miracles, she's the best healer there is. There isn't an ailment she can't treat.

The woman surveyed the sergeant and spoke in a mixture of Portuguese, Txitxope, and Txichangana. Her tone of voice was grave, almost masculine.

This man must come with me. He's broken, his soul has sunk to his feet.

Germano must have understood something, because he staggered after her into the rear courtyard. I followed in order to support his steps and help with translation. Feeling left alone among the men, Bianca decided to join us.

Once outside, our strange hostess looked me up and down, and when she saw my feet, she shook her head and said:

Do you think you're some white woman?

I didn't react. Nor did Bibliana expect a reply. She mumbled between her teeth in Txitxope:

I knew a woman who wore shoes, whose feet caught fire.

After that, I ceased to exist for her as she busied herself with making the Portuguese sit down on a chair in the middle of the yard. Then her hands lingered for some time over Germano's shoulders, while she sniffed his face and neck. She took deep breaths and spat repeatedly. Bianca was sickened and turned her back.

From a bag, Bibliana pulled out some women's clothes and made the sergeant put them on. The Italian woman shook her head disapprovingly from afar. Even I found this behavior strange. Initially, I thought the intention might have been to dress the patient in light, loose-fitting clothes. It wasn't. Bibliana had other motives, suggested by her announcement:

Men may rule over the land. But it is we women who rule over blood.

And, pointing to herself and to Germano, the soothsayer repeated:

We women.

The sergeant's head was beginning to sway as he dozed off, and the healer ordered some boys to go down to the river and bring back the dugout in which we had been traveling.

That boat will be this man's bed, she declared.

It was not long before Germano de Melo was carried into the church in the dugout, in what looked like a funeral procession. Borne on the boys' shoulders, the boat swayed with all the solemnity of a coffin. Terrified, the Portuguese raised his head and must have been assailed by the same disquiet that was tormenting me, because he asked, almost drained of any strength:

Has my time come already?

They deposited the dugout on the altar stone. Once again, the healer summoned the young men and whispered urgent instructions. Hands nimbly rummaged through every nook and cranny of the building, and from the shadows they collected owls' feathers. With these, the soothsayer lined the bottom of the boat.

Take me away from here, Bianca, Germano pleaded. *I'm bleeding to death.*

Tomorrow you'll be going to Manjacaze, the white woman assured him.

However, nothing could placate the sergeant. With his elbows resting on the edges of the dugout and his eyes probing as if overcoming a darkness that was his alone, the Portuguese ranted:

This is how the blacks kill our horses: they cut off their ears and they bleed to death during the night.

He fell silent, exhausted. Then he lay back in the bottom of the boat and continued without pause:

That's how they kill them, those poor horses. The next morning, thousands of flies penetrate their ears, advancing down their arteries, eating away their flesh from the inside, until the carcass is so light that it only takes one man to remove the animal.

The Italian woman stroked the sergeant's tousled hair, smoothed the collar of his dress, and whispered to him:

Tomorrow, Germano, tomorrow we'll be at the Swiss hospital.

Bibliana mimicked the white woman's words mockingly:

Tomorrow, tomorrow, tomorrow.

Then she smiled scornfully and, raising her chin, bade me translate:

This white man will remain here until he's got his strength back. Only then will he go on to Mandhlakaʐi. The very name of that place is steeped in blood. That's what Mandhlakazi *means: the power of blood.*

As soon as day breaks, we shall be on our way to Manjacaʐe, Bianca insisted. And, turning to me, she ordered: *Explain this to that mad black woman.*

Be careful, Dona Bianca, I implored. *That woman understands Portuguese.*

Bibliana pretended she had not heard. With her face turned to the heavens, she half closed her eyes and proclaimed:

This white man isn't leaving here!

And her fingers stabbed the air like arrows quivering in the ground. In despair, Bianca raised her hands to her head and, without waiting for me to complete my translation, answered angrily:

So we leave him here without proper food or the minimum standard of hygiene?

I shall give him food, Bibliana replied. *And we have the river that washes all wounds.*

Tell this black woman, the Italian woman ordered me, *that I don't like her. Tell her I don't trust a witch who goes around in a red gown. And also tell her that tomorrow we'll see who's in charge.*

But the Italian was talking to a wall. Indifferent to the white woman's fury, Bibliana bent over the sergeant to undo his bandages.

Using all caution, to allow the blood to flow into a white basin. If one drop were to fall to the ground, it would be a sign of bad luck.

There is no such thing as someone's blood. With every person who loses blood, we all bleed, the healer murmured.

As the basin became stained with red, it dawned on me how the smell of blood was sour, metallic. The sergeant lay with his eyes closed, while Bibliana added a handful of ash to an ointment made of sap and mafura oil. She rubbed this mixture into the soldier's wounds.

When she had finished this treatment, the woman ripped her red gown in two places and swept around the wide space, still wearing her unwieldy boots. She kicked aside chairs and benches. When the whole space had been cleared, she went out into the yard and brought back some logs, which she deposited on the paving stones of the church. The Italian woman cried out in alarm:

The woman's mad! She's going to set fire to the church!

With one foot on either side of the flame, Bibliana opened her legs as if she were heating her insides. Slowly raising her arms, she intoned a melody. The song became more and more energetic as she executed a succession of virile dance steps, raising her knees high and then stamping the ground vigorously with her feet. She straightened and bent her spine as if she were giving birth. Her hands brushed the floor, raising clouds of dust. At one point, she produced a handful of powder from the scarf tied around her head and cast it into the fire. Her cackling laughter blended with the crackle of the powder in the spluttering flames. Then she revealed, in a tone of voice that was more raucous than ever:

This poisonous powder has spread throughout the world. This powder tears open your throat, devours your breast, and in the end, turns nations blind. This blindness is called war.

With her hand on her hip, her head held high, she began to issue warlike commands. It was obvious: A spirit had taken hold of her.

The masculine voice issuing from her belonged to a warrior of old. This dead soldier spoke in my mother tongue, Txitxope. The dead man made the following exhortation through Bibliana's mouth:

I beg you, my ancestors: Show me your scars! Show me your open vein, your shattered bone, your lacerated soul. Your blood is the same as that blood there in the basin, red and full of life.

Then Bibliana began to move in a wide arc again, in a rhythm that mingled dance and military march. After this, she paused, breathless, and put out the fire with her boots. Approaching the altar, she plunged her fingers into the sergeant's thick hair and, turning to us, whispered:

This white man is almost ready.

What do you mean? I asked nervously.

He's already losing his arms, later he'll lose his ears, and then straight after that his legs. In the end, he'll be a fish. And he'll swim back to the boats that brought him to Africa.

That was what they thought of the Portuguese: They were fish from distant seas. Those who stepped ashore were young, sent by their elders, who stayed on the boats. Those who visited us still had their limbs stuck to their bodies. But in the course of time, they began to lose their hands, their feet, their arms, and their legs. At that point, they returned to the ocean.

Prepare yourself, sister: Soon you won't have this white man's company anymore, she said, pinching my arm.

I fell asleep, dreaming that I too was a fish and that, together with Germano, was swimming across endless seas. This was our home: the ocean. I could have been woken up by a gentle lull. But it didn't happen like that. Shouting and uproar tore me from my bed and brought me to the door. A small, angry crowd was gathering next to the church. In the middle of the throng was a man without any clothes, his hands tied, looking as if he had been beaten.

It's one of Ngungunyane's soldiers, we heard someone shout.

Some claimed loudly that he was a spy, but most people were convinced he was a "night bird," one of those witch doctors who work to order. The supposed wizard was so caked in red sand that he looked like a lump of earth in human form. Maybe that was why it did not pain me much to watch him being kicked.

The priest raised his arms asking to intervene. Then he interrogated the man as to his intentions. To which the intruder replied that he had come to "see women." A clamor drowned out the rest of his explanation. And once again blows and kicks rained down upon him, the wretched man no longer attempting to defend himself. He had ceased even being a lump of earth. Now he was just dust.

This was when Bibliana appeared and took charge of the situation. She led the intruder down to the river and ordered him to be lashed to a trunk. The man silently suffered the violence with which they bound him to the tree, just as they would an animal that is about to be butchered. He did not even close his eyes to avoid the sunlight on his face. At an order from the soothsayer—known to everyone as a *sangoma*—the trunk of the tree, along with the man tied to it, was tossed into the water. Complete silence reigned as the improvised craft was swept away by the current. At that point, Bibliana announced:

You wanted to see women? Well, open your eyes under the water and you'll see nothing but women.

4

SERGEANT GERMANO DE MELO'S FIRST LETTER

*God did not create people. He merely discovered them. He found them
in the water. All living creatures lived underwater like fish. God closed
his eyes in order to see inside the river. At that moment, he saw
creatures who were as ancient as himself. And so he decided to take
possession of all the watercourses. This was how he came to wrap all
the rivers inside his veins and kept all the lakes inside his chest. When
he reached the savanna, the Creator released his load. Men and women
tumbled out onto the ground. Squirming around on the sand, they
opened and closed their mouths, as if they were trying to speak, and
words had not yet been invented. Outside water, they did not know how
to breathe. They suffocated and lost consciousness. And they dreamed.
It was as they dreamed that they learned how to breathe. When they
filled their lungs for the first time, they burst into tears. As if part of
them had died. And indeed it had: the part of them that was fish. They
wept with pity for the creatures of the river to which they no longer
belonged. So now, when they sing and dance, they do so in order to
express this yearning. Song and dance deliver us back to the river.*
—A LEGEND FROM SANA BENENE

Sana Benene, July 14, 1895

Dear Lieutenant Ayres de Ornelas,

Let me begin by thanking you, sir, for having gone to the trouble of
replying to my letter and, what is more, for having sent a messenger

who traveled many miles in order to deliver your most encouraging missive.

My handwriting may be barely legible. I do not even know, sir, how I was able to compose these paltry lines, given that I almost have no hands left, and my fading memory does not allow me to evoke the torments which I have recently suffered. Writing, for me, is so crucial that I no longer feel my pains when I take up a pen. I do not know, sir, where we get this stubborn will to live. I speak for myself, because I am not dying merely in order to be polite.

I struggled so hard to finish this letter that I began to bleed again. For it is difficult to use my hands in their present state, and almost impossible to write with my hands all bandaged. My handwriting is frightful, but I had to write these lines without anyone else's help. This is because I want to express my deep gratitude to you personally for your promise to get me back to Portugal. My happiness, I confess, would be complete, and forgive my audacity in being so open with you, if I could take my dear Imani with me. When I think about living, it is Imani who is at the forefront; when I think about dying, it is Portugal that prevails.

The truth is this: I do not know whether I want to leave, shorn of this woman's company. When I first conceived of this letter, I decided to be honest with you and state that I would not travel without Imani. But now I am not so sure. My greatest concern is not that I might offend you, sir. It is rather that I should not be truthful to myself. The fact is that this girl is now tied to my own destiny, she is my homeland. Will she still be that tomorrow? Can it be that this black woman's love for me is completely devoid of self-interest? Might I not just be a passport for her to escape her place in the world and her past?

These are some of the many doubts I have to face. They are my dilemmas and it is up to me alone to resolve them. I am sure that your insistence that I must travel alone is not the result of some whim or lack of willingness on your part. You, sir, are simply unable to act in any other way. And I can understand this: How can you consider an individual's love problems in the midst of such a cruel war? How can you think of an obscure sergeant's sweetheart in the midst of an entire army?

You may wonder, sir, why I remain so attached to a girl who fired a shot at me, leaving me permanently maimed. I do not know the answer. Was she in fact to blame? Do I have any firm recollection of what really happened?

Bianca Vanzini insists that Imani is innocent. The Italian woman was present at the store when it happened and assures me that I was shot by the kaffir rebels. The truth is that I have no clear memory of that sad moment. And I must admit, sir: I no longer care about the truth. I willingly accept the Italian woman's version of events. For I am not seeking memories anymore. Stories are enough for me. And maybe these letters are just a way of inventing someone to listen to my rambling, solitary thoughts, on the reverse side of this sheet of paper.

In the midst of my febrile raving, I am no longer sure whether I am recalling things or whether I am imagining memories, but I have an idea that during a pause in our journey, I lay with the beautiful Imani on the banks of the river. The girl looked at me with her huge eyes, so huge that they contain all the nights in the world. Then I tore some pages from an old notebook, and laid them on the ground. *Come*, I said, *come and lie down on these papers*. She tried to stop me from dismantling the notebook. *Where are you going to write letters to your superiors?* she asked. And then, with a mixture of defiance and malice, she whispered: *Or is it that I am more important than your superiors?*

I cannot help telling you how much this girl gives my life meaning. Just a short while ago, I had to stop writing this letter because of the acute pain in my hands. Once again, it was Imani who came to my aid. Everything she said, she did so with her eyes poised on the ground. Massaging my damaged arms, she murmured gently but firmly: *More than flesh and bone, our hands are made of emptiness. The space between our fingers, the cup our palm makes, it is in this empty space that our gestures are fashioned. The strength of our hands*, Imani said, *lies in what they lack. If there weren't this emptiness, we would be unable to feel our way forward or hold on to anything. We would be unable to caress*, she added apprehensively. And she finished in a tone that was almost inaudible: *Now that you only have a few fingers left, you will feel things more intensely than when your hands were whole.*

Ashamed of her long disquisition, she hurriedly wrapped my arms with cloth that had been washed in the river and cleansed by the sun. *You are much better*, is what she said. And her youthful optimism helped me to resist the weariness I felt.

It is these trivial occurrences I wished to tell you about. You may find them of little consequence, sir. But in narrating these events, they only gain any significance if they are shared with someone who receives them with the same sense of astonishment with which I experienced them.

P.S. I do not want to end this letter without assuring you of the following: I have no way of avoiding going to the Swiss hospital at Manjacaze. Consider the positive aspect of this matter. Maybe it will serve the interests of the Portuguese. Through our Swiss friend Liengme, I shall come to know what is happening at the court of Gungunhane. And, naturally, I shall not miss any opportunity to tell you what I have seen or not seen, what I have been told and what has been concealed from me.

5

GODS THAT DANCE

At the beginning of Time there were neither rivers nor sea. Dotted
around the landscape there were a few lakes, ephemeral offspring of the
rains. Noticing the aridity of the plants and animals, God decided to
create the first river. It happened, however, that the riverbed kept
extending beyond its banks. For the first time, God feared that the
creation might challenge the authority of the Creator. And he suspected
that the river had learned to dream. Those who dream taste eternity.
And this is an exclusive privilege of the gods.
With his long fingers, God suspended the river on high and clipped its
extremities, severing its mouth and its source. With paternal care,
he then laid the thread of water back in its earthen groove. Lacking a
beginning and an end, the river pushed its banks aside and extended
endlessly. Its two banks became so distant from each other that they
provoked an even greater desire to dream. And this was how
the sea was invented, the river of all rivers.
—A LEGEND FROM NKOKOLANI

They say that Life is a boundless teacher. For me, the greatest lessons I ever learned stemmed from what I had not experienced. Moreover, they were revelations that were not born in thought, but in the dazed torpor of waking each morning. Nowadays, I know that every new morning is a miracle. The splendor of renewed light, the scent of dreams still clinging to the bed, all this revives our instinctive faith. Two days ago, this miracle came to me in the person of a white soldier. His name was Germano and he was waiting for me with the same devotion as a fledgling bird awaiting the arrival of its parents. At that moment, I fulfilled the same parental duties: I fed him some mealie pap with a purée of tangy greens. While I was raising the spoon to his mouth, I realized the situation of dependency to which Germano had been condemned in perpetuity.

When the meal was over, he asked me to uncover his wrists. Germano wanted to air his wounds, as he put it. But he had another reason for doing so: He wanted to examine his wreckage. When the bandages fell to the ground, my spirit sank with them. He had five fingers left, always assuming that some of these could still be saved. Five fingers. Three on his right hand, two on his left. At that point, he asked me out of the blue:

How am I going to make the sign of the cross now, Imani?

Then he fell asleep from that gentle fatigue that follows lamentation.

Halfway through the afternoon, a group of men burst into the church. They came at the orders of Bibliana and lifted the dugout with the sergeant inside.

Put me down, the Portuguese insisted. But these were the soothsayer's orders: The sick man could not leave footprints on the ground there. *Where are you taking me?* the bewildered Germano demanded as they carefully carried him down toward the river.

We are going to say a mass, Father Rudolfo replied.

But why don't you have it inside the church? the Portuguese asked in a panic.

This involves different prayers, the priest answered.

The dugout was deposited in the calm waters of the Inharrime. Seated, eyes agog, in the belly of the boat, the Portuguese watched hundreds of country folk approaching, dressed in white. Under a leafy fig tree sat Bibliana, Father Rudolfo, and my father, Katini Nsambe, on the few chairs that had been brought from the church. The Italian woman Bianca Vanzini walked away from the crowd and sat on one of the ruined steps. During a long introduction to the ceremony, the crowd sang a very beautiful hymn, the meaning of which was completely lost on me.

Dressed in a red tunic with white cloths tied to her waist, Bibliana knelt in the middle of that huge ring of people. Complete silence fell as she evoked the ancestors. She named them one by one, an unending list, as if she were welcoming each one at the door of her house. I learned that there is a basic difference in the way whites and blacks treat the dead. We blacks deal with the dead. The whites deal with death. It was this misunderstanding that Germano had to face when he buried the storekeeper Francelino Sardinha, whose funeral ceremony was a way of asking death's permission to forget the dead.

After her lengthy evocation of her ancestors, Bibliana placed a plaster statue of the Virgin upon her head, wrapped in ribbons of the purest white. The crowd fell silent and prostrated themselves on the ground. The soothsayer descended the slope and hugged the statue before wading into the river with it. She cast a printed cloth of the type we call a *capulana* over the waters, and proclaimed:

We do not wash in the river. It is the other way around: It is the river that washes in us.

And she draped the wet *capulana* around the Portuguese man's shoulders. After an initial shiver, his body began to look more resilient.

Suddenly, the Italian woman opened a path through the crowd of people. She came to a halt next to the priest and screamed at him to put a stop to what she called "this black carnival." Rudolfo placated her; the whole procedure was not very different from Christian rituals. He told Bianca to be patient. The celebration would soon gain in interest. The irascible Italian mumbled something in her own language and returned to her place on the ruined steps.

The soothsayer climbed back up the slope to the open space where the crowd awaited her. With her dress clinging to her skin, she rolled her eyes at the emptiness before her and then swayed her body in a strange dance. Her steps became ever more energetic until they attained a military vigor. Galvanized by her ecstasy, the priest began to tap out her rhythm on the cover of a large book.

What's that book? Bianca asked.

Still keeping time, the priest explained that it was a Bible that the Swiss had translated into the native languages. The local people called this book the "Buku." Bianca's reaction was so aggressive that her voice came out as a screech:

So the sacred book is now used as a drum?

Music is God's mother tongue, Rudolfo retorted.

Neither Catholics nor Protestants, he went on, had understood that in Africa, the gods dance. They all committed the mistake of banning drums. The priest had been trying to correct this error for a long time. In truth, if they did not allow us to dance to our drums, we blacks would turn our own bodies into drums. Or worse still, we would stamp our feet over the earth's surface and, in so doing, open up cracks in the whole world.

Bibliana's tunic of fine cloth, soaked in water, clung ever more tightly to her body. And it was obvious why the priest had allowed himself to be seduced. The woman fell to her knees and spoke with such ardor that her voice reverberated in every nook and cranny. We were all reminded of the legend about the creation of the rivers and of men: *At the beginning of Time there were neither rivers nor sea . . .* And she continued without pause until, in the end, she prophesied:

This white man will return to the first waters and he will learn to dream in them.

32

The entire discourse was recited without an interlude. Exhausted, the priestess dragged herself back to the river and waded into the water up to her waist. Holding on to the edge of the dugout, she kept submerging herself until she was breathless. Then she poured water over the sergeant's head, just as in Christian baptisms. When she returned to the riverbank, she raised her arms and started to dance. This was a signal. Suddenly, the drums began to roll and people bounded onto the *terreiro* with leaps and pirouettes.

Unexpectedly, Bianca joined the dance, swaying around Bibliana. She placed her hands on the black woman's hips and the two women moved together to the rhythm of the music. The priest looked at this scene aghast. And he asked:

So you're dancing as well, Dona Bianca?

The Italian woman, on the verge of tears, shook her head. She wasn't dancing. She was trying to make the witch stop dancing. She was trying to put an end to that blasphemous performance. But then she abandoned her attempt and, struggling for breath, took her place again among the onlookers. When she burst into tears, the priest sought to reassure her:

You do not understand, Dona Bianca. This ritual that troubles you so deeply is what is saving you from being devoured alive. And he added: *The famished of this world, more than bread, seek someone to blame.*

At that point, Bibliana returned to the dugout and raised the sergeant's arms as if they were a pair of sagging flagpoles. Then she took a few sheets of paper out of the bottom of the boat and threw them into the waters. She waited while they drifted away until they were lost to sight. No one was aware then, but what was floating along on the current was later found to be nothing less than a letter to the sergeant from the lieutenant. Ayres de Ornelas's florid Portuguese words dissolved like shadows in the waters of the Inharrime.

Eventually, Bibliana climbed back onto the riverbank and lay facedown on the damp ground. The crowd, enraptured, pressed forward to catch a glimpse of the woman, who seemed to be kissing the ground. But she wasn't: She was pecking the earth as chickens do. Her arms folded over her back reinforced this comparison. It was only afterward that we understood: Bibliana was writing. With her tongue, she was drawing letters, opening grooves in the damp sand. In this way, she was representing Germano's inability to use his hands. From time to time, the woman raised her head as if to admire her work, like a painter stepping back from a canvas in order to gain perspective. And she spat out the grains of sand that had stuck to her mouth. When she had finished, she got to her feet and pointed to the fruit of her labors. She had written a name in the soil. *Germano.*

6

SECOND LETTER FROM LIEUTENANT AYRES DE ORNELAS

Someone said that the tribal throngs from the Vátua empire, when on a
war footing, would be the most fearsome thing when pitched against our
weakness. Someone who had frequented Gungunhane's kraal, came to
tell us he had watched an ominous looking parade of fifteen thousand
warriors. But those who made such claims were forgetting that an
armed multitude is not an army and that the cohesion demanded
by military institutions is incompatible with the mindlessness
of these savages.

—COLONEL JOSÉ JUSTINO TEIXEIRA BOTELHO, "MILITARY AND POLITICAL HISTORY OF THE
PORTUGUESE IN MOZAMBIQUE FROM 1883 TO THE PRESENT DAY," 1921

Chicomo, July 18, 1895

Dear Sergeant Germano de Melo,

You have probably already been told that I am now provisional director of the Royal Commission at Chicomo, charged with an almost impossible mission: to convince Gungunhane to surrender to our conditions of sovereignty. These conditions, as you are no doubt aware, are manifold: the surrender to us of the two rebel leaders, annual payment of a tribute amounting to ten thousand pounds, and the licensing of white Gujarati and Moorish traders in his territory. We also insist that the ruler should allow the establishment of telegraph lines between our military posts. Gungunhane argues that modern communications offend the spirits of his ancestors, his father and grandfather buried in that sacred soil. Our agreeing to wait for his authorization is a good example of our naïve acquiescence. We agreed not to disrespect the beliefs of the natives. Then we discovered that the astute ruler is merely taking advantage of our ingenuousness. It is not the spirits that concern him. It is for reasons of military strategy. Gungunhane is only too aware of the value of rapid communication over long distances.

You cannot imagine how sorry I am for having been transferred from my military functions to a mission of a diplomatic character. I admit, for the good of my honor, that an officer's first task is not to wage war, but to avoid it at all costs. And everything seems to indicate that the king of Gaza also wants to avoid confrontation, now that we have increased our presence in the area where he has holed up. Gungunhane, we are sure, will agree to all our conditions, with the exception of the one which, as far as we are concerned, is crucial: the surrender of the rebels Mahazul and Zixaxa, who, some months ago, had the temerity to lead an attack on Lourenço Marques.

This intervention in diplomatic matters will help in my promotion to the highest ranks, which I am destined to achieve. It was this conviction that led me to agree to accompany the counselor José d'Almeida in his negotiations with the Lion of Gaza. With his long experience and the precious trust that he has established with Gungunhane, Counselor José d'Almeida was to lead the negotiations. This choice did not receive the acclaim of all the members of the high command meeting at Chicomo. The most vigorous objections were expressed by Captain Mouzinho de Albuquerque, who even went so far as to declare publicly that *we can only expect shame from the counselor José d'Almeida*. The same Mouzinho wrote to António Enes lamenting the fact that he had not been chosen to negotiate with the king of Gaza. The text of his letter, to which I had access through means I could never divulge, read as follows: "It would be a thousand times better to lose everything in one catastrophic event, than to withdraw without having done anything." To which he added: "I offer myself for this mission no matter how foolish and dangerous the enterprise may prove to be." These disagreements are sad. As if our war with the Vátuas were not enough. Our internal discord seems far more serious. There is only one solution: to ignore all the envy and rivalry over positions of prestige. A noble spirit such as mine is what is needed. This is what is expected of lucid leadership capable of facing up to the present challenges.

It was with this sense of a mission in mind that I made preparations to leave for Manjacaze in the company of the counselor Almeida. Our accommodation was fully assured: Our counselor's residence was some hundreds of meters from Gungunhane's court.

The Royal Commissioner insisted that we should be accompanied by a military escort. We disobeyed these instructions. The false security of an escort does not compensate for the squabbles caused by soldiers when they get involved with local women. And so we traveled from Chicomo to Manjacaze mounted on two fine horses. At the various places we stopped along the way, my horse always approached me as if it wished to tell me something. Its eyes the color of dark cotton looked at me with an intensity that I found disturbing. And I became so attached to the beast that when we reached our final destination, and despite my exhaustion, I got up in the middle of the night merely to gaze again at those eyes that were also so human.

Once installed in the counselor's residence, we were obliged to wait longer than we wished. The king of Gaza did not appear at the first meeting. A messenger informed us that he was busy at a funeral. The counselor Almeida asked who had died. The messenger answered that it was "one of the king's mothers." I had to stop myself from laughing. One of his mothers? Only a black man could say something like that, I thought.

At the end, the messenger transmitted Gungunhane's invitation to the king of Portugal to visit the State of Gaza, and to bring his many wives with him. The counselor corrected him tersely: *The king only has one wife.* The kaffir graciously assured us of the willingness of his African hosts to help the king compensate for this shortage. This caused much laughter. I mention these exotic occurrences by way of a warning regarding your little dalliance with the girl who seems to have so robbed you of your judgment, my dear young sergeant, that you have failed to understand the consequences of a possible marriage to this woman Imani. By marrying a black woman, you will get the most corpulent brother-in-law there is: all Africa. If you marry a Negro woman, you will marry an entire race. Let us leave it at that, for this affair of yours has left me perplexed, and I have enough problems of my own to face at present. I shall return to the narration of my ordeals in Manjacaze.

The days that followed in that outpost proved the wisdom of choosing José d'Almeida as a negotiator. On the third day, the king of Gaza appeared in person at our residence in Manjacaze. José d'Almeida was the only Portuguese for whom the king waived the requirement that it was he, Ngungunyane, who was the one visited. The royal retinue was so big that it spread in a circle of more than fifty meters in diameter around the tent in which the conversations were to take place. The tent was erected next to the counselor Almeida's house, and this induced in me an illusion of comfort. The more than four thousand unarmed soldiers in attendance formed a human frame that stretched away as far as the eye could see. In the front row sat the most notable figures: the king, his uncles, his principal advisers, and officials.

Here is a curious custom: The king never spoke. An anonymous orator greeted us and presented us with a head of cattle as a proof of goodwill. We had not even gotten as far as beginning negotiations. This was merely a welcoming ritual. But it was also a manifestation of power. The impression of strength they were seeking to show did not merely lie in the large number of soldiers. The chant they intoned left a far deeper impression on me than any bellicose display. In this way, the kaffirs cunningly combine threat and amiability.

At a certain point, a man the Vátuas called "the king's dog" leaped into the circle. He was a short fellow, wrapped in a leopard skin, his head covered with feathers. For a while all he did was rush around, barking and howling like a dog.

This character, to such an extent removed from his human state, struck me so deeply that I was unable to get any sleep all night long. I had read about these performers in a report written by the Swiss traveler Georges Liengme. On various occasions, the doctor had attempted to photograph one of these men. But the image had never been recorded on the photographic plate. That night, I could not get the image of the barking jester out of my head. That man had an animal's soul. Moreover, he had the tremendous advantage of not suffering the misfortunes of the world and humanity. The only things that troubled him were hunger and thirst. In the midst of my sleeplessness it occurred to me that this was what I wanted to be: a dog. Born to nestle at the feet of some master or other. Or maybe a horse to be caressed by some devoted rider.

The following morning, there were four continuous hours of meetings which, as you know, the kaffirs call *banja*. And this was where our adversary's canny intelligence was confirmed. My colleagues curse the savagery of Gungunhane. Well, I have to acknowledge that he possesses the sagacity of an outstanding negotiator. He did not rebuff or even query our nervous insistence on delivering the rebels Mahazul and Zixaxa into our hands. He put forward a counter-suggestion that we should join forces in finding the fugitives. If the search failed, responsibility would not fall solely on his shoulders. And he criticized us for our lack of intelligence—if we were so desperate to capture these fugitives, why were we making such a noise about it? If one is hunting a furtive prey, one should act all the more furtively. And he challenged us with what I thought an even more irrefutable argument: If we were not seeking war, as we were so adamant in claiming, why were we amassing so many thousands of troops and pieces of artillery on the borders of his territory? Even the ruler's mother, Impibekezane, who was ever-present in these negotiations, declared that it seemed strange to assemble so much manpower and equipment just to capture two fugitives. I should add that this queen-mother exercises huge influence over her son, and is therefore one of the most powerful figures in the kingdom. This is why the kaffirs call this lady Nkosicaze, which means "the Big Woman."

At the close of our discussions, when we were taking our leave, my horse suddenly approached the tent in a state of excitement, coughing raucously and frothing abundantly through its mouth and nostrils. It was producing so much foam that the bystanders were spattered liberally with saliva. The animal lowered its huge head toward me as if it wanted to show me its swollen eyes and thus reveal the death that already dwelt in them. The creature dropped to its knees in almost human fashion. It had chosen me to accompany it in its moment of agony. The king and his advisers watched, intrigued, but remained religiously respectful. You, my friend, are no doubt aware that, for these Negroes, horses are almost unknown animals. The word they use for it is copied from the English word *horse*. Well, during this incident, one of the kaffirs present, all covered in adornments—doubtless some type of fortune-teller—leaned right over the horse, placed his hand on the creature's mane, and recited a long litany in the Zulu language. Someone next to me translated the witch doctor's words:

When you arrived, we had no name to give you. You brought with you riders carrying shining swords. But you are a living spear, you run faster than the wind and jump over the tallest trees. On the ground you tread, you leave a trail of fire.

By the time he had completed his assertion, the animal had breathed its last. I was no longer able to remain there. With my eyes brimming with tears, I walked away from the death, which, though that of an animal, was nevertheless to some degree mine as well. Should a career soldier cry in public? And what's more, over an animal?

The High Command at Lourenço Marques has stated that these will be the last discussions with the Vátua chiefs. Time is against us: European nations with colonial ambitions lie in wait. That is why, while we negotiate under a burning sun, while a horse with human eyes dies, and while a little man barks and howls, the two armies are busy preparing for war. It is for this reason that I must end with a warning. It is no longer safe for you to move around without a fully armed escort. Nor should you travel along the rivers. If those lands are not ours, even less so are the rivers. The Angolans who accompany us talk of huge aquatic snakes that cause boats to capsize. Our informers assure us that this is a new type of ambush: The natives lay ropes from one bank to the other, and these are tightened when boats pass by. All these dangers invite the greatest possible prudence. Stay where you are until we can prepare to rescue you with all due safety.

I finish by wishing you a speedy recovery. In a more robust state of health you will, I am certain, see the world through other eyes. Our soul is no more than this: a state of health.

P.S. Let me give you some advice: Do not shower this girl Imani with too much praise. You run the risk of destroying her original purity and humility. I find it hard to say this, but that is how it is with Negroes. You cannot confide in them, for they change immediately in their haste to become like us. There is no solution to this: We despise them for what they are; we hate them when they are like us. Thank God, and assuming your declarations are true, this woman Imani is on her way to ceasing to be black. Let us hope it is no more than this: a fortuitous, passing affair in your long life.

7

THE LUMINOUS FRUITS OF A NOCTURNAL TREE

No one is a person if that person is not all humanity.
—A SAYING FROM NKOKOLANI

I found Germano asleep outside the dugout that had served as his bed on the church altar. He had been bleeding, and his bandages were completely soaked. Bloodstained sheets of paper lay scattered all around him. It looked as if the sergeant had used them to try to clean himself. When examined more closely, one could see that the sheets had been scribbled on: They were the beginnings of a letter. The sergeant had started bleeding while he was writing.

He was so fast asleep that I felt a need to check that he was still alive. I caressed his face to feel his warmth, and listened to his chest to make sure he was breathing. In the end, I crossed myself in front of the altar, and with backward steps withdrew from the church.

I made for the improvised quarters that I was going to share with the Italian woman. I found her at the entrance, combing her long hair. Without stopping what she was doing, she told me:

Germano is confused, he doesn't remember what happened. From now on, the only valid version of what happened is mine: Those responsible for firing the shot were the rebels. You're not to blame for anything, Imani.

I'm not sure, Dona Bianca. I don't want to lie.

You can't lie to someone who doesn't remember anything.

But I remember.

The quarters they had allocated for us consisted of a military tent with one bed at the back. An oil lamp lit up the entrance. On the ground, another lamp caused shadows to dance on the canvas walls. While she was putting her brush and mirror away, the Italian woman declared:

Your father asked me to take you to Lourenço Marques.

The shock of this news pounded me to the point of bringing tears to my eyes. Nevertheless, I pretended that this decision was not unexpected and, above all, that I was completely indifferent to it. My false resignation shone through when I replied:

If that's what my father wants . . .

You'll like it, Imani. Or would you rather stay here in the middle of this savage bushland?

In the face of my despondency, the white woman added:

You'll find it strange at first. In my establishments, we work at night. You'll be a woman of the night. But you'll soon get used to it.

The lamp faded, disturbed by some mysterious puff of wind. It was not my nocturnal fate that was causing me anguish. I was thinking of Germano. I was thinking about our being separated. Bianca noticed this cloud in my eyes.

I'm going to ask you to do something now. Get undressed.

I'm almost undressed as it is, Dona Bianca.

Take all your clothes off, we're alone, no one will see us.

Reluctantly, I undid my blouse and dress. The Italian woman took a step back, seized the lamp next to the bed, and held it up high to take a better look at me.

You're going to drive men crazy before they even touch you.

She put the lamp down in order to feel my hips and my belly. She kept caressing me while she explained: She wanted to know what it was that white men saw in black women. Then she sat down, an enigmatic smile on her lips. She would like to see the look on men's faces when they discovered us naked and sharing the same bed.

Can you imagine it? Two women, and what's more, a white woman and a black woman?

I don't like this conversation, Dona Bianca.

She straightened the straps of her chemise and peered into my eyes as if gazing at herself in a mirror.

I no longer want to have a beautiful figure. Some men are attracted to me just because I'm the only white woman. But you, my dear, what have you done to be so graceful and so free of race?

I'm a black woman, Dona Bianca, I retorted with a shrug of my shoulders.

But I knew how the imprint of my origins had been erased. During my entire childhood, far from my parents, the priest had patrolled my dreams from the moment I woke up, canceling out the nightly messages sent to me by those who had gone before. And apart from this, Father Rudolfo Fernandes would correct my accent as if he were clipping a dog's nails. I was a black woman, indeed. But that was an accident of skin color. To be white was the only profession my soul had been schooled for.

At that point, the beat of drums could be heard coming from the direction of the river. Groups of people made their way along the village paths. I went to the entrance of the tent. And someone told me about a sinister occurrence: The same tree trunk to which the Vátua spy had been lashed had floated back to the landing stage at Sana Benene. The old tree had traveled against the current, and without the body that had been tied to it. Unmistakable marks on the bark revealed what had happened to the intruder: He had been devoured by crocodiles. This could only be the work of Bibliana, which was the reason for all the agitation; the divine powers that protected us were being celebrated.

The Italian closed her eyes and mumbled: *That witch!* I told her we did not use that term. And much less did we talk about such things at night. But she continued:

Well, everyone calls me a witch. I'm a woman, I'm unmarried, and I travel alone in the world.

As a witch herself, she had no difficulty in recognizing another one. When Bibliana was dancing in the *terreiro*, the Italian immediately detected the presence of the devil. The moment she grabbed the black woman's tunic, other hands seized her. They were women's hands. She recognized their faces: They were prostitutes who had been killed in the bars that she owned. But she saw other hands too. They were the hands of people who had given her what she called "dirty money."

I told everyone that I embarked on this long journey for reasons of love. I spoke of my passion for Mouzinho. All that was false. The truth is that I came to collect the debts of Sardinha, the storekeeper.

I recalled the last moments of Francelino Sardinha's life: the kind way he accompanied me home, the story he told me about Ngungunyane and his search for the poison from the *mri'mbava* on account of his having succumbed to forbidden love. And finally, the image of the storekeeper of Nkokolani came back to me, breathing his last in a pool of blood, clinging to a rifle with the desperation of a drowning man. That was how he fell asleep every night, hugging his old shotgun.

So they accused the storekeeper of trading arms with the English? Well, I traded with all of them, Portuguese, Vátuas, English, Boers. They say I have hands of gold? If only they were, may God forgive me.

She held out a piece of blue ribbon and asked me to tie it to her hair, which covered her back. While I rolled my fingers in her perfumed locks, the white woman turned down the flame in the lamp and her tone of voice darkened as she murmured:

The real witch isn't Bibliana. It's you. Germano is besotted with you. And that's got to finish.

Finish? How?

Where I'm taking you, there can't be any wives, husbands, love, or marriage.

She rummaged around in her purse and took out a photograph. Although it was faded and dog-eared, one could make out the image of a tall, gaunt man against the background of a ship.

It's Fábio, my husband, she murmured, as if at a wake. Then she rummaged through the purse again and pulled out half a dozen envelopes. *These are the letters he sent me when I was in Italy. They're Fábio's letters.*

With the utmost care, she put the photo back. And, in Italian, she lamented: *Sono tutti uguali, gli uomini sono tutti uguali.* At first she assumed that her beloved was telling the truth when he expressed his yearning for her. How real her tears were, in that faraway Italian village, as she read the painful messages from her sweetheart exiled in Africa. It was all an illusion. Like the other white men, her companion was busy with other charms, other sweet exiles. And it was in another tone of voice that Bianca Vanzini returned to the thorny matter of my future.

Anyway, this is what's going to happen: I'm going to make a queen out of you. The white men will rush to kneel at your feet.

But what if I don't want to, Dona Bianca?

You will, Imani. You're an intelligent woman. You know what your future will be like with a disabled man who will be more like a son than a husband.

And what if I refuse?

If you do, then I shall remind Sergeant Germano who it was who fired the shot, who it was who crippled him forever more.

She lay down, and with her eyes closed, now repeated in Portuguese what she had said in Italian but a few moments before:

Men are all the same, in Africa, in Italy, or in Hell.

I thought she was already asleep when I heard her once again searching among the envelopes. Her hand, lit up by the oil lamp, suddenly turned much paler as she touched my shoulder.

Read me this letter. Don't tell me you don't know the language. You do, oh yes, it's a love letter.

I deciphered the words letter by letter. I omitted what I couldn't understand, and embellished what I could. But I read quickly, in a low voice, for fear of being heard outside the thin canvas walls. Maybe it was different in Italy. But for us, stories can only be told at night. Only like that can the darkness be distracted. Fortunately, the white woman soon fell asleep.

Lulled by my own voice, I too slipped away into sleep. I dreamed of the tree my grandfather had planted behind our house. During the day, it was scrawny and its shade was sparse. But when darkness fell, it turned into a vast, leafy creature. In the moonlight, its luminous fruits could be seen. It was a nocturnal tree. No one else witnessed its splendor. Only the moon and I.

8

THIRD LETTER FROM LIEUTENANT AYRES DE ORNELAS

*. . . the slightest disobedience or mere delay in fulfilling an order of
mine was punished immediately and harshly—not to say
barbarously—with a hippo-skin whip, and a black convicted of spying
was shot and his body burned in front of some three hundred
Mabinguelas and Mangunis, assembled there at my orders. Do not
think I enjoy seeing natives killed in cold blood, or writhing in agony
under the lashes of the whip, but I realized that Gungunhane was still
greatly feared and respected, due in part to the deaths he ordered every
day, and that was why I did all I could to inspire a similar terror to
that which the Vátua ruler dispensed around him.*

—MOUZINHO DE ALBUQUERQUE, QUOTED BY ANTÓNIO MASCARENHAS GAIVÃO, IN "MOUZINHO
DE ALBUQUERQUE. FROM THE BACKLANDS OF MOZAMBIQUE TO THE POMP OF EUROPEAN
COURTS," OFICINA DO LIVRO, CRUZ QUEBRADA, 2008

Inhambane, July 29, 1895

Dear Sergeant Germano de Melo,

Thank God I have resumed my calling as a soldier. I received orders to
abandon my diplomatic tasks and to prepare, here in Inhambane, for a
powerful military offensive that will take place on the plains of Magul.
Indeed, my stay in Manjacaze had become unbearable. Not only because of the fruitless wait for Gungunhane to change his position, but
because everything about the place was somber and decadent.

Did you, Sergeant, not complain that your military post at Nkokolani was more of a shop than a garrison? Well, José d'Almeida's residence at Manjacaze had been transformed into a bottle store, where alcohol was distributed without any controls. The great and the good of Gungunhane's court, the king's wives and his military chiefs, all pretended that there was a purpose to our official audiences. Then one would watch them leaving, moments later, staggering away with bottles in their hands. Drinking was no longer enough. It was vital that those drinking should be seen doing so by all the others, for they gained social prestige by availing themselves of the alcohol of the Europeans.

The hunger I experienced in Manjacaze was such that even I, who am parsimonious when it comes to drinking, ended up consuming wine without due restraint merely to forget the lack of food. We got to the stage of asking Georges Liengme for food for our people and corn for the horses. He provided us with four sacks of grain.

The saddest thing, the doctor remarked, *is not that one has to give food. But it is not knowing whether this food is for people or for animals.*

Can you think of anything more annoying than this type of comment coming from a European?

I have shared these initial confessions with you, but I should warn you right away that this is not exactly a letter. It is a command that I am drawing up in the intervals between my busy preparations in this pleasant city of Inhambane. As I mentioned at the beginning of this letter, we are on the eve of a major offensive in Magul. This is going to be a crucial moment in my career. The hierarchy has its eyes on me and I cannot miss this opportunity to shine.

I shall get to the point without more ado: I urgently need you to act as my informer on the ground. This is not a request. It is an order from your commanding officer. None of this is related in any way to my promise to arrange for your transfer back to Portugal, for that will be a future favor of no relevance here. This is different. It is going to be vital that I should get firsthand accounts of a strategic nature. The most important of these will concern Gungunhane's movements, or those of the two fugitive leaders. If I am apprised of these before any other Portuguese official—and above all before Mouzinho de Albuquerque—I shall have a golden opportunity to stand out in front of my own superiors. Our correspondence must therefore take on a practical, discreet character. Your letters can and should continue to talk about your personal sentiments, of course. But these should take the form of notes on the side. The most important thing is that you should provide me with useful assets that will serve to boost me and harm my political adversaries. I shall know how to reward you. The moment I am promoted, you, my friend, will be sent back to Portugal immediately. That is my firm promise.

9

AN AGE WITHOUT TIME

The history of the world is a story of three days and three deaths. On the first day, there was a flood and all creatures were turned into fish. This was how my two daughters became submerged in the river. On the second day, a fire devoured the forests, and where clouds hovered, only dust and smoke were left. The sources dried up and rivers disappeared. Then all creatures were turned into birds. That's what happened to your mother, do you not remember her in the tree? On the third day, a violent storm swept through the sky and all the winged creatures were turned into earthbound animals, spreading through valleys and across mountains until they no longer recognized themselves. That is what is happening to us, the survivors of war.

—KATINI NSAMBE, ADDRESSING HIS DAUGHTER IMANI

This is what delights the cook: to see the plates clean as if a cat had licked them. This was what the plate looked like after Father Rudolfo had satisfied his hunger. He was now fanning himself with it. Suddenly, the priest put aside his improvised fan in order to comment on a rumor that was going around. It was said that the queen, Impibekezane, had been seen in the vicinity of Sana Benene.

I hope she's not thinking of coming here, the priest declared quietly.

Rather than an honor, a visit by someone of that rank was a reason to feel insecure. The priest wanted the house of God kept away from politics and wars. The church could be an infirmary. But never a place of ashes and death.

In this, I am in complete agreement with you, Father, Bianca acceded. *Sometimes the worst thing that can happen in a war is to win a battle. The Portuguese won at Marracuene but left a few do\zen dead there. Vengeance is coming.*

The heat was intense at that hour but what we found most stifling was the prospect of imminent tragedy. War surrounded us on all sides with its invisible claws. With so much danger lurking, what worried me was how we were going to get Germano to the Swiss hospital.

Don't worry, my dear Imani, Father Rudolfo declared, adding: *That white man of yours is going to have to stay here a while yet.*

Our departure to Mandhlakazi was delayed. Dr. Liengme had been summoned to Lourenço Marques by António Enes. And no one knew when he would be back.

We sat in silence while Bibliana gathered in the plates and cutlery to put them in a basin of water. Every time the black woman passed by, the white woman would stretch her legs out to try to block her way. Unable to trip her up, Bianca lost her temper and said:

Don't pass in front of people. Keep behind us. Didn't the Father teach you any manners?

When, at last, Bibliana retired to the shadows of the kitchen quarters, Bianca commented in a harsh tone: *That woman was wearing her nightdress.*

Dona Bianca, around here all dresses are nightdresses, the priest retorted irritably.

Women wear those clothes inside the house.

You don't understand, madam: For these folk, the house is all that you can see around us.

The white woman contemplated the disorder around us while the priest continued speaking.

The problem is, Dona Bianca, that you are scared of Bibliana. You don't see her as a person. You see a black woman, a witch.

It's not she who worries me, but you. You've forgotten that you are a priest and that this house is a holy place.

A holy place? Do you want to know why I'm here? They sent me to Sana Benene because this place is in the middle of nowhere. I was punished. I blew the whistle on dirty goings-on, business dealings carried out in the name of important people.

What business dealings?

Slaves.

Now, now, Father, let's get things straight. Slavery finished ages ago!

That's the problem, Dona Bianca. It didn't finish. And you know very well what I'm talking about.

As he entered the church that afternoon, Father Rudolfo was surprised by the presence of three men sitting in the first row of the paltry collection of chairs. The strangers introduced themselves as Manhune, Ngungunyane's general and adviser, along with two bodyguards in civilian attire. It is bad manners for a visitor to state their business straightaway, but Manhune was above such precepts, and without beating about the bush he announced the purpose of his visit. He was there to fetch the women.

What women? the priest asked, all aquiver.

Bibliana and the white woman who has just arrived.

They would not leave without taking the women with them. The *Nkosi* wanted both of them. The black woman because of the powers she possessed. The white woman because of the prestige he would accrue by having a European spouse. The priest implored, almost sobbing: *Please don't take my husband away from me.*

The messengers burst out laughing. Husband? They over-looked the slipup: The white was talking in a language that was not his. And they corrected him patiently. The linguistic misunder-standing stopped them in their tracks momentarily. The messenger agreed that the priest should organize the move before they re-turned in a few days' time. At that point, the women should be ready to leave. And they withdrew, disappearing into the darkness of the surrounding countryside.

Neither Bianca Vanzini nor Bibliana could be found in the church-yard, and so Father Rudolfo took the opportunity to tell me and my father about the visit of the VaNguni chief and Ngungunyane's in-tentions. He asked us not to mention anything to anyone. There was no point in frightening the women who were the target of such threats. And so a heavy silence fell over us, only interrupted by my father's desperate swigs from the bottle. Irritated, the priest snatched the bottle of *nsope* from his hands:

Where is your son Mwanatu?

Katini contemplated the vast expanses of grassland around them as if, rather than searching for his son, he were seeking a lan-guage in which to answer:

He's around somewhere . . .

Around where? This isn't a time to be around somewhere . . .

My father did not reply, for fear of being misunderstood. People spoke of his son in the same terms as they spoke of all madmen: He was prowling through the night putting the wild animals to sleep. He was placating the tiredness and hunger of these beasts. By so doing, he took on the spirit of the creatures of the wild.

The boy is still a simpleton. That's the sad fact of the matter, the priest insisted, concerned.

Katini Nsambe ignored the respect due to a priest and overcame his misgivings in addressing a white.

That's my son we are talking about.

His nervousness prevented him from remaining seated any longer. He walked around the tree and tore off bits of bark until his fingers began to bleed.

The priest spoke to me as if my father were not present:

Your father is happy to take you to the land of the white people. Is that what you want to be? A black woman in a white man's world?

For a second I thought my father was leaning over the priest in order to attack him. And that was what Rudolfo feared too, shielding his face with his hands. However, Katini Nsambe was just reaching past him in order to seize back his bottle of liquor, and he walked resolutely away, clutching the bottle close to his chest.

Do you know that Gungunhane has banned the consumption of alcohol? He decreed the law after his son died from the effects of alcohol last month.

Ngungunyane doesn't tell me what to do, Katini declared. And then he added: *He'll be the first to break the law.*

Stroking his long beard, the priest forgot my father's skinny figure and turned his attention to me.

I can't help hearing what the other blacks say about you. And I must confess, dear girl: It would be better if you were white.

More than to a race, I belonged to some cursed species. I was a friend of the whites. They would hurl this fact in my face just as they do to lepers and the insane.

In the end, he said, *you'll envy your disabled brother for the disdain with which he is treated.*

And there was another lesson he wanted to transmit to me, maybe the last. Our land is an island. Those who arrive here do not want to stay. No matter how much we like them, we should not surrender our souls to them.

Those who knock on our door are passing through. Open up your house but keep your soul shut away.

He was referring to my attraction to the sergeant. But the priest was also talking about himself. A man between worlds, a soul between borders. For whites, he was a friend of the blacks. For the blacks, he was nothing more than a second-class white. For the Indians who shared the color of his skin, the priest was no one at all. He had the language, beliefs, and ways of the Europeans. He wasn't even a traitor. He didn't exist.

This is the sad law of the world: Those who exist in halves end up being doubly hated.

An empty bottle fell in the sand at my feet. It was from my father, who had returned and was seeking our company again, and now sat down in silence. By remaining speechless, he was asking for forgiveness. He rubbed his hands on his knees for some moments before plucking up courage to ask:

Tell me something, Father. That wife of yours, that woman, Bibliana, speaks the language of folk around here, but she's not one of our VaChopi women, is she?

What a question, Katini. Did you ever ask what tribe the Portuguese sergeant belonged to? the priest asked. Then he added: *Bibliana belongs to the women's tribe. That's what she'd tell you if you were to ask her.*

We heard explosions in the distance. Then some shots. And the clatter of horses' hooves receding. And then silence.

I wonder who's doing the shooting now, the priest said.

No one knew the answer. How many wars are there within one war? How many different possibilities of hatred lie hidden when a nation sends its sons to their deaths? I could guess the screams unleashed afar. They were women screaming for sure, and no one paid them any heed, for they were far away, always too far away. The priest sighed, almost out of tedium:

Now for the burials!

And the two men drank. Every time they replenished their glasses, they cursed the king of Gaza:

May his sons and daughters die! And let them lie out in the open air, to be devoured by hyenas.

The inebriated are like prisoners: They create a time that exists only for them and cannot be shared. Feeling excluded, I asked to be excused. But the priest told me to stay. There was a matter he wanted to clear up with my father.

The war is at our doorstep, Katini, my brother. Don't you think it's time Imani knew the truth about the girls who died?

Let time take care of itself, my father said.

It wasn't the river that took your sisters away, the priest declared. *It was because they drank water from a poisoned well.*

Poisoned by whom? I asked, with a serenity that surprised me.

By the devil, the priest retorted.

My old father confirmed this with a nod. In the ensuing tense, dense silence, the most insignificant details assumed the dimensions of an omen: the first drops of rain, the smell that seemed to emanate from the earth, but which came from a primitive recess of our souls. And once again, we seemed to hear the mute screams of women from the great beyond.

These are things from the past, things of days gone by, the priest said, in an attempt to placate his soul.

There are no things of days gone by, Katini declared. *There are things that are empty, like this bottle.*

10

SERGEANT GERMANO DE MELO'S SECOND LETTER

. . . Though great conquerors of lands, the Portuguese do not make use
of them, but are happy to scamper along their seashore like crabs.
—FRIAR VICENTE DO SALVADOR, "HISTORY OF BRAZIL," 1627

Sana Benene, August 8, 1895

Dear Lieutenant Ayres de Ornelas,

You ordered me, sir, to serve as your spy. I immediately began to
fulfill this duty, and through this letter wish to inform you of a
strange incident that occurred here in Sana Benene. Yesterday,
Queen Impibekezane, the mother of Gungunhane, came to this
church. The great Vátua lady was accompanied by a small, discreet
delegation. At the time, I was fast asleep, and did not emerge from
my slumber despite the turmoil. The priest accommodated the
royal visitor in a large shed made of timber and zinc, hidden away
in a bushy thicket. At this point, it is appropriate to talk a little about
these premises. Rudolfo Fernandes's original intention was to in-
stall a printing press there for the reproduction of religious texts.
All that remains of the old typesetter and printing press are a few
bits and pieces scattered around in the corners. And there is still a
wooden box with one or two metal type pieces lined up like soldiers
on parade. It was with all this equipment that the priest had thought
of printing the Bible in Txitxope, to be translated by Imani. But it

never went beyond good intentions. The idea of the Bible in the language of her people dissolved into thin air, just like the smell of printing ink, so strong and prevalent that she still remembered the strangeness of it when everything was still at Makomani.

I was shaken awake with the announcement of the arrival of our strange visitors. Still in a daze, and leaning heavily on Imani and the priest, I slowly crossed the yard, anxious to meet the old lady who exercised such influence over Gungunhane and his court. As you, sir, very well know, Queen Impibekezane is not the monarch's blood mother. His real mother died recently and in accordance with the express wishes of her husband, Muzila, was buried wrapped in the Portuguese flag.

The reason for this unexpected visit, unbelievable as it may seem, was myself! Impibekezane had heard of the arrival of a white soldier at Sana Benene and wanted to meet with the Portuguese in private. This was why I had been shaken awake, for they did not want to keep such an illustrious visitor waiting. At the door to the shed stood two Vátua soldiers who were serving as the queen's escort. They bore no military insignia by which they might be identified. They inspected the cloth that bound my arms. Then, with a nod, they let me pass. At the same time, they did not allow the priest or Imani to enter.

Inside the building sat two women. The queen mother was distinguished by her combed-back hairstyle and the many strings of beads that adorned her wrists and ankles. As I had been advised, I greeted them with a word that was only permitted when addressed to royalty.

Bayete! I said, bowing somewhat unconvincingly.

I confess, sir, that I was attracted to the other woman, who was much younger and blessed with a rare, delicate beauty. I have no words to describe this young damsel. Her skin was coppery in tone, she had a perfect body and well-sculpted face. I was so fascinated by this black girl that, noting my discomposure, the queen told her to sit farther away in a shadowy corner. I spoke in Portuguese in the vain hope that they would allow Imani to serve as an interpreter. The beautiful girl astonished me by replying in my language. She explained that the matters that we would be dealing with were of the utmost secrecy. She said that her name was Mpezui, she was a sister of the king of Gaza, and in her childhood had attended a school that the Portuguese had built at Manjacaze. And she gazed at me with her deep, dark eyes, made to lay siege to a man's soul.

The queen mother was alarmed by the tension afflicting our region. The two armies were bringing together thousands of men on the plains of Magul. She wanted to know what position I occupied in the military hierarchy. I mentioned my rank of sergeant and the two women exchanged a few words between themselves before leaning forward and displaying various signs of respect. Mpezui enthusiastically declared that the king of Gaza held the same rank in the Portuguese army, and for that reason I was worthy of the highest esteem. They were mistaken. They were confusing the ranks of sergeant and colonel, which was the distinction D. Carlos had accorded Gungunhane. I did not contradict them. But the unusual nature of their visit had such an effect on my nerves that I relapsed into feverish tremors. My pulse raced and blood seeped through my bandages. I concealed this leakage behind my back.

My late husband, Muzila, was a great friend of Portugal, the queen announced. The Vátua sovereign had died a disillusioned man. Some of the promises made by the Portuguese had not been kept. But this truth could also be applied conversely: The African monarch had also forgotten to honor his commitments. *You, sir, will raise the matter of these omissions again with both sides. You know well that it is a question of human nature; if we possess memory, it is to forget our own faults.*

The queen mother gazed at me fixedly as she warned me never, but never, to disappoint her. I lowered my head, not as a sign of obedience, but because a moment of giddiness clouded my judgment.

In times such as these, deception is paid for with one's life, the queen intimated.

The land upon which I trod was sacred, she declared. Her dead lived in the ground here. She described Muzila's funeral ceremony in deliberate detail. I heard the narration of his funeral rites as if from far away, in a fragmented form, my auditory senses occasionally failing me. The dead Muzila's corpse had been hung from a tree so that his bodily liquids could be collected in a large basin. These would later be used to fertilize the soil.

We die in order to become a seed, the visitor concluded, straightening her coiffure without appearing to touch her hair. She took a deep breath before speaking once again.

I am queen. But first, I am a mother.

Men, she declared, *are educated to wage war. They fail to recognize, however, that no army is as powerful as a woman defending her family.*

Though not of her blood, Gungunhane—or Umundungazi, as she called him—was her favorite son. And she was determined to protect him at all costs. This was why the queen had come here: She had conceived of a way of saving the emperor. This plan would, at the same time, save the lives and the honor of the Portuguese, who in the eyes of the world would be the only winners. The only people who would never recognize this victory would be the vanquished. And because of this, they would celebrate their triumph in a different way down the centuries.

The queen mother leaned forward toward me as if she were about to tell me a secret. The beautiful Mpezui imitated the sovereign's gesture and her lips brushed my ear in order to translate Impibekezane's murmur:

Listen to me as if you were a son of mine.

At that crucial moment, however, I felt a violent hemorrhaging flooding the ground behind me. I got as far as realizing she was speaking of Sanches de Miranda and the name they have for him in their language, Mafambatcheca, which means the One Who Laughs as He Travels. But by this time, my life was flowing out through my wrists. I tried to cry for help but words failed to reach my mouth. The world was becoming darker as I collapsed into my own blood.

I cannot bear witness, sir, to what happened during that temporary loss of consciousness. Someone must have dragged me out, for I awoke in my own quarters, alarmed by the infernal racket coming from the yard.

I have to stop here in order not to miss the messenger, who is about to leave. I shall give more news soon.

11

THE THEFT OF A METAL WORD

This is what they say before we are even born: Woman's great virtue is to be present without even existing.
—WORDS SPOKEN BY BIANCA VANZINI

I was woken by a great ruckus, and through the sacristy window saw people running chaotically. The first thing that flashed through my mind was that we were under attack. It might be my own people, the VaChopi, with the intention of kidnapping the queen mother.

It was Rudolfo who explained what was happening. After the VaNguni delegation had left, it was discovered that the visitors had stolen all the metal stored in the shed. The boxes were empty. The metal type sets assembled to spread the word of God were now going to be used to make bullets.

At that point, Sergeant Germano emerged from his billet. He was quickly made aware of what had happened, and with a raised finger he warned the priest that he expected a full report on the robbery. He behaved as if he were the proprietor of the church. The priest dismissed the order with disdain. What importance did the disappearance of a few bits of metal have in the face of the news that the Portuguese had won a crushing victory at Magul?

Aren't you celebrating your army's triumphs? Rudolfo asked.

The news seemed to make the sergeant worry. Little did he care that six thousand enemy troops led by the odious Zixaxa had capitulated before a few hundred Portuguese soldiers. Little did it matter to him that his countrymen's machine guns had left four hundred dead on the plains of Magul. The only thing that Germano de Melo wanted to know about was the bits of stolen metal. Rudolfo looked the soldier in the eye and said:

I see fear in your soul, my son.

Then he turned his back. But the sergeant went after him: The priest shouldn't forget that, although injured, he had his sacred duties. And he would have to formally explain what had happened.

Explain? To whom?

I have my superiors.

The priest picked up a bucket to go and fetch water from the river. Halfway there, he suggested:

Go and see Imani, my son. You're in urgent need of someone to comfort you.

At that point, Bibliana passed by and, without stopping, addressed the delirious sergeant in Txitxope:

How many Bibles are there, my young soldier? One for the English, another for the Portuguese? One for the whites, another for the blacks? This God they say is the only god, what language does he speak?

The questions cascaded over him, and the Portuguese understood none of them. When he came toward me, it was obvious how deranged he was. His look was unrecognizable as he stretched out his arm toward my face:

That hair, Imani . . .

What about my hair?

Can't you straighten it?

Is it askew?

From now on, you must straighten it. I don't want it woolly because it's bad for my hands. Those damned curls get into my bandages and infect my wounds.

The fever has come back, I thought. But it wasn't a return to his previous state. There was a harshness in his expression that I had not seen before. Timidly, I stretched out my hand to stroke his hair. But he pushed me away abruptly. The Portuguese looked around him suspiciously, as if to make sure that no one was listening to us. Then he shot an unexpected question at me: Was Father Rudolfo worthy of our trust? In the face of my utter astonishment, he repeated insistently:

Isn't he involved with the blacks?

The blacks? I asked, astounded.

The sergeant did not realize the oddity of his words. And he was even beginning to doubt whether Rudolfo was really a priest.

Do you know this rogue's story?

It was fairly widely known in Sana Benene: Every morning, the priest looked at himself in the mirror. He was convinced that, day by day, his brown eyes were becoming blue. That he was shedding his race just as snakes shed their skin. And that he was becoming more and more like his Portuguese mother, whom he only knew from what people had told him.

I don't believe this fellow has a Portuguese mother. To tell you the truth, I don't know whether he has a mother at all, Germano declared.

Do you want to know who Rudolfo Fernandes is? There is no one better to tell you this priest's story.

Rudolfo Fernandes's mother was one of the so-called orphans of the king. After she was taken in at an orphanage in Lisbon, the Portuguese king sent her to Goa. In India, she was supposed to marry one of the few Portuguese men serving there. The intention was to maintain what they called "racial purity." In the case of Rudolfo's mother, this objective was not carried out: The orphan girl didn't choose a white man, but an Indian of much darker skin. The son of this unusual couple was placed in the seminary in Goa, which was where he received his religious education. When he had completed his education at the seminary, the Portuguese authorities sent him from India to Mozambique, for there were no more than half a dozen priests in the whole territory capable of evangelizing in Portuguese, a civilized and civilizing language. The other Christians, the Swiss Calvinists, were spreading an erroneous version of God's word. They were encouraging the blacks to write in their own languages. They were teaching them to be Africans.

It was with the mission of counteracting these influences that Father Rudolfo landed at Makomani, a village on the coast. And this was how he landed in my childhood as well. At first the Goan was enthusiastic. The church was packed with people at mass on Sunday. The so-called natives keenly received their alphabet primers so that they could learn to read. The missionary believed that the Africans were diligently attempting to decipher the letters. How naïve he was! The older residents resorted to tearing pages out of the books to light fires in order to fry fish.

My father, Katini Nsambe, viewed catechism as more than just a religious conversion. It was a door that opened onto the white world. This was his intention: that I, Imani, should free myself from my origins, escape from myself and seek another destiny, without a return, a race, a past.

There was something of me in that stolen metal, I said, interrupting my long narration.

In order to counter the influence of the Protestants, Rudolfo decided to translate the Bible. For months I helped him convert the Portuguese into Txitxope. On one occasion I was even impertinent enough to doubt the book's holy character. Whoever wrote it and printed it, were they not mere mortals? For Rudolfo, the answer was simple and straightforward:

Books are never written. When we read them, we write them.

That book might not be holy. But it made people holy. This was what the priest taught us at catechism. However, neither the book nor his faith helped him preserve his lucidity and integrity. Far from Goa, and his people, the young clergyman began to lose his sense of reality. Various women slept with him in the church. He explained that this was the best way of administering their first Communion. His laxity, however, was not limited to carnal pleasure. The beach was the guardian of an accumulation of empty wine bottles along its waterline. The sea would seize these bottles round their midriffs and leave them bobbing, like solitary ballerinas, on the crests of the waves. According to the missionary, they were setting out on the journey back to the beaches of Goa. Empty, as empty as the man who had drained them.

Then one day he ordered me to stop my task of translating and return the Bible to him.

We don't need translation anymore. Nor do we need any more books.

Pointing to the river, the dunes, and the sea beyond, he declared: *This is my library.*

12

SERGEANT GERMANO DE MELO'S THIRD LETTER

The worst form of suffering is not defeat. It is not being able to fight.
—A PROVERB FROM NKOKOLANI

Sana Benene, September 9, 1895

Dear Lieutenant Ayres de Ornelas,

I know, sir, that following the Battle of Magul you returned to Inhambane, and I imagine that while rejoicing at such magnificent
news, you have not been aware of the events that I shall now relate.
It all began last night when the presence of an intruder roused the
dogs. People rushed outside to see what was happening. A black
man of the VaNdau group had staggered into the village. He was
wounded and bleeding from his chest and legs. Just imagine, sir, he
had survived a firing squad at Chicomo. He pretended to be dead
after falling to the ground. The soldiers were bending over his body
to make sure he was dead when a huge snake appeared from the
darkness, causing them to flee in chaos. Gravely injured, the man
climbed into a dugout, letting the current take him as far as Sana
Benene.

It was Mouzinho de Albuquerque who had sentenced him to
death, believing him to be one of Gungunhane's spies. He was told
to take all his clothes off so as to certify that he had all the traditional tattoos of our enemies. This was merely a minor delay in

carrying out the sentence. Whether or not he sported the insignia proving the guilt of his ethnicity, the wretched man was doomed. The mere fact that he had dared stray into the area abutting the garrison was sufficient proof.

It was a miracle that the kaffir managed to make it to Sana Benene alive. When Bibliana appeared, I noticed that there was something special happening between her and the survivor. The healer was dumbstruck as she contemplated the intruder, and then suddenly threw herself into his arms. *It's my brother-in-law, Manyara*, she announced tearfully. And arm in arm, the two of them went into the church. Everyone knew what they had to do: Imani went to boil water, Bianca went to fetch bandages and clean clothes, and the priest remained seated, looking at me with a fixed stare. *What's wrong, my son?* he asked me in a tone of paternal irritation. I reminded him that the kaffir was a prisoner who had been sentenced and should be escorted back to Chicomo and the judicial process. *To go back and get killed?* the priest asked with irony.

I further reminded him that, in allowing this to happen, we were the accomplices of a criminal. Rudolfo turned to me with unexpected aggressiveness:

This man was never here, do you understand? Bibliana is going to tend to him just as she tended to you, and afterwards he will go on his way just as you will go on yours.

I entered the church and smelled the aroma of infusions that I knew so well. The wounded kaffir occupied the bed in which I had spent my convalescence. I ordered the black to tell me what had happened at Chicomo. I was trying to establish whether he had admitted to being a spy when interrogated. It was Bibliana who, in her limited Portuguese, translated her brother-in-law's muttered statement: *My brother-in-law tells me he spoke his language, Xindau, and none of the Portuguese understood him.* Then the soothsayer commented that a similar mistake occurred more generally between whites and blacks:

Those whose language we do not understand are already confessing their guilt.

I could not stop thinking of your new instructions, sir. This was why, in spite of the healer's opposition, I insisted that the mistreated Negro should give me an account of the circumstances surrounding his arrest and subsequent flight. Amid groans and grimaces, the man recalled his hellish experience at Chicomo. When they dragged him over to the wall, Mouzinho de Albuquerque made his soldiers stop and reminded them that only whites could make up a firing squad. After the shots, the kaffir really thought he was dead. *I didn't have to pretend, I'm here because I was restored to life*, he mumbled. And he added, with just a flicker of a smile: *I returned thanks to my sister-in-law*. For two days he dragged himself along painful paths in order to give thanks to Bibliana, the widow of his late brother. It was she, with her spells, who had protected him against the bullets. And it would be thanks to the treatment of this *sangoma*—which is what they call healers around here—that he would recover from his grave wounds.

Exhausted and in pain, the man asked to be left alone. But before we withdrew, he muttered something that Bibliana translated. He was advising me to flee the area. He said that war was coming. And this was no place for either whites or those of his tribe, the VaNdau. We were both phantoms, and we stood out in that wilderness.

Dona Bianca agreed with the stranger's message and she gesticulated furiously, as if we needed to see her words rather than hear them:

The man is right. Run away from the army, Germano.

Do you know what they do to deserters? the priest warned bitterly.

But, Father, in the midst of this turmoil, who even knows of this man's existence? Bianca asked. *If no one paid him any attention before, when he was at his post, who is going to notice him now?*

Bianca and Rudolfo went on talking as if I were not present. I looked at Imani, but she averted her eyes. I understood. To be honest, I was barely aware of my own existence!

So these, sir, were the turbulent events that occurred here. I returned to my room and began to scribble this letter. And I spent the rest of the morning in an inexplicable state of inertia. I have to confess that I felt a deep yearning for Imani. At noon, I was told that Bibliana's brother-in-law had not survived his injuries. The last thing he asked for was for someone to come and sing to him in his mother tongue. I attended the initial preparations for his funeral. The priest called me aside to tell me that, as he was giving him the last rites—which, for kaffirs, is their baptism—the black had confessed to him that the charges against him were true. He had been working as a spy for weeks beforehand. He was sending Gungunhane information in exchange for the safety of his enslaved family at the court of Gaza. And this, sir, was when the priest made an extraordinary comment. I am writing his exact words: *There is certainly no shortage of spies out there. If we were to shoot all of them, maybe you would no longer be with us.*

There was, in the priest's words, a veiled suggestion I found unpleasant. It may have been due to my guilty conscience, but I was unable to sleep that night. The fact of the matter is that I was a spy by trial and error. What was more, I had failed in my trial. Rudolfo's words left me feeling truly helpless. Having regained the use of my hands, I now lacked my soul.

As night fell, when the rituals for the intruder were over, I knocked on Bibliana's door. I wanted to be shielded by the African spirits. I wanted to be protected from bullets, from loss of love, from my past, and from myself. No one should know what my intentions were, which is why I was desperate for Bibliana to attend to my muffled taps on her door with all possible haste.

The soothsayer was in a state of undress when she half opened the door, her firm breasts and thighs revealing themselves through the slit in her *capulana*. What happened after that, sir, will be of no interest to you. I shall, nevertheless, alert you to our need to keep a close watch on this polemical, charismatic figure. You cannot imagine the powerful influence that this witch exerts over the natives. You can be sure: No army can offer us more of a threat than this woman with her prayers and prophecies. I recommend that we keep this black woman under surveillance. It was not for this reason that I visited her, and I have already admitted to that. But the execution of her brother-in-law, the spy who ended up dying here at Sana Benene, does not place us in a favorable position. All we can assume is that Bibliana must feel considerable hostility toward the Portuguese.

In a word, we must keep a close eye on this woman. We need to know something about her past in order to see how we can turn her into our ally. In the following lines, I provide a brief outline of the life of the person in question.

Bibliana was born and until recently lived in a village near Chicomo. As is quite common here, she had another name, which is of no interest to us. Her father was taken as a slave, and her mother was killed trying to defend the family. For weeks the slave hunters searched the village to be sure that no one had escaped from their captivity and returned home. The slaves and slave owners were all of the same race, the same language, and had the same gods.

This was how, while still a young girl, Bibliana was left with only her maternal grandmother by way of family. The old woman had deformed legs and would be unable to escape in the event of an attack. At the end of each day, her granddaughter would place her in a gunnysack in case she had to be dragged out into the bush in an emergency. One night, the village was set on fire and Bibliana was obliged to abandon her grandmother whom she had vowed to protect. The girl fled and disappeared into the forest.

She was taken in some days later by the first Protestant missionaries to visit the region. None of them was European. The two Negroes were from the Transvaal and spread the gospel in African languages. During her catechism, Bibliana saw that her story was written in the sacred book. With the permission of the missionaries, she changed her name from the one she had been given as a child to the one by which she is known by everyone today. With the blessing of the missionaries, she married a fisherman in the village. Years went by and she never became pregnant. The husband had a right to abandon her. But he did not do so. Nor did he ever accuse her openly of being a barren woman. To demonstrate her gratitude, Bibliana worked tirelessly, hunting snakes and crocodiles in order to sell their skins. Her husband suspected that she might be a tamer of crocodiles. But she proved her truth by exhibiting her cutlass and traps.

With the money she saved, Bibliana bought her husband two new wives. These spouses produced children and the family began to take shape. During an attack on the village, her husband was killed by Ngungunyane's soldiers. As a widow, she thought the family would disintegrate. But this did not happen. The other wives remained with her, together with their children. Funnily enough, the little ones began to call Bibliana *Tate*, the word for "Father." The wives feared that the dead man's soul would be angry. But nothing happened. And Bibliana thought: I've had more good luck than I could have hoped for. Her sex, age, and widow's status did not permit such good fortune. Before long, people would accuse her of being a witch. So she made her decision:

Keep my house and possessions. I'm the one who's leaving.

Then she left for Sana Benene, where she met Father Rudolfo. And the certainty that her story was included in the Holy Book was no longer enough for her. She gradually came to assume that she was Our Lady:

The children I reared were not the other women's. They were mine. I'm like the mother of God: I was made pregnant by men I never went to bed with.

That was how this unusual woman settled at Sana Benene. The only mystery lies in how she came to be the queen of this place and of the priest's heart. But I shall explain that in another report.

13

BETWEEN BULLETS AND ARROWS

The river is a tear on its way back to God's eyes.
—WORDS SPOKEN BY CHIKAZI MAKWAKWA, IMANI'S MOTHER

My sleep was gnawed through by jealousy. I know of no more effective ruminant of one's soul: Jealousy is a windmill that turns even when there's not a breath of wind. The curious enthusiasm with which the sergeant told me about Mpezui some days ago was a false breeze. But now there was a real reason. My recollection of the previous night was a knife thrust into my chest: Sergeant Germano knocking at Bibliana's door late at night. Not a moment goes by without me remembering it. It was then that I heard the Portuguese begging to be treated, in a tremulous voice. Haughty and provocative, the woman asked:

But haven't I already treated you, my white friend?
I'm asking for another type of treatment.

Germano went in and the door closed. I stopped watching and listening. And I started to guess what was going on, knowing that the imagination is the sharpest of the senses. However, I had no time to torture myself. For moments later the same door opened again and Bibliana emerged into the yard dressed in the sergeant's uniform. She hesitated in the darkness and then, with a firm step, walked toward me. She offered me her hand and then led me over to her quarters, where the ashamed sergeant crouched gloomily in a corner covered only in a *capulana*. *We exchanged clothes*, Bibliana murmured, explaining the obvious. I immediately started to ask myself if they had exchanged anything else.

He came and asked me to shield him from bullets, Bibliana declared, pointing at the Portuguese. *This young brave of yours is scared.*

I'm in a panic, Imani, the sergeant stammered. *I've made enemies everywhere. I need help.*

Well, I'm not going to shield you, Germano.

And before the sergeant could protest, the *sangoma* continued:

Do your sums, my white friend. How many soldiers have died in this war? And how many women have been assaulted, raped, murdered? Now answer me this: Who has a greater need of protection?

And she stamped on the ground with her boots as if in the process of turning from a soothsayer into a soldier. Her hand clasped my shoulder firmly as she declared:

You don't need any ceremonies, my girl. You've long been immune.

Then, before our very eyes, she took off the uniform and returned it to the sergeant.

And you, my white friend, can keep that capulana, *which looks as if it was made for you*, she joked.

Then she told us both to leave and take advantage of the night, as she put it, to immunize ourselves even more.

I led the shivering Portuguese by the arm, making sure that he didn't stumble over the *capulana* wrapped around his body. *If the lieutenant saw me like this . . .* , he moaned, as we walked along. Once in the sacristy, I helped him lie down in his improvised bed. He held out his arms and asked:

Am I still bleeding?

I never found out. If his bleeding hadn't been stanched, he had certainly started to bleed inside me. And we fell asleep, our bodies touching each other.

The following day, the church was empty. The sergeant had gone out in the direction of the river. He had been fishing ever since the early morning. He had made a fishing rod out of an old rifle. He had been there for hours without catching a fish. But that mattered little to him. *Fishing* is a verb with a wide range of meanings. As wide and deep as the river.

I waited for the priest in the sacristy. And as the waiting grew longer, I lay down on the mat where we had slept. The places where we dream eventually become part of our body. In that bed, I still felt part of Germano. I was torn from these daydreams by the sound of footsteps inside the church and chairs being dragged around. I peered, apprehensive. I immediately saw that they were VaNguni soldiers. The one who appeared to be the chief sat down next to the altar. The others remained standing. It wasn't long before Father Rudolfo appeared, more hunched and demure than I had ever seen him.

Ngungunyane told us to come and fetch the two women: the white one and the other one you said was your husband, the leader of the delegation announced in Txizulu.

The intruders laughed so long and loud that the priest also smiled, pretending to join in the mocking of which he was the target. And his voice was so gentle that no one could understand what language he was speaking: *No one is leaving here* . . . And he repeated it, this time more spiritedly, adding: *not even over my dead body*.

Tie him to a chair and call the vultures, the leader of the group commanded.

It wasn't courage but some unknown force that caused me to emerge from the sacristy into the middle of the church. The men tying up the priest halted what they were doing, surprised. I recognized those strange figures as members of the feared *timbissi*, the so-called hyenas, the emperor's death squads.

Can you hear an arrow as it flies through the air? It is not by chance that they call the VaChopi the bow-and-arrow people. A Chope woman like me can hear the hiss of an arrow up to the point when it pierces a man's chest and he falls into the final abyss. Then, straight after this, a second arrow, and another fallen body. All this in fact happened as if in a dream.

It was then that reality burst into the church of Sana Benene with an almighty crash. Before our astonished eyes Xiperenyane, the most charismatic VaChopi warrior and the most feared of Ngungunyane's enemies, appeared. With his own hands, Xiperenyane freed the priest while giving the order for the bodies of the VaNguni to be removed.

The house of God cannot receive the blood of the devil, were his words.

Ever since I was a child, I have learned to distinguish that unmistakable sound of a body being dragged along. It was as if the friction of the act robbed the ground itself of life. The priest, freed from the ropes, but still sitting on the chair, seemed even more lifeless. Xiperenyane walked up to the last of the brigade's survivors and challenged him face-to-face, saying:

Do you remember me, Manhune? I grew up alongside your king, I lived in your domains until I reached manhood. And I escaped in order to continue being a person.

He had been the victim of the age-old tactic used by the VaNguni to make an effective army. They seized young boys and took them away from their native land, making them forget their families and the bonds of love they once had. And from among their oppressors, they concocted the only family left to them. This tactic had not worked in the case of Xiperenyane. The Chope warrior was passing through Sana Benene on his way back from the Battle of Magul, where he had fought alongside the Portuguese.

I've still got the blood of your people on my hands. You're going to have to take great care when you count how many of your soldiers made it back home.

And he made fun of the most bellicose squadrons of VaNguni soldiers who, according to him, arrived full of plumes and left with their feathers plucked. Then he addressed the emissary of the king of Gaza in Txizulu.

So you came to steal women for your king, did you? Well, so that you shouldn't leave empty-handed, take him this message from me: Tell him my nails are long like the claws of a lizard. Wherever I am, and without having to take so much as a step, I shall tear at his sleep every night.

You know that I cannot take that message, the other answered. *No one can.*

You're a slave, Manhune. It isn't a king that's your master. It's fear.

Manhune was an eminent military commander and adviser to Ngungunyane. He did not abandon his haughty demeanor when he withdrew. As he passed the Portuguese priest, he joked:

You can relax, Father, we shan't be taking your husband away for the time being.

14

FOURTH LETTER FROM LIEUTENANT AYRES DE ORNELAS

Ayres de Ornelas himself admitted his ignorance, for as he himself
wrote: "Although this may seem strange, no mention was made
whatsoever of colonial campaigns during my time at the Military
School. The Provisional Regulations for the Service of Armies on
Campaign, of 1890, had nothing to say on the matter. How were we to
wage combat, how did our adversaries wage combat?
We had not the faintest idea."
—AYRES DE ORNELAS, "A COLLECTION OF HIS PRINCIPAL MILITARY AND COLONIAL WORKS,"
VOL. 1, GENERAL AGENCY FOR THE COLONIES, 1934, CITED BY PAULO JORGE FERNANDES IN
"MOUZINHO DE ALBUQUERQUE: A SOLDIER IN THE SERVICE OF
THE EMPIRE," A ESFERA DOS LIVROS, LISBON, 2010

Chicomo, September 16, 1895

Dear Germano de Melo,

Our good friend Xiperenyane will be the bearer of good news, my
dear sergeant: we won the Battle of Magul, and in no uncertain fashion! The secret of our success lay in a prior detail that no doubt few
will remember. This detail has a name: the local headman Chibanza.
Let me now tell you what happened. When we drew near to Magul,
we took four days to cross an inferno of pools, mud, and mosquitoes.
With the few men we had at our disposal, and using just two donkeys
and two horses, we were obliged to pitch camp in a spot that had no

shelter or vegetation, and which was saturated with water. Groups of enemy soldiers could be seen in the distance. But they seemed unaware of our presence. We sent out a few Angolans to provoke them and try to force them to attack our position. This was something I had already learned—the only way we could move with any security among those multitudes was by pretending to be a tortoise with a shell on all four sides. And we certainly could never take the initiative of openly marching against our adversaries. On the contrary, they were the ones who should attack us.

At Magul, however, neither one thing nor the other occurred. Our forces remained at a standstill. And the enemy forces would not budge either. As I have already said, we obliged the Angolans to make an incursion by way of provocation, but this plan did not have the desired effect. Or rather, it had an effect, but not the one we expected. Apart from the two thousand soldiers we had caught sight of, we began to hear a crescendo of chanting and the syncopated crash of spears striking shields. And suddenly, the entire skyline was filled with some seven thousand warriors advancing towards us in a kind of war dance. Their intention was obvious: to lay siege to us in the middle of that swamp and watch us starve to death. Never had a platoon wanted to be attacked so much. Then, when we had already lost hope that anything would change, we saw the local chieftain Chibanza emerge from our ranks carrying a rifle. With a firm, solemn step he advanced toward the Vátua hosts. Next to me, a soldier commented: *That black son of a bitch is going to give himself up to his brothers!* To our growing surprise, he climbed to the top of a huge termite mound. And from that improvised platform he launched into a violent speech, laden with insults against Gungunhane. The Vátuas protested and jeered but they allowed the chieftain to continue his tirade of invective. When he had finished, Chibanza fired seven shots into the Vátua horde. Then he spat on the ground and hurled the ultimate abuse: *Cowards!* After this, he returned to our lines. Chibanza's display of bravado had the desired effect. A rabid human wave rushed toward our position. The Vátuas were unleashing their assault. The blacks threw themselves, bare-chested, against the crackling of our machine guns. And the fighting was all over in a few minutes. Enemy casualties were so many that it was impossible to count all the bodies scattered among the grass. But I was unable to count our own dead either. I was told that there were no more than about thirty and most of those were Negroes from Angola. Nevertheless, when the time came to collect them up and lay them in the ground, there were not enough tears in my eyes for so much pain. Each one of those young men was part of me and the guilt of losing them will weigh upon me for the rest of my days.

And then there was more pain to add to my guilt. As soon as the enemy had retreated, the forces of the local headmen of Matola and Mahotas, on seeing the fragility of the defeated army, pillaged the houses, women, and cattle belonging to Mahazul's and Zixaxa's people. It is impossible to imagine the desolation in which the ravaged territories were left. It was a quarrel among themselves, the blacks, but I cannot help thinking that it was we who facilitated such devastation. For my colleagues, such gruesome pillages were greeted as encouraging news. As far as they were concerned, the desire for vengeance on the part of Mahazul's and Zixaxa's folk had now become greater than the hostility they previously felt toward the Portuguese.

The most experienced military commanders in Africa were, after all, completely correct in their argument for a slow, cautious advance. At first, I confess, I did not understand (or I understood but I did not respect) the wise counsel of that old fox who goes by the name of Caldas Xavier. According to this experienced strategist, one should not engage the Vátua army in open attack, for it was preferable to surround it with a belt of fortified military posts that would gradually squeeze the life out of it. If the enemy, realizing the threat, elected to react, all the better, because, as Xavier assured us, the Vátuas did not need to be feared when they went on the offensive. It was even good to provoke them. And Caldas Xavier even recommended that these posts should be built in such a way as to appear vulnerable, to encourage the enemy to attack them. Who knows whether that post of yours at Nkokolani wasn't in such a degraded condition in order to conform to this tactical recommendation?

However, this whole plan, no matter how sound its basis, had one fatal flaw as far as I was concerned. It was going to take time. And I was in a hurry. I was recently qualified and young, and had just arrived in Mozambique, with an aspiration to rise in the hierarchy as quickly as possible. I was one of those who argued in favor of an attack at Magul. And I am proud of my gamble. But that final battle proved another principle: In war, those who are in a hurry, die in a hurry. Caldas Xavier was right; we are not facing an army but rather a people armed with weapons.

Let me give you a piece of advice, Sergeant. Do not reveal yourself as being so fragile, so human, and so equal to the kaffirs. You, my dear sergeant, are a white, and for the time being, at any rate, you are still a soldier. You are wounded, and in isolation. But you must not open your heart to the natives, weep or laugh with them, and above all, you must not show love for a black woman.

Caldas Xavier was correct in his long-term strategy. Magul should never have happened. But it did, and we emerged from it with tremendous advantage. For we need to carry out daredevil actions. These audacious deeds are not only to intimidate rebellious kaffirs. They will also impress public opinion in Portugal, which has a dim view of the fortunes being spent on a distant, remote war. And of course, other European nations will be made aware of our effective dominion in East Africa.

We no longer need envy our own past, were the words of one soldier after the Battle of Magul.

15

WOMEN-MEN, HUSBANDS-WIVES

I had a dream.
But it was a sightless dream.

I saw a path
But it was a craggy path.

I lived until I was old.
But I died before starting to live.

—A SONG FROM NKOKOLANI

That night, Father Rudolfo Fernandes came looking for me so that
he could tell me about his linguistic oversight when he had referred
to Bibliana as his "husband." We laughed, and I tried to make light
of the matter. *Don't worry, it was just a mistake.* But the priest admitted that his relationship with Bibliana was very strange. He made a
point of sharing with me the secrets of his liaison with her.

Our dear Bibliana, he began, *looked after the church the moment she
arrived at Sana Benene. There were a thousand versions of how she came
to be here. Some claimed that she had emerged from the waters of the river,
others that she had come out of the earth like a blind snake. What is sure
is that the woman came to me, offering her services as a domestic.*

The priest accommodated her in a shed at the back of the church. They spoke in Txichangana and they would pray together on the banks of the river. Bibliana always addressed God in an un-Catholic way, which was perhaps why the priest at first did not allow the woman to say her prayers inside the church. In the house of God, the black woman just saw to the cleaning of the building.

Late one afternoon, Bibliana heard chanting coming from inside the church. She entered quietly. With his back to the entrance, the priest was standing in prayer before the altar. Bibliana approached him, and embraced the man from behind, as if she were a shadow returning to its body. She allowed her hands to wander over the clergyman's cassock. She anxiously sought the bulge of his sexual organ. But she found nothing, no bump, not even the suggestion of a protuberance. She decided to look farther up and as she was fumbling his chest, she found two unexpected outthrusts. She took off his cassock, pulling it over his head. When Rudolfo appeared stark-naked before her, she did not look at all surprised: The priest had the body of a woman. Terrified, Rudolfo stammered:

I'm not really like this, my daughter. I'm like all the other men. I don't know what's happening.

But I know, Father. You have turned into a woman because of me. You became like this when you touched me.

May God protect me, but this can only be a punishment.

It's the opposite, Father. This is the only way we can make love.

She added in a whisper: The priest was an *impundulu*, a man who loves like women. He was one of those men who, when they make love, change into a woman.

Don't say any more, Bibliana. God has abandoned me to the most obscure of fates.

But his strange visitor did not stop talking. An *impundulu*, she explained, is a prince, but he has no sexual organ. Instead of a penis, he has a tongue that sticks out of his body like a slow, dark river. This tongue was made for kissing, licking, sucking. The *impundulu* is like a wingless bird but which has soft, abundant plumage. If a woman is caressed by so much as a feather, she lights up like a torch. And her fire can only be placated by a fire of equal force.

Am I one of these creatures, then?

You are one of my creatures.

The woman moved her hand to the gap between Rudolfo's legs. Alarmed, the clergyman held his breath. Then Bibliana muttered the following pronouncement in the perplexed missionary's ear:

Now you're going to bleed. Every new moon, you will see your own blood.

The priest fell to his knees and closed his eyes, as if this were the only way he might contemplate Heaven.

The following morning saw Bibliana bustling around in a state of great animation. She even asked me to help her in her tasks as an exorcist. Xiperenyane had stopped by at Sana Benene on his way to Zavala, with a view to subjecting himself and his men to the rituals of purification that Bibliana called *kufemba*. They had come from the Battle of Magul contaminated by death. There would be no return unless they were cleansed internally.

It involved a whole day's work. One by one, the warriors sat down next to the soothsayer's mat and watched her throwing her little magic bones to see whether they bore the spirits of those they had killed. The bearers of other people's spirits were then seated on the riverbank. The blood of a goat was poured over them, and the *capulanas* that they wore around their waists were cast into the current. In this way they were unbound from the past, and the dead could not return from death to avenge themselves on the living.

By the time all these ceremonies were over I was exhausted, as if some of those spirits had dug their claws into me. Divesting myself of my clothes, I washed in the river. It was a pity Xiperenyane was not there to see me. He was a handsome man. For a moment I forgot about my desire for Germano de Melo.

16

FIFTH LETTER FROM LIEUTENANT AYRES DE ORNELAS

The black does not obey us, or respect us, or even know who we are in most of that province. This is the truth in all its crudity and so many and such frequent occurrences demonstrate this fact that no manner of protest or invocations to past glories can invalidate this.
—J. ALBUQUERQUE, "THE ARMY IN THE EASTERN COLONIES," 1893

Inhambane, September 24, 1895

Dear Sergeant Germano de Melo,

I am deeply disappointed in you, my dear sergeant. You are one of the reasons why I have not yet become sufficiently known to my superiors in the hierarchy. Let me ask you this: Despite all the letters you have sent me, what useful information of the sort I requested have I yet received? Spies have passed your way without you alerting me to them in time; you are going to be tended by a doctor who is our enemy; you spend your time in a church full of black heretics. Is all this just the result of lapses in concentration, mere inattentiveness? And to make matters worse, you persistently call a black a "king" when he merits little more than the epithet of "headman." You talk about "dynasties" and the "royal blood" of the Vátuas, as if the concept of an aristocracy could be extended to Africans. I assume that for you, an out-and-out republican, all these observations make little sense.

You must be made aware that you are not only insulting the monarchy, which both I and Mouzinho represent along with so many other officers. In truth, we are an army of poor, humble folk commanded by aristocratic monarchists. I would like to put the following on record: I am a descendant of the Lords of the Estate of Caniço on my father's side and of the Count of Ponte on my mother's. Our families are proud of the ancient military traditions of which they are the bearers. You, I imagine, benefited from a very sound education. But there are ways of behavior and customs, the possession of which cannot be put down to effort but to the distinction of breeding. To aggravate this whole world of differences, you got involved in a love affair with a black woman. As if this weren't enough, you have been ignoring my instructions and persist in maintaining a liaison with a girl who, as well as being of too black a race, is too young. And I am concerned to see that your romance has gone beyond a merely casual encounter.

Let me say this without beating about the bush: As a soldier, you are a disaster. You spend too much time thinking, you ask yourself whether the war is a legitimate one, and you are devoid of any career ambitions. Moreover, you have lived for so long and so intimately among Africans that you have even discovered traces of humanity in them. I myself have to admit that on the occasions when I have allowed myself to get near these people, I have ended up making mawkish confessions, such as in the letter I wrote my mother telling her of my intense emotion on hearing the sublime chants of the Vátuas. I can therefore speak from my own experience when I say that all these emotive situations weaken a soldier by rendering him feeble and indecisive. And this is all the more serious because, by occurring in the middle of a war, this type of promiscuity eventually blurs the borders between our territory and that of the adversary.

For all this, let me formally communicate the following to you. You are released from having to send me any more reports, and your functions as my informer are suspended forthwith. With the clumsiness you have already displayed, you would only cause me problems.

I sincerely lament that our epistolary relationship should end in this way. Do not write to me again. Any messenger reaching me under your orders will be immediately detained and receive due punishment.

P.S. Two days have passed since I composed these brief paragraphs. I have had the opportunity to reconsider and I acknowledge that I exceeded myself in the curt and intransigent tone with which I addressed you. I shall not delete or make any alterations to what I wrote. However, now that I am less impulsive and more discerning, I shall make the following recommendation: From time to time, but only very sparsely, you may share your adventures and misadventures with me, Sergeant. No more than this. And no longer as sergeant. Germano de Melo will suffice. Please abstain from spying on the enemy, whom you have difficulty in distinguishing anyway. It will be enough for you to speak to me as a human being.

17

SERGEANT GERMANO DE MELO'S FOURTH LETTER

Such is our wretched fate: We end up yearning for the previous tyrant.
—THE WORDS OF FATHER RUDOLFO FERNANDES

Sana Benene, October 1, 1895

Dear Lieutenant Ayres de Ornelas,

You are right, sir. As a soldier, I am worthless. Still less talent have I as a spy. Thank you for your letter, even though your comments on me as a person are not flattering. But when you, sir, present yourself to me only as Ayres de Ornelas, that is when I benefit from being in the noblest company. That is why your words did not discredit me. On the contrary. When I read the closing words of your brief missive, I received the most precious of prizes.

I am eternally grateful to you for having dismissed me from my duties as a spy and for having encouraged me to continue sending you these clumsy personal messages. That is the purpose of this letter. And you will see that my accounts will enable you to envisage the African interior as something more than a mere landscape. Maybe I am a second Diocleciano das Neves, the white man who mingled in the world of the natives and who never returned from that world. They called that pathfinder Diocleciano "Mafambatcheca," the One Who Laughs While He Travels. I do not laugh or travel. But I shall embark on a journey into the depths of the African soul. See my letters as an account of this journey. The continuation of my letters will save me from dying and disappearing forever from the memory of men.

On this occasion, I shall tell you of a mysterious meeting I had this morning. I was strolling along the riverbank with Imani when a little boy came up to us to ask when my wings would grow back. I thought I had misunderstood him, given my paltry grasp of the kaffir language:

My wings? I asked.

The ones that got cut off, he explained.

Imani sat down next to the child and I cannot tell you what was said. But I could tell that they were talking about me and at one point the boy imitated a bird flying around me, while he called me a *chapungu*. My companion took the kid's hand and made his little fingers brush the sparse bandages that are still left on my arms. The child was scared at first, but then burst out laughing. The pieces of gauze dangling from my wrists had been interpreted as the remains of my wings. I was not, after all, a *chapungu*, one of those eagles that never lets go of its feathers. And the boy laughed, half relieved, half disappointed.

Those bursts of laughter made me realize that you, sir, are right. As a soldier, I am a complete failure. But let me tell you this. If, in order to be a good soldier, one cannot have any doubts, I would rather my career stopped right here as a lowly sergeant, who was so utterly forgotten by the army that he ended up oblivious to the purpose of the uniform he wore.

The incident of the boy who took me for a bird is a mere preliminary to the account of a more serious and urgent matter that came to light later in the day. I surprised Katini Nsambe and the Italian woman, Bianca Vanzini, in the middle of a conversation. Katini was asking her to take his daughter Imani to Lourenço Marques and get her to make some money off white men. He argued that the girl was pretty, docile, and light-skinned. The Italian woman would not regret it. Bianca answered that she was not in a position to agree to his request, for she was only the proprietor of some bars. To which Katini replied imploringly: *Well, take her to one of your bars.* But the wretched kaffir had never been in a city. In those bars, the prostitutes were all white. The black women only worked in liquor stores out in the native areas.

Gradually the Italian woman became less adamant, and promised to give the matter some thought. The following day, she openly brought the subject up with me, as if she owed me an explanation. She confessed that it had also crossed her mind to take Imani with her to Lourenço Marques. And all the more so on that first night, when she had seen her without any clothes on. Katini's request made complete sense; white prostitutes were losing ground against colored women who were competing with them. When she saw me horrified and lost for an answer, she encouraged me to visit the lively bars of Lourenço Marques. She told me the names of establishments, the International Music Hall, the Tivoli, the Trocadero, the Bohemian Girl, the Russian Bar, and so many others.

In this part of Africa, European visitors felt as if they were in Lisbon, Paris, or London. With a few pounds, one could purchase the sympathy of women of a thousand nationalities, even if most of them were exhibiting a fake identity. Bianca mentioned names as diverse and exotic as Dolly, Kitty Lindstrom, Fanny Scheff, Helen Drysdale, Sarah Pepper, Blanche Drummond, Cecília Laventer. If she were to contract Imani, she repeated, she would be contravening the established rule: white women in the city bars; black in the suburban liquor stores. But Bianca was amused by the idea of disobedience, in a world that was already so disobedient to the laws of God. *I'll call her Black Lilly,* she announced. I told her to stop. She didn't understand my reaction. She thought I didn't like the name. I complained that Imani, the interested party to all this, had been forgotten.

Has anyone heard Imani's view on this? I asked.

Since when have women been consulted? she retorted. *Imani would be much happier on her own. In your hands, if that is what one can call those appendages at the end of your arms, the girl would merely be a white man's wife. In my hands, she'll be a queen.*

And she added that we both knew—from our own experience—that white men would lose their prejudices when they saw black women sparkling in the city bars. As for the white women, they would be the ones to worry, swept aside by competition. The only problem, Bianca declared, was that black women soon grow fat and flabby. They need to be recruited very young, before they bear children and go to seed. Young, beautiful, and single, Imani fulfilled all the requirements to have a long, lucrative career.

I listened to her plans with my heart in tatters. If I were not now disabled, I would seize this woman and take her off to a place I suspect does not exist.

You are still right, sir. I have no idea what it would be like to be married to a black woman. In spite of this, I allow myself to dream of it. Yesterday, when I was broaching the subject with Imani, she said something that seems irrefutable: Our two worlds were not after all so different. And she is right. Whether in Africa or in my little village in Portugal, women share the same meager expectations of what it might be like to be married. Nothing is expected of a husband. So he can never disappoint. When it comes to a woman, she is expected to be a mother. Not to any children she may choose to have. But to those who, by God and Nature's command, are born to a man from whom nothing is expected.

You might wonder, sir, what children we would have. How would we introduce them to their Portuguese relatives? The person who gave me the answer was not Imani, but Bibliana, who proclaimed with the certainty of a prophet: *What does the skin color of those who are born matter? Gungunhane will have white Portuguese grandchildren and the Portuguese will have African grandchildren! To seek to hinder this inclination is like trying to stop the wind with a sieve. Time, my son, Time is a great blender of seeds.*

For all these reasons, the first thing I shall do in the morning is to ask for a mass to be said so that God, from whom I have distanced myself, may guide me and help me to recover from my fevers. The church at Sana Benene may be small, solitary, and decrepit. Its priest may be a deviant. But a church, wherever it is, is a little piece of home. Even I, who am not a practicing worshipper, find in the peace and quiet of churches the place where my original soul is born again.

18

A MASS WITHOUT A VERB

You will live forever with these thick scars. But the truth is this: Scars protect far more than the skin. Were I to be reborn, I would ask to come into the world covered in scars from head to foot

—THE WORDS OF FATHER RUDOLFO SPEAKING TO SERGEANT GERMANO DE MELO

The sergeant's voice was barely audible as he stood in front of the priest, who was sweeping the floor of the church. Even I, who was holding him, had to lean forward to hear what he was asking. When Father Rudolfo eventually understood him, he could not contain his astonishment:

A mass?

The priest looked closely at the sergeant as if not recognizing him. He hadn't been asked for prayers for years. He stopped sweeping and leaned the broom against the wall with such care that it seemed as if he were positioning a buttress. And then he gazed in rapture at the clouds of dust that still floated in the musty air of the church. This was the only reason why he swept the temple: in order to see the rays of light flickering in the building. They are my windowpanes and they are alive, he thought.

Father, did you not hear my request? Germano insisted.

Some natives are fascinated when they look at the windows, the priest thought. They've never seen a pane of glass. They are captivated by something that can be touched without seeing it, this vertical water, this pure transparency. Rudolfo had been born in a modern city, and had become used to glass windows from an early age. However, the first time he really *saw* a sheet of glass was when he watched the rain trickling down the windowpane one day. And now the sergeant's words were trickling down the pane of his inattention.

Father Rudolfo? Can you hear me? I'm asking you to pray for me, Father, the soldier repeated.

My son, after all you have been through, do you still think God is alive?

The priest turned his back and was on the point of leaving, when I threw myself onto my knees before him and begged:

If you won't pray for Germano, then ask God to allow me to do it.

Surprised, the priest took a deep breath and then bade me help him. I still clearly recalled the times when, as a child, I helped in the rituals of the mass. And so I did what I had done before: I took a missal from the sacristy, a bell, a metal cup, and a bottle of wine. I helped the priest up onto the pulpit overlooking the altar, a task he fulfilled as if he were scaling the steepest slope. Leaning over me, he whispered that the person who normally used this for conducting services was Bibliana. The crowds who, every Sunday, filled the building, came only to attend the black priestess's cult.

Once up on the platform, the priest's eyes roamed around the empty space. He still remembered the first time Bibliana contemplated Christ nailed to his cross. She seemed concerned, and remarked: *He should have got married, that man Jesus, just look at how thin he is.* Then Bibliana's gaze lingered on the feet of the crucified man. It was in his feet that the Son of God began to shed his race and assume the kinship of the meek.

I rang the little bell, more to summon Rudolfo back to reality than to begin the mass. With his back to me, the priest waited for the echo of the bell to cease before raising his arms before Christ on the cross. He remained like this for some time without uttering a word. Until he turned around and faced the sergeant, who was waiting on his knees, with a puzzled look:

A mass?

Yes, please, Father . . .

Let me ask you, my son: Didn't Bibliana alleviate your pain?

The sergeant's despair must have eventually convinced the priest, who opened the missal and leafed through it slowly, from back to front and from beginning to end. Until, with an extravagant gesture, he put the book down on the lectern. He looked up at the pigeons flapping up in the roof and sighed as he declared:

Not a psalm or a prayer. I'm not going to read anything. And he concluded in a tired voice: *Life must be read through the scars, like those scars you now carry on your body and in your soul. If I were to be reborn, I would want to enter the world covered in scars.*

On hearing these words, the sergeant burst into tears. The priest descended from his pulpit in order to comfort him:

Are you unhappy because you've lost your hands? It wasn't just now that you lost them. You lost your body the moment you arrived in Africa.

On days of infernal heat, Rudolfo continued, it is not we who sweat through the pores in our skin. It's the devil. Was the sergeant not recognizable from the smell emanating from him? And why not? Because the sweat wasn't his, that sulfurous odor didn't belong to him. It didn't belong to him or to anyone else. There hadn't been anyone inside the soldier for a long time now. In this way, the less body we have, the lighter the death we'll have to face. *Do you understand, my son?* Bewildered, the poor sergeant didn't understand a word. But no matter how obscure all this seemed to him, it came laden with a kind of divine allure. The Portuguese nodded his head respectfully.

There was, however, no need to feel depressed. While all this might have the resemblance of misfortune, it had its benign aspect as well, the priest declared by way of a conclusion. He should think of the obvious advantages: He would be released from his military service. And he would be sent back to Portugal without his uniform and the obligation to kill.

Isn't that what you want? Isn't that what any soldier dreams of? To go home?

I don't know, Father. I've been so confused, the sergeant replied, holding back his tears.

What for Rudolfo was a word of comfort sounded to me like a punishment. The thought of Germano returning to Portugal hurt like a dagger thrust to my chest. *To return* is a strange verb. One who returns does so because he is awaited. And the sergeant did not have anyone waiting for him on the other side of the ocean.

I don't know what I want anymore, Germano added. *I want Imani, I want my hands, I want to return, I want to stay.*

With all these doubts of his, it was essential that his evacuation to the garrison at Chicomo should be avoided at all costs. If Germano turned up there, at the military post, damaged and debilitated, he would be transferred immediately to Lourenço Marques. And from there they would repatriate him to Lisbon, far away from me. This was what I argued with heart and soul before the hesitant sergeant. The priest calmed me down:

We're not going to send him to the garrison at Chicomo. He will be safer at the Swiss hospital. There are no Portuguese *there.*

Even Bibliana considered this the best course of action. Although noticeably better, Germano de Melo was still assailed by fever and delirium. The sorceress had done as much as she could. The patient bore with him spirits from across the ocean.

Send the patient to those who pray, Bibliana declared.

Throughout the region, the Swiss Protestants were known as "those who pray." Local folk listened to their singing in large, tuneful choruses during Sunday services. According to Bibliana, the great energy of those sonorous voices can be explained by the fact that whites only worship one god. In their songs, they are comforting their god condemned to eternal solitude. And it is out of shame that they close their eyes when they sing his praise. So that God isn't revealed to them as being fragile and wanting.

There was an additional reason for hastening Germano de Melo's departure from Sana Benene. The priest mentioned it as he tore a page from the missal in order to roll a cigarette. It was not tobacco that he was preparing, but *mbangue* leaves and seeds, which he smoked without any remorse, arguing that it was God who had sown this miraculous plant.

The first puffs flooded the church with a sweet, intoxicating aroma. With a voice masked by coughing, the priest declared:

There are soldiers coming . . .

I sighed resignedly. There were too many soldiers there already. There were nothing but soldiers in those bushlands: blacks, whites, children and the elderly, the living and the dead, all of them carrying weapons. The priest guessed my silent doubts and explained:

They are our soldiers, the Portuguese. They arrive tomorrow, led by Santiago Mata, a man devoid of a human soul.

Then he held out the weed for the sergeant, who refused the offer energetically, raising his truncated arms as if a revolver were being pointed at him. The priest smiled indulgently. And he spluttered rather more than he spoke as he said:

Tomorrow, you'd better hide in the sacristy. Your superiors are going to want to take you to Chicomo.

My brother Mwanatu looked like a ghost when he appeared at the door of the church. He was excited, his eyes seeming bigger than his face. Before coming in, he did a kind of military salute and then, standing before the altar, he did the sign of the cross over his stomach. After this, he opened and closed his mouth without producing any sound whatsoever. The priest scolded him impatiently:

For God's sake, Mwanatu, you don't even cross yourself correctly!

Father, my brother stammered, *I want to say you something* . . .

It's not "say you something." It's "tell you something" . . .

Our father joined us, approaching from the rear of the building. Dragging his feet, he walked up to his son and examined his face with the curiosity of an eagle. He was obliged to wait until my brother managed to articulate a word.

Sergeant, something terrible has happened, Mwanatu eventually announced. *Nkokolani no longer exists. They killed everyone, they burned everything.*

The shock of this news caused me to collapse on the stone paving of the church. During the long silence that ensued, I lay on the floor as if searching for some earthly remnant of reality. I crumbled flakes of paint between my fingers that had fallen from the wall. To everyone's surprise, Mwanatu spoke again in a voice that was firm and serene:

I'm going there.

Where? my father, Katini Nsambe, asked.

I'm going to Nkokolani to bury our dead.

You are a man, but I am your father. I'm the last of the Nsambes. I'm the one who must go and lay the land to rest.

However, Mwanatu had everything planned. He had spoken to some fishermen who were waiting for him down at the landing stage. He had a bag, packed and ready, at the door. Our father could go later. Father Rudolfo would get a place for him in another boat.

Now let's pray for those who died, my brother urged.

I looked at Mwanatu as if I no longer knew him. Something must die in order for us to reveal ourselves reborn and integral. My weak, doltish brother now reemerged as a calm, eloquent man.

Returning from his feverish ravings, the sergeant took his young sentry in a leisurely embrace. Then, in a fraternal tone, he advised him:

Take that uniform off, Mwanatu. It could be dangerous. You could be taken for a Portuguese soldier.

I am a Portuguese soldier. I'm not going to abandon my weapon, and he pointed to the rifle leaning by the entrance to the church.

Did you bring that from Nkokolani? the sergeant asked. *Why on earth did you do that? That weapon doesn't work. It never did.*

Yes, it does. Who said it doesn't work?

My father held out his arm and helped me to my feet. It was only then that I noticed the tears streaming down my face. *Wipe that face of yours*, my father ordered. *Crying in a church shows a lack of respect.* Then he addressed my brother:

If the VaNguni have already buried our dead, you know what you've got to do. Dig them up and proceed according to our traditions.

I shall do that, Father.

We knew how the VaNguni treated those they had defeated. They were to be humiliated even in death. They buried us, the VaChopi, just as they did with slaves: They would wrap them in a mat and throw them into a common grave. The bottom of this anonymous hole was covered with other slaves in their death throes, legs broken. On top of this heap of dead and dying, they threw earth which, in the end, they stamped on persistently, to leave no indication that the soil there had been disturbed. This was how they proceeded. And there was a purpose to it: Without a grave, they made sure that the slaves left no recollection. Otherwise the living memory of the dead would haunt their masters forever.

And what shall I do with Mother? Mwanatu asked.

With Mother? I asked, astonished.

If they killed her, where shall I bury her?

Mother had died months before. I didn't correct him. At that moment, reality was of little importance. And our father, Katini Nsambe, seemed to share my reaction when he solemnly declared:

If they killed her, I am the one who will bury her. Leave that task for when I get there.

Mwanatu was sitting polishing his boots. This was the last of his tasks before departure. He looked at me lingeringly and commented that, seen against the sunlight, I reminded him of our mother.

It wasn't the first time Mwanatu had confused me. He was inventing this likeness to protect himself from his inexplicable fears. The greatest of these fears was an old one. When he was little, he was scared I would go away. When I read him stories, he, overcome by a sudden fit, shouted for me to stop.

I never told you why, Mwanatu commented, putting his boots down. *I was scared you would disappear into the book and never come back.*

Didn't you enjoy the stories?

Stories always have an end.

It might be a nice ending.

But it was always an outcome, he commented. Then the vast silence of leave-taking gripped us, that full stop that ends all stories we never tell.

I've got a favor to ask you, sister. Let me take your shoelaces. I'll give you mine.

I agreed. I slowly undid my laces, ignoring the strangeness of his request. When, at last, we completed the exchange, Mwanatu declared:

Now you'll show me the way, sister.

Then we joined the others in order that we should all go down together to where the boat was moored. Mwanatu went in front. I followed in his footprints as if no one had ever passed that way before.

On the little wooden jetty, as Mwanatu and I hugged each other, my voice failed me. Farewell is never a word. It is a bridge built of silence. The dugout disappeared around the bend in the river, swallowed by the dusk. I stayed on the bank waving, wrapped in a sudden shiver of cold.

And then everyone began to walk back to Sana Benene. I remained on the landing stage with the sergeant. For the first time, I took the initiative:

Come with me, Germano.

In silence, we waded into the tepid waters of the Inharrime. I told him I wanted a river to weep in. He hugged me clumsily and my shoulders shuddered, insecure but happy. Then the Portuguese suggested that we plunge into the river and remain underwater until we could no longer hold our breath. And that was what we did. When our lungs were bursting, we both returned to the surface. The Portuguese murmured: *Now kiss me.* I hesitated. A drop of water glimmered on the lips of the Portuguese. Our lips touched.

This is what the first kiss should be like, Germano said.

It was a kiss of hope and despair, as if each of us sought in the other a last breath of air.

This is what the first kiss should be like, he repeated.

The first?

All kisses. All kisses are the first.

19

SERGEANT GERMANO DE MELO'S FIFTH LETTER

There is an old legend in Goa that tells the story of an island and a boat. A fisherman was wrecked and sought refuge on a desert island. There he remained for years, shrouded in a permanent mist that robbed him of his horizon. One day, he realized that there was in fact no island. He was living on a boat. He hadn't noticed it before because he was blind. So blind that he hadn't even noticed he'd stopped seeing. Some time later, the fisherman was bitten by a gigantic fish. Then he realized that the boat where he was living was, in fact, the remains of one at the bottom of the sea. He discovered that he wasn't just blind. He was dead.
That was what was happening to us. We were dead in our exile in the African interior.
—A TALE TOLD BY FATHER RUDOLFO

Sana Benene, October 2, 1895

Dear Lieutenant Ayres de Ornelas,

For over two months now I have been stranded in the place, which, as the priest says, isn't a place at all. Bianca announced that she cannot take it anymore, and that she is going to leave at the first opportunity. I am also sick of it, tired. Yet I do not want to leave Sana Benene. Imani's sweet company holds me here. I cannot say that I have completely given up on my dream of returning to Portugal, the gift you so generously promised me, sir. I am divided. And these letters constitute the bridge between my conflicting desires.

Maybe this is why something strange and new is happening to me. Whenever I sit down in front of my papers, I find myself making the sign of the cross before writing. As if writing were a temple in which I found shelter from my inner demons. Do not therefore worry about answering me, sir. *To write* is an intransitive verb, my way of praying. And whoever prays knows there is no answer.

I spoke to Imani, sir, about your promise to take me back to Portugal as soon as you gained your promotion. She wanted to know what I had replied. I told her the truth. That I had first said yes, and then no. At first, Imani's reaction was surprising. Whispering, her lips brushing my ear, she asked: *Don't you want to go back home?* I replied that, for me, home no longer existed. For that reason, there was no going back. Then she added that if my love was strong, I should devise a solution that would enable her to travel as well.

My heart was stifled by an age-old suspicion. Without mincing my words, I asked her if her love for me was greater than her desire to escape. The girl smiled and answered evasively that those two desires were one and the same. Then she walked off, smiling to herself, leaving me with a doubt, the uncertainty I have already told you about. Am I being used so that Imani can get away from her native land? Is her surrender to me, along with all the dreams she had given me, merely make-believe? I can guess your answer, but would prefer that you keep it to yourself. I shall preserve my beliefs and passions intact. I learned from Bianca that love is a fire. When it's good, you come out of it singed.

I shall disobey you because of love, whether or not that love is false or true: I shall go to the Swiss hospital in spite of your wish that I should not, sir. That is what I shall do. And I am already aching from an anticipated yearning for the people who became the family that I never had. When I told Father Rudolfo about my nostalgia, he wrinkled his nose. And he said he no longer believed in love, yearning, or unselfish surrender. He didn't believe in anyone, even less so since he had made my acquaintance. Offended, I asked him to explain.

I read the letters you left scattered around in your room, the priest revealed. And then, his arms folded inside his sleeves, he asked: *Is there nothing you want to confess to me?*

I was still recovering from the shock of the priest's revelation when he took from the sleeve of his cassock something that I assumed at first to be a crucifix. Only afterwards did I realize it was a pistol. I raised my arms while Rudolfo contemplated the heavens and spoke:

God gave me this weapon. Even the Creator knew that words were not enough in lands that were so full of dangers and transgressions.

You can't have read my mail! I still dared to exclaim.

With his finger on the trigger, he twirled the gun clumsily around while he reminded me of our correspondence.

You revealed secrets about this parish, you denigrated people whose only concern was to look after your welfare. You even got to the point of suggesting that the Portuguese should keep a watch on Bibliana. You should be ashamed. That woman gave you back the hands you now want to stab her with?

I confess, sir, that I have never felt greater grief. And the priest didn't stop there:

Your boss asks you to find the rebels. Do we call rebels those who fight us in order that we shouldn't steal their land? Have you never asked yourself whether that is not the precise reason why we are here: to steal these peoples' land?

These peoples' land was stolen a long time ago.

The priest didn't seem to have heard me. For he kept gazing upward while upbraiding me sarcastically:

Now you can certainly tell your friend the lieutenant that there are weapons in this church.

All of a sudden, he tossed the pistol into my arms.

Keep it, he advised me. *You had better be armed, because here everyone wants to kill you. And if they let you go on living, it's because they need you to help them kill others like you.*

I got up and as I was about to walk away, I realized I didn't want to go anywhere. I fell helplessly to my knees, and cried my eyes out on that red sand. I cried as I had never cried before.

I found succor at last in Father Rudolfo's words. During his entire priesthood in Mozambique, he had witnessed incidents of such atrocity that one would need a whole new language to describe them. He had seen blood flowing down the swords of the Europeans. He had seen blood being wiped from the spears of tribes massacring other tribes.

Our attire is of no use, he concluded sadly. *Let us throw away our cassock and uniform.*

Then he invited me to sit down again. He had a memory he wanted to share with me. He recalled that a long time before, when he still celebrated mass, a Portuguese soldier passed through Sana Benene and sought confession. But the man was not forthcoming, and with a furtive look merely said, *I don't know.* And he shook his head as if trying to escape from bad thoughts. Then he got up and went to the door, avoiding any eye contact with the parish priest of Sana Benene. As he left, his face fell, and he muttered: *I don't know how many I killed, I lost count.* With their heads hung, the priest and the penitent remained without moving, incapable of looking at each other or exchanging a word. When we lose count of how many we have killed, there is no longer any sin, no longer any God. The soldier tried to cross himself but halted mid-gesture as if he had given up. The moment he turned the corner, a shot was heard. That was the first time Rudolfo saw the young soldier's eyes. After that, the priest never again had the courage to receive anyone's confession.

That was what had happened. And perhaps somewhere in the priest's soul it was still happening. That was that, and he slapped his hands on his knees, bringing that particular story to a close.

Fortunately, God has brought us other gifts by way of compensation, Rudolfo declared. *Take my Bibliana's body, have you had a good look at Bibliana?*

I cautiously avoided an answer. The priest challenged me: *Let me ask you, my friend, to take an imaginary journey with me*. First, I should picture an attack on a village. In the midst of this imagined scenario a woman, in panic, was attempting to escape from the fury of the attackers. At the height of her despair, the only refuge this woman could find was in a burning hut. By turning herself into a flaming torch, she escaped her assailants.

The priest was, of course, talking about Bibliana. Underneath her old clothes, her body was all burnt, a large area of her skin was lifeless, like a lizard's scales. This was the expression he used while he rubbed his fingers together as if the words were burning his hands.

The priest got up at last, and an odor of decay seeped from his vestments. Noticing my wry expression, he explained his grubbiness, saying he did not have water to wash with. For it was the inside of him that was rotting away: He was made of two halves that did not fit easily together. In India, he had been taught from birth to recognize the caste of the untouchables. The filth that he carried in his soul had now become a contagious illness. He had turned into an untouchable himself.

They say we are surrounded by enemies. But it is not the presence of others that threatens us. It is our own absence. That is what Father Rudolfo most lamented: the nonexistence of our authorities. He had traveled the vastness of the African interior from end to end, and all he had seen was a vast emptiness. Throughout these bushlands, the only people who in fact governed here were

Gungunhane's *indunas*. Apart from anything else, these kaffir agents of authority were the only ones who collected taxes. And it was they who received foreign emissaries. It was to these native authorities that Portuguese officials—such as the intendant, Counselor José d'Almeida—directed their requests for mining concessions. The Portuguese presence was so nonexistent that the intendant addressed Gungunhane as "Your Majesty." For his part, the African king called the Portuguese "chickens" or "white Shangaan."

I shall not take up any more of your time, sir. This account is already long and exhaustive. And I tell you all these things to show you how indifferent I have become to all these heated debates. I do not care who is in charge. For I am governed by other forces. The only law I obey is called love. It goes by the name of Imani Nsambe.

I do not know whether I shall be able to maintain this correspondence. The tiny stock of ink I found in the sacristy is running out. At Nkokolani, the only request I had for visitors was that they should bring me new pots of ink. Who can I ask now? I thought of using water. *Writing with water?* you may ask, sir, believing me to be still in the throes of some feverish hallucination. The truth is that the water at Sana Benene is so dirty that my handwriting would be easy to read. But yesterday the problem was solved when Imani brought me a pot of liquid of undefined hue, but which looked like some form of scarlet dye. She asked me to keep it a secret, but I cannot resist telling you: These letters have been written with an infusion of leaves and bark to which Imani told me she had added her own blood. In reality, what you are reading, sir, is the blood of a black woman.

20

THE WANDERING SHADOWS OF SANTIAGO MATA

Having reached its zenith, the kingdom of the VaNguni is on the point of collapsing completely. Nor could it be otherwise. This is the history of all dynasties founded on crime and terror. But in spite of everything, I am fond of Ngungunyane; in spite of his cruelty, I cannot but feel attached to him.
—GEORGES LIENGME, SWISS DOCTOR

We awoke to the sound of gunfire. We quickly crowded under the protective roof of the church. The priest placated us:

They must be Portuguese soldiers. They are killing heads of cattle.

In the beginning, Portuguese soldiers would even trade food for clothes. Now they would point their rifles at the owners of herds of cattle and tell them to choose between life and death.

It was strange that the Portuguese used the term "heads of cattle." For we also call slaves *tinhloko*, which means "heads." Stranger still was my getting used to the notion that the VaNguni had less regard for a human being than for an ox.

The priest's explanation allayed our fears. If they were Portuguese soldiers, there would be no danger. And we were beginning to disperse when a young boy with a startled expression rushed up with the news that one of those Portuguese boats, a blockhouse, had attacked the dugout in which Mwanatu was traveling. All the occupants had been killed. My brother's corpse was floating in the waters of the Inharrime.

Terrible though it was, I was hardly surprised by the news. I felt the same shiver run through me as when we had passed the *nwamu-lambu*, on our own journey up the river. My eyes clouded over, but I knew that my brother had sought this end. It wasn't the dead of Nkokolani that Mwanatu was going to bury. He wanted to feel the embrace of those who had already departed.

My self-control contrasted with the emotional reaction of my companions. My father wandered aimlessly around the yard like a blind man facing the heavens. After a while, he paused, leaned against the trunk of a tree, and sobbed out loud. Father Rudolfo tore off his cassock and threw it to the ground. Dressed only in his drawers, he stamped on it and kicked it. The sergeant forgot his physical discomfort and used what was left of his hands to conceal his tears from the others. Bianca, the Italian woman, asked us to gather together and pray. Attracted by our lamentations, Bibliana abandoned the kitchen and came over to the yard to comfort us.

This was when we heard, first, the sound of footsteps on the march, and then an order given in Portuguese:

Stay where you are!

A group of three white and six black Portuguese soldiers emerged from the trees. They had the arrogant bearing of those who own the world. Leading them was a captain, who identified himself as Santiago Mata. They had just disembarked from the blockhouse and immediately admitted that it was they who had fired on Mwanatu's dugout. They had confused the boat and assumed its crew to be VaNguni fugitives. In the face of Rudolfo's desperate protest, the captain argued:

This is a land of tigers and hyenas. Do I have to ask whether there's a cat by any chance among the wild animals?

There are no tigers in Africa, Captain.

There was an armed black in the dugout. What did you want me to do?

It was a fake weapon, the priest answered, yelling. *Didn't you see his uniform?*

I thought it was fake, goddammit! Round here, my friend, everything looks fake. For instance, do you look like a real priest?

He was preparing to enter the church but the priest openly blocked his way:

There are people who are unworthy of entering this house.

The captain felt for his pistol. He was indignant with the order, offended by the lack of respect. He took a deep breath and adopted a conciliatory tone:

These guys are all the same. Can you tell one from another, Father?

I can tell human from inhuman. I can tell the meek from the powerful, I can tell the poor—

What's all this? the captain interrupted. *Are we now defending the niggers like those Swiss bastards do?*

I can tell those Africans who are worthy of the Kingdom of Heaven, I can tell these poor blacks—

Well, don't tire your eyes, and take a look at these white soldiers with me here. Take a good look at them, mister priest! This poor wretch had never put his feet in a pair of shoes until recently; and that one there, just last month, was watching over a flock of goats. None of them ever parked his ass on a school bench.

With his hands on his belt, his eyes flashing in the shadow cast by the brim of his hat, the soldier looked closely at the bystanders for several long moments before turning to address the priest again:

Are you looking for purity in these savages? You can be sure that Paradise isn't here. These folk are devils. What gets these kaffirs going isn't the prospect of tearing the shirt off your body. It's tearing your shirt along with your body as well.

He paused in front of the dispirited sergeant, who, more sad than tired, was leaning against the doorpost for support. He looked at the filthy trousers and ragged singlet of the young soldier. Only then did his gaze turn to Germano's arms:

The kaffirs bound you! That's what they do. They bind their prisoners' hands together until they go gangrenous.

I supported the tottering sergeant while he stepped forward from the group and presented himself:

I am Sergeant Germano de Melo.

Sergeant? And in what bloody army?

Ours, Captain.

You don't look it. Because if you were, you would already have saluted me in the proper way.

With a wince, the sergeant gave a clumsy salute. Thick drops of what looked like perspiration ran down his face. But it was soon apparent that the soldier was of no interest to Santiago. What occupied his mind was his contest with the priest:

Do you consider you can tell races and disgraces apart, mister priest? Well, let me explain how you can tell a black from a white. It's not the color of the skin, my dear father. It's in the eyes.

We were all enthralled by the words and gestures displayed by this histrionic captain. With the skill of a conjurer, he clicked his fingers next to the sergeant's face and declared:

Take a good look at this man, look him in the eyes. If you look carefully, my dear father, you'll see deep inside the eyes of this poor wretch the burning heat of smoke from the kitchen of days gone by. No matter how white his skin, this guy's a black. He spent his whole childhood blowing into the embers of the hearth.

He knew he was right. He was a military chief, and he delved deeper and more quickly into the souls of men than any priest. Then the tone of his voice rose when he yelled: *Do you hear what this Portuguese captain is saying?* And he took out his pistol and fired a shot at the church tower. A whole horde of crows rose like a cloud into the sky. The shot seemed to calm the captain down. With his head held high and his back straight, he turned back to Sergeant Germano:

What did you say your name was?

Germano de Melo at your orders, sir. I was stationed at the Nkokolani military post. I was injured during an attack on the garrison.

Don't lie, Sergeant.

It's the truth, Germano replied, holding up his bandaged arms.

The injuries are real. But there is no garrison at Nkokolani. The military post is no more than a store.

For me it was a garrison, the only garrison in this world. And Mwanatu, the young man we are mourning here, was my sentry.

Sentry? The captain smiled disdainfully, rolling his eyes. *I'm sick of this bloody charade, of soldiers who aren't soldiers, of garrisons that are stores. I'm sick of wars that politicians plan back in Lisbon.*

Then, raising his arms as if in prayer, he bemoaned:

Oh, Mouzinho, Mouzinho! Why are you taking so long?

He looked for some shade next to the wall, and, leaning his back against the stone corroded by time, he contemplated us as if we didn't exist. Unlike his compatriots, he didn't seem uncomfortable at the sight of other white people. Indeed, those pale faces seemed to provoke outright aversion in him. The only exception was if one of those other whites happened to be female, which was the case of the Italian woman, who was gazing at him with a mixture of fear and fascination.

I have seen you somewhere before, Santiago probed.

Maybe so, Captain. I'm Bianca . . .

The Italian with the hands of gold? What a pleasure, my dear lady. And he made a grotesque attempt at a bow.

You must understand, Captain, the reason why we are all so concerned here, Bianca declared. *The boy traveling in that boat was the son of our friend here*, and she pointed to Katini, who was hiding behind all the others.

Dona Bianca, the soldier replied, *you cannot imagine how sorry I am. We are at war, what more can I say? I'm a Christian, I had the unfortunate travelers in the boat buried.*

So where did you bury them? I asked.

I hardly recognized my own voice. Pushed forward by some invisible hand, I found myself confronting Santiago Mata. And I repeated the question. The man smiled and asked:

Well, now! Who is this young beauty? Don't tell me she's one of your girls, Dona Bianca?

Where did you bury my brother Mwanatu? I insisted in a sharp, stubborn tone.

Wow! This cat's got sharp claws! And Santiago's voice gained a malicious candor. *Where did you learn to speak my language like that, my little dove? Could you maybe teach me yours?*

I shut my eyes and remembered our late mother's advice. *Their insults aren't directed against you*, she used to say. *It's against your people, your race. Pretend you're water, imagine you're a river. Water, my daughter, is like ash: No one can hurt it.* This was the lesson taught me by Chikazi Makwakwa, my mother, who died but a short time ago. For I, in the eyes of the world, would never be exempt from guilt. The color of my skin, the texture of my hair, the width of my nose, the thickness of my lips, I would have to carry these things forever as if they were some sin. All this would prevent me from being who I really was: Imani Nsambe.

I glanced at my father in the vain hope that in some rare display of courage he might confront the man who had openly confessed to murdering his son. But Katini Nsambe remained as he had always lived: submissively good-mannered, eyes down, his feet indistinguishable from the dust. Maybe there was an almost imperceptible tension in his pulse. Nothing more than that.

With a click of his fingers, Santiago Mata summoned his soldiers to line up in military formation. *We need some order here!* he declared. And he ordered the Portuguese flag to be raised over the church tower. The priest made as if to show his displeasure. In vain, Germano offered to help the soldiers, but the captain opened his arms in a magnanimous gesture and said:

You are exempt.

Lined up, we watched the blue and white flag being hoisted. Standing down from his salute, the captain felt in his pocket and, waving an envelope in his left hand, exclaimed:

Germano de Melo, is that what you said your name was? Well, I've been carrying this letter around for ages to give you.

The sergeant received the envelope, placing his wrists together as if they were two pincers. He glanced at the seal and gave a frown that signaled either curiosity or disappointment. The only letter he expected was from Lieutenant Ornelas. But this letter was from Portugal.

We'll spend the night here, Santiago announced. *We won't take up any room, Father. We'll use our tents. All I ask is that you provide us with a head of cattle early tomorrow. What we don't eat, you can share among your people.*

Are you asking for one, Captain? Or are you going to threaten me with a weapon like the kaffirs do?

The captain gave a deep sigh while the soldiers romped off, their laughter confirming their takeover of what had until then been our place.

At this point, Bibliana emerged. She had waited for the right moment to make her appearance. She passed through the intense light of the churchyard with the dignity of a queen. She was wearing her customary boots and a cartridge belt around her waist. She walked with a military step and a defiant demeanor, and came to a halt in front of the Portuguese captain, who asked:

Hey! Where did you cook up this creature?

He examined every inch of the priestess. He peered suspiciously at the cartridge belt. The woman stood there impassively while the soldier emptied the contents of one of the cartridges. What he saw was tobacco, which she kept there. He trod on it with a thoroughness that bordered on anger.

And what about those boots? Where did you steal them? Did you kill a soldier? Was that how you got them?

She doesn't speak Portuguese, the priest hastened to explain.

Bibliana guessed what was going to happen. So she anticipated the humiliation of the order she was about to receive. She took off her boots, without taking her eyes off Santiago. The Portuguese watched scornfully as the woman undid her boots. Shaking his head, he commented: *Poor thing, she doesn't know that the socks they never gave her are more important than the shoes. Without them, the boots are torture.*

This was why, he added, the boots given the natives by the Portuguese were left hanging up, unused.

But there was another reason why the sorceress took off her boots. And that was what they now saw.

Taking a deep breath, Bibliana hurled the boots through the air with such force that they rose in a spectacular arc toward the top of the mango tree. They did not fall to the ground, but were caught on a branch. They remained hanging, swaying gently, until, all of a sudden, they started to spin frantically, and the captain watched in astonishment as two sinister black birds of prey emerged from them. This was when he fired blindly at those errant shadows that only he could see.

21

SERGEANT GERMANO DE MELO'S SIXTH LETTER

Beware of those defending the castle against barbarian invaders.
Without knowing, they have already turned into monsters.
—THE WORDS OF FATHER RUDOLFO

Sana Benene, October 5, 1895

Dear Lieutenant Ayres de Ornelas,

The arrival of Captain Santiago Mata reminded me that there was a world out there to which I belonged. I confess that the captain is probably not the best emissary in this world. It would have been better if he had not appeared. However, his appearance in some way allowed me to see how empty and heavy-handed our arrogance is around here. Perhaps the days are passing more quickly than I think. Maybe there is another time advancing silently underneath the everyday lives we live.

In the meantime, my dear lieutenant, this is the truth of my situation: I have a whole church as my bedroom. I and the house of God both slumber in a peace and quiet that is only interrupted by the fluttering of doves and owls. I awaken to the rustling of mice hurriedly gnawing the remains of candles. I am terrified that when these meager resources have been chewed up, those big fat mice will turn to my injuries. And that I shall wake up one day without any eyes, which is how I found Sardinha the storekeeper just a few moments after he had died.

I am delaying opening the letter that Santiago Mata brought me this afternoon. After all, everything in my life is subject to strange delays. I was supposed to stay only a few days in this place, which was to be a mere pause on my way to a hospital. I have been here for weeks now. That is why I look at the letter without haste and choose to deceive myself: It has not come from my village, and was not sent by any relative of mine. I have no other home except for this one. I have no family except for these folk here.

I know how assiduous you are, sir, in writing to your mother. You cannot imagine how much I envy you. For, nowadays, I would not know what to say to my mother. I am writing all this down while nevertheless aware that it is not true. But I shall refrain from amending or deleting anything.

Our current familiarity with each other permits me to transcribe line by line the extraordinary letter sent from my homeland. On various occasions, sir, you have asked yourself the reasons that led a country boy like me to seek to perfect a refinement in his use of language and to heighten his sensibility. Well, this letter speaks of two women who cultivated these qualities in me: my mother and my teacher, Dona Constança, a learned woman who, in order to escape political persecution, exiled herself in our village.

Without so much as a comma changed, what follows is the letter dictated by my mother, Dona Laura de Melo:

Germano, my dearest son,

This is your old mother writing to you. After so many months without hearing from you, I have sad news to bring you: Your father has just died. He died because of his heart, as all men do, according to Toneca at the pharmacy. I am dictating this letter to our neighbor, Constança, who was your teacher at primary school. She sends you her best wishes but is angry that you have never sent us any news.

I want to tell you how your old father left us. I have repeated it so many times that I seem to have put a distance between myself and that sad day. It was late afternoon and your father was sitting on the front step. It grew dark and he was still sitting there, without eating his dinner or supper, and without saying a word. Halfway through the night, I took him a blanket to cover himself. I didn't ask him anything, because that's how things were between us. That was when he said he was going to stay there until the sun came up. In the early morning, when I went down to let the animals out, I found him stiff and cold. Your uncle Arménio helped me pull the body into the house and confided in me that the men of the village had got hold of secret information that soldiers would be arriving from Africa. If they did, it wasn't to our village, and your father died waiting for you to come home.

It was a very modest funeral. In attendance were the few folk we have left either in our family or in the village. The ceremony was so brief that I didn't even have time to weep. It is a great sin, I know, but I am still waiting for a tear to come even now, just one simple tear. Instead of crying, all I do is sigh. The thing is, my dear son, I was so tired of not being a wife, tired of not being a mother, tired of not living!

And do you know why not a single tear comes to my eyes? The truth is that I have been a widow ever since I got married. How often I would rub my arms with basil in order to smell like a lady! But your father never smelled my perfume. Countless times, as soon as night came, I loosened my hair. And your father would ask me to tie it up again with my headscarf. He only ever touched me in the dark.

His jealousy wrecked our home. He was even jealous of you. Above all, of you, my son. From the moment you were born, that man only had one purpose in life. That was to punish me. First with silence. Then with words. And eventually with kicks and blows. I thought about running away, I wanted to die.

But then what happened to me was what befalls all women in our part of the world. I gave up on everything, I gave up on myself. I consoled myself with the idea that his jealousy was the only gift he was able to give me. Poor thing! What happened to him was what Father Estevão mentioned in a sermon: He who has never loved, doesn't know how to be jealous. And even in his jealousy, your father was clumsy. Ever since we got married, he spread it around the village that he was going with Julinha Five Cents. He took his time coming home in the evening, just to annoy me. But I knew he was alone, sitting under the great mulberry tree that scatters its fruit all across the square. Your father's trousers were full of sweet, dark stains. I sniffed his clothes. That was the only perfume he ever wore. Sometimes I miss the smell of mulberries.

Now I'm going to make a confession to you that only God should hear. There were times when that father of yours, may God be with him, went as far as to pray that you would die when you were a child. Not out of malice, but because of the privations we went through. And if God took you when you were still small, it wouldn't have been you who died. When children die early, they are just little angels. And when angels die, there is no weeping, no sadness, no death. There is merely a heavenly creature that God gives us and that God takes away from us. That was why, I confess hand on heart, I said nothing when your father prayed like this. Fortunately, God never heard him. And from then on, as if by miracle, you began to belong to me more and more, blood of my blood, life of my life. And I clung to you so strongly that the scorn which your father showed you grew ever worse.

The next thing I am going to do, my son, is to go to a hairdresser's. There is none here in the village. But I shall go to the town, where they say there is a very skilled lady, Perhaps it is vanity, and maybe it is a sin. I just want to see myself through my own eyes, because up until now I have only known myself through my husband's eyes. When you come back, I don't want to be taken by surprise like your father was, your father who is still waiting by the front door.

You'll see, my son, that I've also done some work on the house. I've made it cozier. With the small amount of inheritance money I bought three chairs, to offer guests and absent ones somewhere to sit. When you get here, you'll have a chair to sit on and do nothing, because they say chairs help one to forget the past. That's according to my friend Constança, who spent a lot of time sitting at school. And she also says that those coming from wars have a lot to forget.

We begin to plan a few amusing escapades while she is scribbling the letter. Do you know what we are going to do? The two of us are going out and we are going to whistle as we walk down the street. For whistling is something that women are forbidden to do. That's what people say in this land of yours: A woman who whistles is summoning witches. Well, Constança and I are going to whistle for witches.

I pray to God that you will come soon and in good health to be near this mother of yours, for you are now all I have left in this vale of tears. And I hope they have fed you well, for in my dreams you always appear very thin. Accept the thousand kisses I never gave you when I held you in my arms. From this, your loving mother.

I have transcribed this letter in its entirety because, more than just its content, I wanted to share with you just how much I both feared and yearned for this moment. It is not the gravity of the event that moves me. But it is a feeling of guilt. Not for having forgotten my family and my past. I am assailed by further guilt involving a secret about which I can only tell you, Lieutenant. In my locker at the Military College, I kept a photograph of someone I told everyone was my father. Except that it wasn't. It was a career officer whose picture I cut out of an almanac. The image was false but my pride was real. In everybody's eyes, I, like you, sir, was the inheritor of a noble family tradition. From lying so much and feeling the eyes of that unknown individual looking at me, I eventually forgot my real father's face. I brought the photo of this unknown progenitor to Africa with me, and still have it in my sparse baggage. As you can see, sir, I am not lacking in an aristocratic past. I just invented that past for myself. Whether I hang it on the wall or keep it in my baggage, that other life of mine is, with all due respect, no less real than any other.

And I think that is all for now. Tomorrow, Imani will leave with her father to try to locate the place where they supposedly buried her brother Mwanatu. I hope what Santiago Mata told them is true. I hope they did bury him and that they find his grave. I even offered to accompany her, but neither Imani nor her father wanted my presence. Katini now does everything to prevent Imani and me from being together. He wants to prove to Bianca Vanzini that his promise to deliver his daughter up to her remains in force.

I made a remark to the priest on the insistence of the kaffirs in communicating with the dead as much as, or even more so, than with the living. Rudolfo explained what I already knew: The difference between the living and the dead lies purely in the extent of their presence. The dead man is cared for in order that he should never die. Whether one is above the ground or under it is no more than a minor detail. The soil of Africa is so full of life that all the dead want to remain buried. And I agree with him: In this part of the world, the earth isn't a grave. It is just another home.

I confess that it was odd listening to such beliefs coming from the mouth of a priest. Then I recalled the inflammatory speeches of those who, in the name of the Homeland, sent me off to war. Successive generations, in the name of the sacred soil, have been hurled towards their deaths. I couldn't resist proclaiming the following words: that I too had been taught to love a cemetery.

To have a homeland is something different, Father, I said.

The clergyman wanted to know what this was. I did not answer. I was busy thinking, more than anything else, about Imani. When she returns from her final farewell to her brother, we will travel together to the hospital at Manjacaze. Then we will go on to Lourenço Marques after my hands have been completely cured. Now that my father has died, my fate will be that of the angels: My arms will grow back again and I will have the same number of fingers that God gave me.

One of these days, I'll answer my mother. And I shall announce that soon one of her other chairs will be occupied, with the arrival of her new daughter-in-law.

22

A LOCUST DECAPITATED

*Such is the effect of hatred: not to recognize ourselves
in those we despise.*
—THE WORDS OF GRANDFATHER TSANGATELO

As evening fell and we finished our meal, Captain Santiago approached the great fig tree, where we had sought shelter. And he apologized for his previous behavior. He had been nervous, after weeks of traipsing around the bushlands in a fruitless search for the rebels Zixaxa and Mahazul. Ngungunyane had hidden them. According to him, in Africa they didn't need thick forest to make someone invisible. People hid themselves within people.

That is why, the captain declared, *it is necessary to kill hyenas and cats. And tigers, even though they don't exist.*

Santiago circled our table, catlike. No one spoke, no one raised their eyes. Countering our feelings of antipathy, the Italian woman pulled up a chair and invited the captain to join us. Dona Bianca didn't understand that our silence was not a way of being absent. It was a prayer. In our silence, we were conversing with our dearly departed Mwanatu. Bianca Vanzini smiled at the Portuguese, and, pointing to the empty chair, said:

Sit down, Captain. My mother used to say, No one grows old sitting around the table.

The captain helped himself to a drink and remained silent, watching the clouds of insects fluttering around the oil lamps. I remembered our house at Nkokolani. The darkness was the same and from it emerged the same winged creatures, dazzled by the same lights. Here, however, there were so many that one could hear the crackling of bodies as they came into contact with the flames.

Have you ever eaten them, Father? Santiago asked. *I'm told these locusts are good when grilled over a fire. I thought you, as a good pastor, would have shared your folks' food.*

The priest received this ironic comment with muttered curses. The captain asked him not to take it so seriously.

Don't be like that, Santiago urged. *At heart, we are all Portuguese and we are all in the same boat, waiting to be rescued by our cavalry.*

No one here is waiting for a savior, the priest shot back. *I'm a man of faith, but I can guarantee one thing: Here, even Christ would have thrown in the towel.*

What a devil of a thing for a man of the cloth to say!

When you arrived, did you see some poles with fishing nets hanging from them down by the landing stage? Rudolfo Fernandes asked.

Until some time ago, there were human heads stuck on the ends of these poles. This was what the priest recalled in unhurried detail. They stayed there for days on end, exposed to the heat and flies as if they had been born like that, detached from the body and the life to which they had belonged.

Were they blacks or whites? Santiago asked.

Guess, Captain, guess.

It wasn't me, my dear father, don't blame me. He paused for a moment and then continued. *And while we're at it, between you and me, it's much more comfortable for a dead man to have his head stuck on a pole than to have his body hanging on a cross.*

Blinking hard, the captain laughed. But we all saw the fear his laughter concealed. Never again, the priest assured him, would the place be free of the smell of putrefaction that had poisoned it.

Santiago got up to walk over to one of the lamps. He seemed oblivious to the cloud of locusts flickering around his face.

So they want to find Zixaxa and Mahazul in order to punish them? Well, I think they should be given a reward. If it weren't for the rebellion of those kaffirs, our army would still be away with the fairies.

Do you know what I would like? Bianca cut in, with a timid, conciliatory smile. *I would like to live like this all the time, with all these soldiers here, but without there being a war at all.*

In that case you're in the right place at the right time, my dear lady! Santiago volunteered. *The thing about wars is that there's always a problem with them, Dona Bianca: To wage them, one needs an enemy. And we, thanks to that bunch of crooks in Lisbon, have an internal enemy that is much bigger than the one out there . . .*

Everyone else said they didn't want a conflict. As for Santiago, he prayed for a fight that would engulf all that sleaze and corruption. Father Rudolfo retorted:

No war has a big enough mouth to swallow so much corruption. Wars are carpets, he added. *All the dirty dealings of the powerful are swept under them.*

We were preparing to retire to our quarters when we surprised Santiago Mata kneeling in prayer, his head almost touching the ground. When he saw us, he hunched his shoulders, embarrassed. Then he asked us to gather around him. He placed his hat on the ground and, lifting its brim, covered some locusts. Next, he scratched out a map in the sand with its compass points. A large circle showed Lourenço Marques; another farther up was Inhambane; and in the middle, a smaller circle represented Mandhlakazi. Then, sliding two fingers between the ground and the brim of his hat, he pulled out a first insect, to which he gave the name of António Enes. He placed it on Lourenço Marques, while addressing us:

What's this creature doing? he asked, as he tore off its head. And he answered: *He's not doing anything. Or rather, he writes reports for others who don't do anything.*

With another locust struggling between his fingers, he proclaimed:

This one here is the commander of the Northern Column. It's that faggot Colonel Galhardo. What's this locust up to? Before giving his answer, Santiago pulled off the insect's legs one by one. *This is what's happening, the scum isn't moving. He's scared stiff.* He picked up his hat, shook the dust from it, and shooed away the remaining insects. Then he clicked his heels as if he were ordering us to disperse. But at that point a praying mantis landed on his gaiters. And as of one, we all rushed forward to protect the creature. The priest explained:

Not this one, Captain! This is an envoy of God.

Santiago Mata retorted with irony:

Then it must be Mouzinho, it must be him at the head of the column coming up from the south.

The mention of Mouzinho de Albuquerque brought a glint to Bianca's eyes, and she begged him enthusiastically to describe this dashing dragoon, this prince she had been dreaming about for so long. Santiago Mata did not need to be asked twice—but he did not say who Mouzinho was; he limited himself to what Mouzinho was not. For instance, Captain Mouzinho was not like the other officers who proliferated in this part of the world, fat-necked and big-bellied. His gaunt, angular face stood out among the crowd. His demeanor, as he was mounted on his horse, was that of an angel of fire.

You would like him, dear lady.

You have no idea how much I like him already. But you, sir, are no less a man than this prince.

Then Santiago continued with his description of the cavalry officer. Apart from all these attributes of his, this great Portuguese was no novice in colonial affairs. Mouzinho had already been in Mozambique four years before as a district governor. And he was not like the others, who reconciled themselves with the widespread apathy. He asked to be exonerated from his post because he could not take the politics of "the slower the better." He himself, Santiago Mata, had been contracted directly by him for an armed intervention which, as Mouzinho put it, could not be undertaken by the army.

So you were a mercenary, then, Rudolfo cut in.

There are terms we should avoid, my dear father. Let us say I was a member of a volunteer force that was directed to attack the encampments of Cecil Rhodes's British South Africa Company.

And Ngungunyane? I dared to ask, going against the flow of the conversation.

The captain gazed at me, perplexed. I was a young black woman. How did I dare to speak in that meeting? I changed the pronunciation and said the name in the way the Portuguese did: Gungunhane.

Do you know Gungunhane, sir? I persevered.

He replied that he did, but he didn't feel like talking about that at the moment. Partly, he added, because it wasn't the blacks who were the real enemy, with all due respect to those assembled here. The real adversary, according to Mata, was inside the fortress. And it was António Enes, the Portuguese Royal Commissioner.

Do you know what Mouzinho calls António Enes? Well, he calls him "Tsungo Khongolo," which is the term that the blacks of Inhambane use to designate whites who think themselves important. This António Enes is the big chief of that band of parasitic locusts.

The discussion went on into the night. My father gradually

slumped over the table, looking ever more closely at a glass of wine that had not been emptied. Bianca seemed to be nodding off, and only the sergeant was still following the dispute between Santiago and Rudolfo. According to Father Rudolfo, it wasn't Mouzinho who would capture Ngungunyane. It was the blacks who would deliver him on a silver platter. The people who heaped praise on him today would stab him in the back tomorrow. And the priest concluded:

The emperor's capture won't be a feat of courage, but the product of betrayal.

The captain feigned not to hear, and said this to the sergeant:

They've been tending your injuries the kaffir way. Do you know the best cure? It's called a machine gun.

It was with this cure that the Portuguese were going to blow away Ngungunyane's warriors. It was a pity the sergeant was disabled. And the captain, still addressing Germano in the same defiant tone, added:

If you hadn't been crippled, you'd come with us and sniff the gunpowder. There isn't a better drug, my friend. We sniff it once and we're addicted.

23

SERGEANT GERMANO DE MELO'S SEVENTH LETTER

What is said of our cruelty
is not so much that we kill
but that we prevent people from living.

—THE WORDS OF FATHER RUDOLFO

Sana Benene, October 12, 1895

Dear Lieutenant Ayres de Ornelas,

I do not know, sir, what I can say in answer to my mother. What does one say to a mother when one loses a father? What is there to say when that father never existed? There are some who say distance causes sentiments to fade. It is not true. Far from home, everything is born anew. And there are pains that I do not want born again.

What my mother hopes I will say is that I shall soon return. I do not know, though, what my fate may be. As I have already said, I do not want to return without Imani. And if my homeland is still the way I left it, then the only thing that would make me return would be my mother. Who knows whether I can't arrange for her to come to Africa and enable her to find herself again as a mother and grandmother of the children I shall have with Imani?

However, for me, sir, all skies are cloudy and nebulous. For if Portugal does not appear auspicious, the same somber doubts begin to form when I think of making my life in Africa. What will I do in these backlands, in a war that will continue even after it seems to have finished? Parading before me, I see Father Rudolfo, who has forgotten about God; Captain Santiago, who has forgotten about the army; Counselor Almeida, who runs his affairs as if he himself were Portugal. I see all this and I ask myself what other choice I have but to become like them. Or whether, in spite of the circumstances, I can become the father I never had myself.

I imagine you do not want to waste your time with these trivial digressions. Nevertheless, I cannot resist telling you of a fantasy that I constantly relive. In the dream, I see myself as clearly as if it is really happening, following the course of the River Inharrime on foot from its mouth to its source. I am making the journey with the sole purpose of bringing a gift for the emperor Gungunhane. This is how things are done in Africa: Gifts are brought for the great chiefs. For days on end, I carry in my arms an enormous jellyfish, whose watery body scintillates under the burning sun. I hurry because I want to deliver the animal alive and still moving its gelatinous tentacles. I am aware of the terror the Negro has of creatures from the sea. My intention is that the almighty Vátua ruler will not survive the surprise and will surrender in the face of this fearsome creature. With the aid of this gift, at once deadly and delicate, I shall defeat the greatest enemy of Portugal without arms or bloodshed. It is this patriotic purpose that causes me to march for days and days, aware of the advance of turbulent waves behind me, flooding the African hinterlands with an endless ocean.

When I kneel at the emperor's feet, I realize that the medusa's venom has dissolved my hands. My fingers flop to the ground along with the jellyfish's tentacles. The monarch smiles disdainfully, and orders me to collect my bits and pieces and return to the ocean. He tells me to enjoy myself while I am awaited. I reply that no one is waiting for me. Then the king of Gaza makes the following declaration: *Someone is always waiting for you even though you don't know it. The sea is vast, one enters and leaves it without having to ask for authorization. There is no law nor lord in all that immensity. That is why I hate the ocean and curse all its creatures.* Those are Gungunhane's words, words that invariably bring my dream to a close.

Forgive me, sir, for these garbled confessions. But if my soul is already weakened, I am also taking leave of my body now. I repeat what I have already mentioned to you, namely that I shall not present myself at Chicomo, in spite of the risk of punishment. I shall go to Manjacaze with Imani, and await the judgment of the Swiss doctor. Later, I shall tell you what happens. It will be a miracle if the remains of what were my hands are ever any use to me again. In order to treat me, Georges Liengme, the missionary and doctor, will have to resort to God rather than to science.

24

ONE TEAR, DOUBLE SADNESS

The world is a river. It is born and dies all the time.
—THE WORDS OF CHIKAZI MAKWAKWA

Monotony increases time's girth. It was enough to have the company, however unwelcome, of Captain Santiago Mata, for that day to pass by more speedily. The first night, birds could be heard and people were already bidding each other good night when the captain decided to call Bianca Vanzini to one side. I heard the soldier's honeyed voice:

And now, my sweet Bianca, this gentleman wants his just reward.

Do you want me? I'm very expensive, Captain.

A man like me needs a great deal of sustenance. I want you and one other woman. One to light the flame, and the other to douse the fire.

I understand. I'll go and speak to Imani.

No, not that one. I want a real black woman. Do you understand?

No, I don't.

I want the other one, the black woman with the boots.

Ever since he had watched Bibliana parade in her red gown, her black gloves, and her cartridge belt, the captain had thought of nothing else. A mischievous smile lit up Bianca Vanzini's face. The captain's interest confirmed what she had already confided in me: A macho man prefers a masculine woman.

I don't know whether I'll be able to persuade that woman. We've had our differences; I think Bibliana hates me.

I'll pay you double, Dona Bianca.

I'm very expensive, Captain. I'm made of gold, or have you already forgotten?

Well, between you and me, let me tell you something: It won't be long before I discover where Gungunhane has buried his fortune in pounds. And I know where that storekeeper Sardinha has hidden a hoard of ivory tusks.

In his case, I only want what he owed me.

He owed you a debt?

All men owe me a debt, Captain.

Leaning against the trunk of the mango tree, Captain Santiago Mata was the conqueror who, from the heights of his fortress, watches the trophies being gathered together. From where he was standing, he could only guess what was being said by the two women he had chosen to satisfy his desires. What they were saying, however, was very far removed from what he might imagine. Not even I could guess the contents of the dialogue if I weren't standing behind the tree where they were talking.

Never, the sorceress complained. *That money's hot, it'll burn my hands.*

The captain's summoned you. If you don't go of your own free will, you'll be forced to, you damned witch.

Suca! Famba khaya ka wena.

The answer in a language she didn't understand infuriated the white woman. And she launched herself against the other. They fought, scratched, and ruffled each other. I tried to separate them, but to no avail. The Portuguese captain was grinning, thinking that the scuffle was some sort of an erotic performance put on especially for him. And the confrontation got louder until Bianca, exhausted, collapsed on the ground and burst into tears. At that point, Bibliana suddenly hugged her in a gesture of maternal warmth. Then she laid Bianca's head on her breast and caressed her hair.

Why are you so aggressive toward me, Dona Bianca? This is the second time.

Sobbing, the white woman confessed what she herself had not understood previously. At the moment when Bibliana was dancing during the ritual in the yard, she had been struck by a strange feeling: That woman could not possibly be, as people were then proclaiming, a black Our Lady. She could not be, as was being heralded, the Mother of the Word. The truth was, however, that the black woman had caused her to experience an epiphany and the Italian woman had felt the ground disappear under her feet.

Suddenly, my only son appeared before me, the child I lost when he was one year old.

Her son's death seemed to her to signal the end of her life. When Bianca decided to return to Africa, she was merely looking for somewhere to extinguish herself. The opposite had in fact occurred. Life had embraced her with the arms of a boundless mother.

I wasn't able to die, the Italian admitted.

Do you feel guilty? Bibliana asked.

Incapable of articulating a word, Bianca Vanini nodded, her expression drained like that of an orphaned child.

Let's go to the river, Bibliana suggested. *At nighttime, it's another river, a nocturnal river that is the domain of women alone.*

As if no longer in control of her body, the white woman followed in her footsteps. She looked back over her shoulder, and saw the flag drooping from the cross at the top of the church tower. And she got the feeling that underneath that church, another church had been established. It was this subterranean temple to which she was now descending, led there by a heretic priestess.

Santiago Mata watched, puzzled, as the two women walked off, hand in hand. He was sure they were exhibiting themselves erotically in order to heighten his appetite. On the banks of the Inharrime, the two women danced, clinging to each other. The white woman, shaking her head, hissed: *I'm drunk, dancing with a black woman by the side of a river.* But suddenly, the black woman stopped her in her tracks:

These hands, sister. I see grains of sand under your skin, I see earth under your nails.

Could it have been any other way? the Italian retorted, her voice no more than a delicate thread. Can a mother see her little son being buried by strangers? A woman gives birth, a mother opens and seals closed the earth. That winter's morning, Bianca Vanzini pushed aside the gravediggers and dug the cold, stony ground with her own fingers.

I put my little boy to bed. As I do every night.

In silence, the priestess plunged Bianca's hands into the river. And she saw how Santiago was swallowed up by the darkness.

25

SERGEANT GERMANO DE MELO'S EIGHTH LETTER

Anything of gravity you have to say to an enemy, you must say it in his language. No judge passes a sentence in a tongue the defendant cannot understand. No one dies unless it is in their own language.
—A SAYING FROM NKOKOLANI

Sana Benene, October 22, 1895

Dear Lieutenant Ayres de Ornelas,

This time, I bring you substantial news. At last, my dear lieutenant, something is moving in this lifeless land. You are absolutely right, sir: something out of the ordinary is altering the fate of this Portuguese territory. And it was in the context of such change that Xiperenyane passed through here yesterday morning. He made a brief stop on his way to his lands at Zavala. The man is unstoppable, constantly roaming through the bush on campaign. He is an extraordinary fighter, a Negro of proven loyalty to the Portuguese crown. I only hope that this time we know how to repay him with due generosity. Strangely enough, Bibliana confessed to me that she had seen Xiperenyane in her dreams, skinny and in rags, sweeping the streets of Lourenço Marques. This was the pitiful future that awaited him. No more than the premonition of a witch, you will say, sir. Perhaps. Time will tell.

I know that our forces are preparing for a huge battle at Coolela. Part of me would like to be present at what will certainly be one of the most glorious events in the history of Portuguese Africa. Another part of me hesitates. Maybe there is more glory in these letters that are written independently of military confrontations. Maybe this unlikely encounter between such different people is nobler. Who knows whether Portugal may not achieve more for itself in this interweaving of such different people than in these bloody wars?

Were you concerned, sir, about my presenting myself at Liengme's hospital? Did you fear that I would avoid appearing at the Chicomo military post, as my situation as a soldier requires me to do? Well, as things stand now, both destinations are out of the question. The military tension felt around here does not permit anyone to leave Sana Benene. At the moment, it is not even safe to travel down the river. We are surrounded, sir. And I suspect that we are besieged more by fear than by any real threat.

The person who suffers the most from this confinement is Bianca Vanzini. Between you and me, what worries her most is being away from her business interests in Lourenço Marques. Yesterday, however, the sun once again gleamed in the eyes of the Italian woman when our friend Xiperenyane promised to accompany her back to Inhambane after the upcoming battle at Coolela. From there, she would return to Lourenço Marques by sea. At one point, she even came up to me and asked me, in that evasive way of hers, whether it would not make more sense for her to go to Chicomo instead of Lourenço Marques. *At least I won't die without seeing Mouzinho*, she said. I pitied her, but all I did was to shake my head, smiling like an idiot.

I have talked about Bianca, but the one who is going through a period of deep sadness is Imani Nsambe. The death of her brother has pitched her into a colorless abyss. My whimsical changes in mood and hesitation over my future make her melancholy still more intense. Last night, the girl was assailed by a nightmare that had been recurrent in the past, but which had not visited her since leaving Nkokolani. The truth is that once again she dreamed that she had become pregnant. After nine months, nothing had happened. After a year of being pregnant, her belly became immense, so much so that her legs could barely support her. Her breasts burst through her blouse, spilling abundant fountains of milk. Until at last she went into labor. In her first spasm, a machete emerged from her belly. The midwives stepped back, horrified. Then they returned quietly and cautiously in order to peer at the ghastly spectacle. After the machete, a spear emerged from her insides, and when her contractions seemed to have finished, a pistol popped out. The weapons came out of her body one at a time, and she hadn't even recovered from the spasms when the news spread throughout the whole area. Warriors turned up and wanted to take her weapons away from her, but she resisted them firmly: *No one lays a finger on my children!*

So this is what happened: Wherever she went, she took her death-dealing babies with her, treating them with a motherly care that deeply moved other women. Men reacted differently. During the months that followed, various men queued up to make her pregnant. If that woman was capable of giving birth to weapons, there was an opportunity for them to accumulate power and wealth. And never again would blacks need to fear their enemies.

This was Imani's dream. The following night, the poor girl must have relived the nightmare, for she woke up shouting and sobbing, begging that no one should touch her children. I calmed her down with my usual clumsiness. Imani got up and walked around and around in confusion until her father, Katini Nsambe, burst into the room. I remained by the door as a precaution. He ordered Imani to get ready, for as soon as morning broke, they would set off downstream. They would take with them one of the black soldiers who had arrived with the captain. Katini said that the purpose of the journey was to make sure that Mwanatu had been buried in accordance with the precepts of their folk. He had lost faith in everyone, blacks, whites, Chopes, and Machanganes. Imani's father complained bitterly that life had become a whole string of betrayals. His daughter asked him to explain what particular instances of disloyalty he was talking about. Katini replied that they would talk about this matter when they were in the boat.

Imani had known for some time of the ghosts that tormented old Katini Nsambe. She was always aware of them, but pretended not to know. It all had to do with the name she had been given in her early childhood. Everyone knew what was hidden behind that choice. Imani is the name given to girls whose father is unknown.

At that moment she suspected that this was the ghost now haunting Katini Nsambe. And she gently sought to put his mind at rest: He was her only father, the only one she had ever known. *I've already told you*, Katini snapped back. *We'll talk when we get back from Mwanatu's burial.*

Old Katini Nsambe asked me to pour him a glass of *nsope*, for he needed to bless their mission. The term *mission* seemed a bit strong to me. He guessed my uncertainty. And with an emperor's pride, he declared, *I am the last of the Nsambe. It falls to me to preside over the closure of our ancestral home.*

I offered to go with them down the river. Katini refused. It was a family matter. Imani would be the only one to help him, his only company. Up until some time ago, he said, he would have gone alone. But now he was beginning to be as fragile as a little bird. At the least sign of rain, he didn't take to his wings.

I accompanied father and daughter to the landing stage. I followed the old man's steps through the gloom. His footsteps were light, as if there were some studied delicacy in his gait. And I pondered on the courage of that man who, for all those years, had had to cross the terrain of his own humiliation. His daughter told me how he avoided the company of the other men in the village. And how he lowered his eyes every time the name Imani was mentioned. Everyone considered him a coward. But it would be hard to find similar bravery. Katini Nsambe forfeited his dignity and defended his daughter, regardless of whether he was her progenitor. I wasn't therefore surprised that his steps were so light.

We passed the ruined steps in front of the church and noticed how they had slid farther toward the river during the night. *Did it rain last night?* I asked. Imani's father commented evasively that the stones were merely returning to where they had been born.

When we reached the wooden jetty, Bianca and Father Rudolfo were already there. They had come to say goodbye. Each of them had brought something by way of a gift. Bianca wrapped a scarf around Imani's neck. And the priest gave Katini an iron crucifix. So that he could place it on the grave of his son Mwanatu.

I took a few steps back. Bibliana came and joined me, watching the flowing current of the Inharrime. It was the healer who broke our silence:

Your mother was here.

Here at Sana Benene?

It wasn't just African forces that had cured me. I too had brought my medicine from afar, the soothsayer said. *My medicine?* I asked, astonished. My dreams had been my most effective cure. For, according to her, they came full of cargo, like ships. And many relatives had visited me without my knowing.

Your mother was here with me, tending your wounds.

Then we went and joined the others sitting on the landing stage, feet dangling in the waters. The swirl around our ankles gurgled gently, like the most ancient of lullabies. We almost failed to hear an approaching raft, pushed along by the current. Riding it was an unclad man, with matted hair and the look of an animal. The priest sighed and commented: *That's all we need!* The intruder, he explained, was a madman called Libete who traveled the river constantly, carrying with him his foul-smelling bag.

The craft hadn't yet reached the bank and the area was bathed in a nauseous stench. The priest addressed the man in Txichangana, asking him to throw his stinking bag away. The intruder refused, pulling toward him a large leather bag, in which he claimed he carried his children. Sensing that the priest doubted his word, he offered to spread the entire contents along the landing stage if he were permitted. The priest reacted in alarm: *No, for the love of God, don't do that!* He should continue down the river, for the priest would give him his blessing. The raft drifted farther away, dragged by the current. And the man could still be heard shouting:

It was Ngungunyane who killed them! He killed my children, he killed me.

Katini Nsambe got up and we thought he was going to head for the dugout to start his journey. But he stood watching Libete's raft zigzagging along on the current. Eventually, he murmured:

Don't call him mad, Father. That man is me.

26

A LIQUID GRAVE

*The recruitment of soldiers in Angola to fight in Mozambique began in
1878 and finished in September, 1879. The bearing and discipline of
these soldiers from Angola caused surprise in Mozambique. Soon,
however, their splendid qualities began to be obliterated and within a
year, no one would have recognized those fine battalions recruited in
Angola. Either because of the lack of any regime of beatings, to which
they were accustomed, or because their generous leave caused them to
lose the rigors of discipline, or, the most likely, because the officers
assembled in the Province neglected their duties, the Angolans, from
being orderly, became unruly brawlers and a danger to the peace and
security of the capital.*

**—COLONEL JOSÉ JUSTINO TEIXEIRA BOTELHO, "MILITARY AND POLITICAL HISTORY OF
THE PORTUGUESE IN MOZAMBIQUE FROM 1883 TO THE PRESENT DAY," 1921**

I watched the sergeant waving from the landing stage, with his
large white handkerchief fluttering, somewhere between a pennant
and a mirage. I waved too in order to fulfill our false farewells. And
we continued downstream, looking for the grave of my brother
Mwanatu. Guiding us was a black Portuguese soldier who had been
assigned us by Santiago Mata. He was dark, much darker than those
from our part of the world. He was a *mangolê*, one of those soldiers
originally from Angola. On the journey, he remained silent, cautiously keeping his distance from my father.

When we stopped for a rest and my father walked off into the bush, the soldier opened up. He spoke Portuguese like a white and only his skin color and his name reminded me he was African. His name was João Ondjala because he had been born in the year of hunger. We laughed because that is how we say hunger in Txitxope. He spoke quickly, as if the end of the world were peeping at us from around the bend in the river. He said he wasn't to blame for the death of our relative. For he was a poor wretch, unable to exert any control over his own life. He said that a month before, he had been captured by Ngungunyane. He was brought into the presence of the emperor and one of his sons, named Godido, had served as interpreter. Godido had studied in the School of Arts and Crafts on the Island of Mozambique and could speak Portuguese fluently. The Angolan laughed as he recalled how terrified he had been as he knelt in front of the king of Gaza.

Don't harm me, Ondjala stammered as he knelt. *I'm your brother, I'm black like you.*

A brother? Ngungunyane asked. *A brother who kills us?*

Ondjala invoked his situation as a victim of discrimination in the Portuguese army and recalled the way the *mangolês* were sent to the front as cannon fodder.

So you're one of those mangolês, *then?* Ngungunyane asked.

The Angolan pointed to the flagpole planted in front of the VaNguni emperor's house.

I am like you, Nkosi, *we both obey the same flag.*

At the time, the blue and white flag of Portugal hung limp and soulless. When it droops, a flag is no more than a pathetic piece of cloth. Ondjala thought: It isn't the cloth that makes a flag, but the wind. That was how his soul was: empty, far from any wind.

I don't understand, the emperor retorted. *I asked you whether you were Angolan. What has the flag got to do with my question?*

Here, we all venerate the same sovereign: the king of Portugal.

The emperor raised his eyes skyward, diffusing the anger caused by the prisoner's insolence.

That flag is a piece of cloth, which I have hoisted and brought down whenever I want, he growled.

I also take off my uniform when I want, argued the Angolan.

The king didn't like what he heard. With a twig, he cleaned the long nail of his little finger, a habit of his when he was irritated. He muttered between his teeth:

Someone go with this man.

This was his way of announcing a sentence. The emperor uttered these words and the wretched man's fate was a foregone conclusion. He wouldn't even reach the outer limits of the village. The victim would be speared to death, his body lying where it fell, unburied and forgotten. But God was on his side. For Godido, who was leading the executioners, allowed him to escape. He untied him and told the others: *Let's leave him be, he'll be eaten by wild animals.*

On that occasion, he had gotten away. But the *mangolê* knew that he was serving another, longer, more deadly sentence. *When the war ends, the Portuguese will go back home. But we Angolans will remain prisoners here forever.*

While Ondjala recounted his troubles, my father was busy gathering pieces of bark and wood. To these improvised keys, he added some *nsala* gourds. Out of almost nothing, he fashioned a marimba. With the crucifix, he tapped the wooden keys and a ragged melody caused us to stop talking.

I like him, said the soldier. *He's a musician, he doesn't live in this world.*

Katini abruptly stopped playing his music and bade us hurry so that we could continue our journey. And we returned to the dugout. My old father's face had a peculiar expression and he didn't speak until he dug an oar in against the current, causing the boat to stop in midstream. With the tip of his oar he prodded the soldier's shoulder and asked:

Who fired the shot?

What?

Who killed my son?

I don't know, we all fired at the dugout.

All?

Then my father suddenly got to his feet, causing the boat to rock perilously. Seen from below like this, he gained the loftiness of a giant. He raised the oar high above his head and brought it down fiercely on the Angolan's head, arms, and whole body. Then he pushed the soldier's body overboard, holding his head underwater for a time. When the Angolan offered no more resistance, my father brought out his metal crucifix and did what is done to fish: he plunged it, like a hook, into the man's neck. The soldier's arms and legs spread out like wings on the surface of the water and our boat was surrounded by a bloodstained slick. Katini stood motionless, watching the body drifting weightlessly.

Father, let's go! I wailed.

I grabbed the blood-covered oar. In my haste to get away, I was unable to get the boat back on course. Whichever way I turned, I saw João Ondjala's body floating as if seeking its own shadow on the riverbed. With unusual decisiveness, Katini Nsambe ordered:

We are going back to the church!

But Father! What about Mwanatu?

There is no grave. My son was thrown into the water, that's what they did to him. The river is the only tomb he has.

Standing at the prow, as stiff as an ancient statue, he raised his cross and a thousand flashes glittered in his hand.

With this crucifix, I'm going to kill the others.

What others, Father?

He didn't answer. He merely added:

When we get to the church, we'll say the soldier fell into the river and was eaten by crocodiles.

With a nobility he had never shown before, my father confronted the surrounding landscape like a corsair who had taken possession of the river he was navigating. He held the crucifix up against the sky again and declared:

Some see a cross, but I see a dagger. This is the blade God has placed in my hands. Vengeance is the justice of the weak. Well, my daughter, I am the weakest of the weak. There will be no greater vengeance than mine.

The sparse meager lights of Sana Benene were twinkling when we moored the boat to the landing stage. In times of war, the fires remain lit day and night. This is done so that the warriors, wherever they may be, always remain in the light. I was preparing to climb the slope when my father grabbed my arm.

Wait, I need to talk to you.

I sat down in the boat again. I looked at Katini's bloodstained hands still clutching the fateful crucifix.

I've changed my plans, he declared. *I'm going to give you to the* Nkosi, *you're going to be the king's wife. You're going to be Ngungunyane's principal spouse.*

Don't do that, Father, for the love of God!

Life has deceived me, the Portuguese have betrayed me. Now it's my turn to betray them. You're going to be his wife.

His words were a double-edged knife. In one go, he was tearing me away from my love for Germano, and delivering me up to the creature I most detested. I wept as if I were speaking, as if each tear were a word, each sob a sentence:

I shall do as my mother did: I'll kill myself.

My intention was to appeal to his sense of compassion. The

opposite occurred. Overcome by an uncontainable fury, my father ground his teeth together and upbraided me:

Never compare yourself again to your mother! Your mother was full of life. That was why the tree received her in its embrace. You cannot kill yourself. And do you know why? Because there's no life in you at all.

Whereupon he fell on me as if he wanted to hurt me. But then he stopped himself. When I opened my eyes again, I received the blurred image of my father bent over me, his arms shaking my shoulders:

Stop crying. You'll summon evil spirits.

Don't do this to me, Father. Are you going to betray those of our people who were murdered by Ngungunyane?

I'm fighting for those who still have to live. The others . . .

There's no difference, Father. There are no others . . .

Hatred was growing in me and I couldn't contain my weeping. I slapped the oar against the water as if I were beating myself. Smacking the river was a way of hurting old Katini Nsambe.

Think of one thing, my daughter . . .

I'm not your daughter!

That doesn't matter much. I'm your father.

Apart from anything else, I made a promise. I promised on my mother's grave that I would kill that cursed Ngungunyane.

You haven't understood, Imani. That is my intention: You marry him first. Then you kill him. Who, other than a queen, can hold a king's life in her hand?

What Katini Nsambe was saying at that moment was too much for me to comprehend.

Let me go, Father. I need to say goodbye to Germano.

You've already said goodbye.

I want to be with him. It'll be our last time together.

That sergeant of yours left for Chicomo this morning. Go and get your things ready. Tomorrow we'll go to Mandhlakazi.

27

SERGEANT GERMANO DE MELO'S NINTH LETTER

*It's not enough for us to walk unshod. Our feet need to tread the ground
until they lose their skin. Until the soil's blood circulates in our veins.*
—THE WORDS OF BIBLIANA

Somewhere between Sana Benene and Chicomo, October 28, 1895

Dear Lieutenant Ayres de Ornelas,

I am dead, sir. I have been deprived of my past, and my dreams have
been torn away. In the early morning, Captain Santiago Mata forc-
ibly pulled me from my quarters at Sana Benene. He uttered only
two words: *Come on!* While I hurriedly put on my clothes, the captain asked me: *Why do you think I came to this bloody place?* He raised
his arms as if the whole world were obliged to hear him: *I was told to
come and get you.* And he did not need to add that I was to be taken
by force to the garrison at Chicomo.

This is a sad way, sir, of reminding me that I am, more than
anything else, a soldier and a Portuguese. Farewell Swiss hospital,
farewell Imani, farewell to my dreams of a life in Mozambique. I am
writing these lines with the same despair as those who are buried
alive and hopelessly beat on their coffin lid. This is the source of my
lassitude. Never again will I have romance, friends, or neighbors.

You cannot imagine, sir—or maybe you can imagine it better
than anyone—the circumstances in which I am scribbling these

lines to you: seated in a cart, the world swaying all around me. I take this opportunity to tell you of the adventures I have been through ever since I began this journey by oxcart early this morning. I am traveling in the company of Santiago Mata and his seven soldiers who are plodding along as an escort. Apart from myself, the cart is loaded only with weapons, some boxes of biscuits, and two pots of water. I am seated in the devil's position, with my back to a path that opens up endlessly in front of us. We are bound for the garrison at Chicomo, where I am due to receive medical treatment.

Swayed by the movement of the cart, I cannot help feeling that I am once again rehearsing for my own funeral cortege. First it was in the belly of a boat. Now in a dusty oxcart. On the day of my real funeral, I shall be dressed in this uniform that I always hated and that now covers my soul more than my body. Take note of this request, sir: Bury me as if my skin had been transformed into the foul-smelling uniform. It was in this predestined funeral shroud that I set out on this journey. Or, sadder still, this is what I am: A piece of cloth that I have been wrapped in, whether in life or death. First a uniform, and then a shroud. I am a soldier, I do not belong to myself. At my funeral, other soldiers, ignorant of the fact that they too have lost their souls, will fire a salute of blank shots. They will be unaware that their shots will be killing the very sky.

Throughout the journey, I have been the butt of Santiago's insults. Far from troubling me, they distract me from other, greater pains. And besides, my mother used to say: *He who utters a lot of insults can't be a bad man.* Judging by the way he reels off his derisive comments, Santiago must be an excellent person. *Thanks to you*, he confronted me, *thanks to you, my little faggot, I never got to take part in the Battle of Coolela. All because I had to come and fetch you, because our little prince here couldn't walk through the bush on his own. Tell me something, my little sergeant: With those little arms of yours, how do you manage to wipe your ass? Was it that lovely little black girl who washed your nether parts? Wouldn't you like one of these black soldiers to wipe your little butt? You can be sure, they're very good at it. They'll make such a thorough job of it, you'll never shit again in your life.*

At first the soldiers contained their laughter. Then gradually they stopped listening. The captain merely began to talk to himself in his endless rosary of insults:

With your hands in the state they're in, there'll be no more tossing off for you. I can just imagine how you've found your fun spanking the monkey out in the bush. Anyway, no more fun and games with those five little dwarves of yours. Now you're going to have to screw those wily kaffir women. I hope you've made a start with that cute little black girl who was with you in the church. Or shall I check her out for you, you crafty little piece of scum?

Eventually, he fell silent. Despair caused him to hunch his shoulders as he walked on in silence. In his swarthy face, however, his eyes continued to gleam, as they scanned the countryside. The man guiding us through the bush must have been terribly lonely.

When darkness fell, he ordered us to stop and pitch camp far from any path. While he was spreading out the canvas that would serve as our bed, the man addressed me in a civil tone for the first time to tell me that I was in luck, for Dr. Rodrigues Braga was passing through Chicomo.

The following day, after a cumbersome climb up slopes covered with thorny shrubs, we encountered a kaffir, whom we asked for food and water for our oxen. He led us in silence to his hut and there offered us some roasted corncobs, which we devoured. Then he warned us that some Vátua soldiers had assembled not far from there. They had arrived in groups and were concentrated by a small lake, where they were getting ready for a ceremony to bless their fighters.

A group of these warriors had visited him early that morning. The oldest of them went to his corral and chose a bull ox. He infuriated the animal by hitting it on the nose with a rod. At this, some younger ones jumped on its back and brought it to the ground. While they were holding it down by the horns, the leader of the group slit its throat with an ax.

Look, you can see the blood here. The farmer pointed at a black stain covered with flies.

In little more than a few minutes, the warriors had cut up the carcass and carried chunks of flesh away on their backs. The kaffir pointed to a valley down which they had disappeared.

Follow me, the man invited us. *They're not far off. If we're careful, they won't notice our presence.*

Are there many of them?

About fifty.

What battalion, what impi *are they from? Don't tell me they're the Ziynhone Muchopes, the White Birds?*

No, these are older. They looked to me more like the Mapepe, the Wily Ones.

We'll ambush them! Santiago ordered.

You're crazy, Captain, I said.

In any other situation, my insolence would have been harshly punished. But at that moment Santiago merely glared at me before handing me a rifle.

We're going to make a soldier of you, my old son of a bitch. With the fingers you've got left, or with your old cock, you're going to fire this gun.

Another weapon was given to the poor farmer, who stood there stock-still, such was his astonishment, unable to bear the gun's weight.

And you too, nigger, if you don't kill them, we'll kill you.

We advanced in complete silence as far as a clearing in the forest. The kaffir was right: There were some fifty men arranged in a circle around a witch doctor, called a *nganga* around here, and a military commander. Smoke rose from a huge pot where they had cooked the meat of the ox. Hidden behind a clump of bushes, we peered at this extraordinary ritual. Each down on one knee, the soldiers were chanting and beating out a vigorous rhythm on the ground with their shields and spears. Then at a certain point the commander got to his feet and held up a human finger. A cold shiver went through me. The appendage could have been one of my missing digits. Noticing my alarm, our kaffir companion explained that this was some old trophy torn from a VaChopi military leader. Such were the rules followed in this magic ritual.

When he had finished exhibiting the desiccated finger, the commander scraped it with the blade of a large knife, allowing the dust to fall onto the ox meat. This condiment was called war medicine, the potion that would make any qualms of conscience disappear. By eating meat seasoned like this, the soldiers lost their heart. For conscience dwells in the breast. This is what the farmer whispered to us.

Santiago was far from paying attention to those words. He was studying the surroundings in order to plan a surprise attack. Using only gestures, he ordered us to spread out in order to create the illusion that there were many of us. At his order, we launched the attack. Taken by surprise, the Vátuas fled in disorder, leaving behind their spears and the few firearms they had. Three of them fell by the great pot, dying next to the potion that was supposed to render them immune to the bullets of the enemy.

The Vátuas seemed to have vanished into the forest when, all of a sudden, our position was sprayed with a salvo of bullets. One of our soldiers, a black private, fell next to a boulder. I even saw his fingers buried in the sand as if he were trying to resist some dark force dragging him away. As he lay dying, he turned to look at me and his eyes were as dark as bottomless wells. I recognized him. He was one who had not spoken a word during the entire journey, because the only European language he spoke was English. And this, for Santiago, was an unacceptable slight.

Next to me, Santiago was horrified. The ambush had gone into reverse and the hunters had become the prey. In a frenzy, the captain assembled his soldiers and, with yells and kicks, urged them to advance against the enemy. He kept calling them cowards until he saw them eventually advance, open-chested, against the invisible Vátuas. The captain and I remained in the rear guard. Suddenly, I saw him bend double as if he had been shot in the stomach. He was waving at me to come to his aid when I noticed that the stain on his trousers was not blood. It was urine.

Then the shooting stopped abruptly on all sides, and a complete silence ensued. Santiago Mata ordered us to return to the hut where we had left our effects. Once there, the first thing the captain did was to pour a whole pot of water over his body. The soldiers were puzzled by this wastefulness.

Fearing that the kaffirs would prepare some ingenious counter-attack in revenge, we grabbed all that was indispensable for us, tied the oxen up in the middle of the bush, and cut some branches so as to hide the cart. It was crucial that we set out as light and as speedily as possible on a forced march to Chicomo. Realizing what our intentions were, the farmer declared almost in tears:

The only thing left for me now is to go with you.

Santiago ordered him to tether his oxen and bring his things. It wasn't a question of returning a favor. His presence as a guide would be vital:

My things? he asked, with a sad smile.

And off we went, handing the luckless, barefoot farmer the task of guiding us through the inscrutable landscape. Under instructions from Santiago, we passed an abandoned military outpost where they had arranged to meet the Angolan soldier who had guided Imani and Katini down the River Inharrime. But the post was empty, without any sign of anyone at all having passed through the place. Santiago didn't seem surprised at his absence:

Black son of a bitch! There's no point in trusting these people . . .

At that point, the farmer told us what he had heard from a traveler he had met that morning. This traveler had told him that the body of a black man had been washed up on the riverbank, half eaten by crocodiles. And this black man was wearing the uniform of a Portuguese soldier. Santiago Mata's reaction was immediate and forceful:

We're going back, we're going to find him.

Are we turning back, Captain? one of the white soldiers queried. *Isn't it there we're running away from?*

Toninho's right, Captain, the other white protested. *Are we going to pick a fight with a pack of wolves?*

There are no wolves here. No wolves and no tigers. We're turning back and we're going to give our comrade the burial he deserves.

Faced with the captain's conviction, I joined the protesters. If we altered our route, it would be the end of all of us. Once by the river we would be all right, but to get there was dicing with death.

I'm not abandoning my men, the captain persisted. *Alive or dead, white or black, I won't abandon them.*

Then he turned around suddenly and asked me for my pen. He scribbled a few quick, crude lines, folded the paper, and gave it to one of the black soldiers:

Take this message to the garrison. It says we are going to be late.

And I asked Santiago's messenger to also be the bearer of these untidy, scrawled jottings. Perhaps they will be the last lines I ever write. Santiago came as my savior. The same Santiago is leading me to my perdition.

P.S. I took advantage of another traveler to get a message to Imani. Right there on the spot, I scribbled a few heartfelt lines laden with yearning, and conveying my intense desire to see her again. I had already thought of the most poetic ways of reminding her of my love. But faced with the blank page, the only things that came to mind were the most ridiculous turns of phrase. Then, at the precise moment when I was carefully handing the letter to the messenger, Santiago appeared and demanded that I give him the pieces of paper. As I expected, the captain summoned the soldiers and read the contents of the letter out loud, while scoffing at my sentiments. Even worse, in an unbelievable display of cowardice, I eventually joined in the laughter directed mockingly at me. The messenger looked into my eyes, shook his head, and left empty-handed.

28

THE DIVINE DISENCOUNTER

Women weep, men lie.
—PROVERB FROM NKOKOLANI

That night I slept like the fishes: in a sleepless dream, my body awake in a bed replete with life. I couldn't get the image out of my head of the Angolan jerking in the waters, the crucifix soaked in blood in my father's hands, his fingers trembling as if petrified. And Germano's absence pained me as if there were no bed and I were lying on stones. My chest was heavy with so much crying. And my wailing didn't stop even after I fell asleep. I slept weeping, such as only the dead are permitted to do.

First thing in the morning, my childhood ritual was repeated: I awoke to the gentle lull of a broom sweeping the backyard. It was the priest who was sweeping. *Where is Bibliana?* I asked. He didn't reply. In front of the broom, the sand turned to water. In the priest's hands, the broom was an oar sweeping the waters back to the river. As always, Rudolfo Fernandes swept in order to dream. And he was bound to be dreaming of somewhere beyond all journeys. But the dogs snuffling around on the ground brought him back to reality in all its sadness. And once again, we were suffocating in the persistent dust of a poor, aimless world.

I waved away the dogs that were busy breathing by the entrance. *The dog's shadow is its own tongue*, my grandfather used to say. On a hot day like this, I'd give anything to be able to gasp like a dog. Or better still, I'd like the ground to turn to liquid. And it almost happened like that: Throughout the entire village the sands steamed, creating the illusion that we were walking over some endless lake.

Father, I need to talk to you.

This is what I murmured as I took the broom from his hands and began to walk up the path leading to the church. The priest followed me, shooing the dogs. Then he walked beside me, his hands hidden in the sleeves of his cassock.

I know what is happening, my daughter. But there is nothing I can do. It's not me you must talk to. It's you alone with God.

I hurried my step, for I didn't want him to see that I was crying. I passed a group of men playing *ntxuva*. They stopped their game to watch me pass by. They stared at my shoes accusingly. They thought I couldn't understand them, and they commented out loud: *Damned VaChopi, they spoil their women with gifts.*

I knelt down in the church as if I were never going to be able to get up again. My hands together formed a cup in which my words echoed:

I have come, my God, to offer up my own feet as a sacrifice. Here they are, immaculate, without blood or wounds. As if life had never existed in them, as if they were mere things, worthless objects.

The priest nervously asked me to withdraw.

Come, my daughter, he urged. *Let's go outside.*

Can't I pray?

That's not praying. No one speaks to God like that.

And he tried to force me to my feet, tugging at my arm. I resisted. At this point, the rosary that hung from his belt broke. Its fifty-nine beads fell noisily to the floor, and, bouncing willy-nilly, scattered everywhere. In the beams up in the roof, the doves stirred. They peered curiously at this unexpected commotion.

Where is Bibliana? I asked.

She went up north, for her dead brother's funeral rites. She's going to stay there for a few days.

I asked the priest to leave me alone. I wanted the church all to myself, I wanted to feel the silence embracing me. As he left, the clergyman stumbled over his rosary beads. And I listened to him cursing angels and demons.

Then I slowly became more serene in the midst of that peace, as if time had never invaded the interior of the church. I curled up on the seat and fell asleep. And I sensed that God was agreeing to listen to me. At first his divine words reached me swaddled in the cooing of the pigeons. But then they began to take shape and it became clear that the Creator was addressing me directly. I was mad, but my madness was beating a path for me toward God's voice:

Your choice was a sad one: a pair of shoes instead of bare feet. Because of your preference for them, you will forever remain incomplete. In exchange, the shoes will become part of your body. This was the choice you made and it will have its price, for your steps will never again belong to you alone. With your leather soles, you will follow paths that will lead you far from your own self. You will be different from other black women. And when you dance, your legs will no longer be yours. And every time you tighten your shoelaces, you will be constricting your soul.

The priest was waiting for me by the church door. He said that he had heard me crying, speaking, and praying inside the church. There was no point in making myself suffer so much, the priest continued: My father would never back down from his decision. I would be offered to the king of Gaza. Nsambe had grown tired of being a good man in a world that only favors the malign. When he tried being deceitful, all he could muster was the primitive art of revenge. The docile man, the affable musician, the tolerant father figure. All this was now part of his past.

I sighed deeply. Yearning does not stem from the past. It is born in an empty present. No memory could come to my rescue.

They say that the church at Makomani, the church of my childhood, has collapsed and been swallowed up by the waves. I miss the sound of the sea. Don't you miss it, Father?

Do you want to know the truth? I always hated that time next to the seashore.

He had difficulty in even recalling it. Every night he had lived on the coast, the sea had flooded into his head. The priest never fell asleep without being submerged in the ocean that flooded the darkness of his room. Fearing that his eyes would jump out of their sockets, Rudolfo slept with his hands covering his eyelids. He would wake up with a stream of tears flowing down his face and salt stinging his skin.

The sea told me there was a return. That is what pained me. For at the time I no longer knew how to wish for such a journey. I was like you are now, my dear girl: not knowing how to sleep, and not knowing how to live.

29

SERGEANT GERMANO DE MELO'S TENTH LETTER

*Gungunhane is the most cosmopolitan man I know: He speaks various
languages, does business with various nations, dresses in cloth from
Asia, adorns himself with bijouterie from the Middle East, surrounds
himself with black and white advisers, has African spouses and
European mistresses, and by day drinks local liquor while
at night he gets drunk on port wine.*
*His memory will live on among those who have no written records. And
he will live in the books of those who have no more dreams.*
—WORDS OF FATHER RUDOLFO FERNANDES

On the way to Chicomo, October 29, 1895

Dear Lieutenant Ayres de Ornelas,

Can I tell you, sir, of the yearning I feel for Imani? Would my dear
lieutenant have the patience to provide a shoulder for me to lean on
in my infinite sadness? You will ask me, sir, whether I write to this
woman. The answer is no. When I get to the moment of trying to
put my feelings down on paper, something within me snaps, a kind
of fulfillment of some anticipated end.

Do not worry, now, sir: I shall not use our messengers to get
you my letters. These are exclusively for the use of the military.
And it was only a day ago that a messenger left with two letters.
One of them was a laconic message from Santiago. The second,

which was mine, was needlessly long, and I have no doubt that you didn't have the patience, sir, to read beyond the first paragraph. But if you did by any chance read it to the end, you will know that we turned back in order to carry out the funeral of one of our soldiers. And we buried the unfortunate Angolan there, on the banks of the Inharrime, or rather the little that was left of him. The crocodiles had spared his trunk and head. I didn't have the courage to gaze at this horrific spectacle. Santiago also moved away from the macabre sight. But he ordered one of the black soldiers to examine the corpse before burying it. And that's what he did with the utmost rigor. At one stage, he paused at two perforations on the right hand side of the wretched man's neck:

It wasn't the animals that killed him.

After the funeral ceremony, we washed ourselves and our stinking clothes. We were all half naked while our gear dried in the sun. One of the white soldiers climbed onto the top of a rocky cliff on the other side of the river to act as a lookout. Down by the river, the other soldiers lit a small fire to prepare coffee. And the captain and I rested in a generous patch of shade. Santiago Mata amused himself by scratching grooves in the sand with a twig.

What are you writing, Captain?

I'm not writing, I'm drawing. I'm drawing a country. Let me show you. You always start with a flag. See? This rectangle here, all full of stripes, is the goddamned flag.

That's a fine flag, Captain . . .

I'm not your captain. Tomorrow we'll reach Chicomo and I'll leave you at the entrance to the garrison. And you'll never see me again.

Won't you come in with me?

I don't know. We'll see.

Then he explained that the soldiers who were with him were not part of the regular army. I recalled Father Rudolfo's use of the term *mercenary.* He answered, shaking his head:

We are—how shall I put it?—an independent unit. We carry out operations that the others can't.

I tell you all this, sir, on the assumption that you already know. But for me, all this came as a complete surprise.

Then, once again, the captain started to scratch in the sand. *There's a garrison missing here*, he declared, surveying his work. Then he added: *You, who never were a military man and who spent a long holiday in a store, perhaps you can draw me a garrison . . .*

In the ensuing pause, we could hear the wind rustling the leaves. Santiago, however, was listening to other things. *Here, we are like animals*, he said. *Speech and silence take their turns.* He signaled to the lookout, who responded from the other bank by calmly folding his arms. I remembered our encounter at Sana Benene and the moment when Bianca had asked Mata if he knew Mouzinho. I recalled, at that moment, the interest Imani had shown in that conversation back at Sana Benene.

Do you remember Imani wanting to know whether you had ever met Gungunhane, Captain? Well, let me ask you now: Do you know the king of Gaza?

Santiago Mata had indeed visited the court of the king of Gaza at Manjacaze. And he recounted the details of his meeting. At the time, he was escorting the counselor José d'Almeida on one of his endless diplomatic missions in which you yourself, sir, participated. As he entered Gungunhane's domains, he felt the same surprise as all the other European visitors to the palace. Instead of an imposing palace, there was just a grouping of simple huts. Instead of a magnificent court, he was faced with a yard of spartan simplicity: the queens sitting on the ground, with barefoot, half-dressed children. What impressed him most, though, was the king of Gaza. According to Santiago, the king does not say much, expressing himself only in monosyllables, and although an inveterate drinker, he always appeared sober during the negotiations. Gungunhane possesses a quality of pretending not to understand what is being said to him. He acts as if he understood no other language apart from Zulu, the language of his court and empire. In meetings with his officials, rather than an autocrat who monopolizes the dialogue, the emperor allows his advisers to speak without ever interrupting them.

In Africa and in Portugal, the same thing applies. The attitude of advisers veers between adulation of the king and wanting to kill him. To which Santiago added: *Allowing these representatives of the people to have a voice is the best way of keeping the nation quiet.*

And now let me tell you, sir, the conclusions Santiago drew from everything he had seen and heard. He believed that that black headman with his simple ways was more of a king than our monarch with all the medieval sumptuousness of his retinue. That man without a uniform was a greater military tactician than our generals who strut around like peacocks at parades. He recited all these impressions with his eyes closed and then, with a tired sigh, concluded:

The kings of this world, both black and white, can go and fuck themselves.

I'm a republican, Captain.

It's all the same shit. Don't you think the republicans will go and romp around in the kings' palaces once they've ousted them?

You will now understand, sir, that this is not a simple account of a mundane incursion into the African backlands. For at a certain moment, one of the black soldiers called us. On the cliff from where the lookout was watching the horizon, our sentinel had fallen asleep. We laughed, amused by the negligence of Toninho, the white soldier. Only Santiago suspected that there was another reason for his slumber. And he was right. Toninho was dead. A trickle of blood ran down his neck. The captain had no doubt: There were the same two perforations that had featured on the body of the Angolan, the same death, the same killer. And he ordered us to make a thorough search of the surrounding terrain. Perhaps the murderer was still in the vicinity. But our search was fruitless.

So we had come to the place to bury one, and we ended up burying two. There was no prayer, nor words to commend the dead men's souls. We closed their graves and left two improvised crosses on each. And all we could hear was the river and one of the soldiers weeping.

Santiago remained detached from all these sad proceedings. He put out the fire and told us to resume our journey to the garrison at Chicomo. He smoothed the sand with his boots, extinguishing the ephemeral country he had invented in that little patch of ground.

If you want to find a true soldier, the captain told me, *look for him outside the army and far from military careers. Because I, my dear soldier . . . I've forgotten your name . . .*

Germano.

Because, my dear Germano, I admit that if I were to formally join the army one day, it would only be for the pleasure of deserting.

Do not be offended, sir, for I am just reproducing all the excretions of that deranged captain's heart. I do so in order that you should be aware of your subordinates and be sure of the loyalty upon which you can rely.

Once we were on our way again, Santiago cursed those who view military life as a career one might pursue with the hope of an early retirement. He talked about this and then said no more for the rest of our journey. I suddenly felt like showing the captain my old mother's letter. I carried it more in my thoughts than in my pocket. I wanted the captain to understand the affection that motivated my dedication to this strange fate of mine. When I was left an orphan, I became a son for the first time. Fortunately, I didn't yield to the foolish urge to share these mawkish musings. Only with you, Lieutenant, do I feel at ease to share matters of this nature.

And do you know what happened during the course of our march? Strangely, it suddenly dawned on me that my mother was not the author of that letter. For that woman abandoned her home when I was still a child. She abandoned home without ever managing to leave it. I was in fact adopted. But I was adopted by my own mother. Do you understand, sir? The woman who gave birth to me was called Mother. Afterwards, she took on the name of Spouse. It was this latter woman who nurtured me. With a love that was supervised, with a residual affection and whispered words. I was half a son, and so how can I be a whole man? And maybe it is better like this, to only half exist. The yearning I feel for my beloved is thus less painful.

30

SIXTH LETTER FROM LIEUTENANT AYRES DE ORNELAS

Upon approaching Gungunhane, we feel an inexplicable sympathy.
With his docile expression and tone of speech, we discover a set of
attractive qualities that predispose us to be favorable towards him from
the outset. It must be understood that underneath those amenable
manners, he has an iron will that will not bend to any pressure.
—RESIDENT MARQUES GERALDES, "REPORT OF 1888"

Chicomo, November 1, 1895

Dear Sergeant Germano de Melo,

I received your letter brought by Santiago's messenger. By an irony
of fate, I shall already be in Inhambane when you get here. I was
directed, along with other officers, to coordinate the final offensive
against the Lion of Gaza.

How strange are these misencounters of ours, which seem to
repeat themselves endlessly, as happens in the case of platonic love.
Santiago Mata is a man of boorish manners. I ask you to be patient
with him. I have also had to revise my perceptions of others. Much
of that which is ascribed to emotion is in fact prejudice. This was
how I became reconciled with Mouzinho de Albuquerque. We need
the ability to ponder just as much as we need single-mindedness.

Do not worry about disobeying my orders. By refusing to fulfill
the functions I assigned to you, you enabled me to gain a much

better understanding of my own duties. By continuing to send me your colorful personal letters, my dear sergeant, you performed an invaluable service for our army. I now have a much better acquaintance with the people of Mozambique than most other officers possess. You refused to act as a spy for me, my friend. So what? You can be sure that Portugal would find it hard to find a better spy in Africa. From your picturesque accounts, I gradually came to realize how far we are from understanding the territory that we aspire to conquer. How do these people think of themselves? How do they describe themselves, their nations and their leaders? For example, no one apart from ourselves uses the term *Vátua* to describe the VaNguni. No one uses the name *State of Gaza* anymore. What do the kaffirs themselves call it? And what do they call the man we call king? The name they give to Gungunhane is *Nkosi*. They use the same word for God. And they are right to call him that, for he behaves with divine authority. He punishes and rewards like some great Father. Our war does not just have a military dimension. It is a religious war.

Finally, the purpose of this missive is to validate your often repeated claim. If we want to defeat the Africans, we are going to have to get to know them better, penetrate their world and live among their peoples. They have been doing the same with us for decades now. They observe our way of life, usurp our way of thinking without our knowledge, and learn our language. And they do not need to write letters to divulge this wealth of information among their fellow men. As if conveyed by silent drumbeats, news of our power, and above all of our weaknesses, has spread across the African interior.

By way of conclusion, I must tell you that the same messenger brought me news that your beloved Imani and her father had left Sana Benene. They both left for Liengme's Swiss hospital, goodness knows why. Be careful, dear sergeant. As a future husband you must remain vigilant of your young fiancée, who is both beautiful and, apart from this, black. I give thanks to God that I did not leave a female heart waiting for me back in Portugal. One can only rely on a mother for absolute loyalty over and above all other contingencies. For the rest, for wives and sweethearts, the longer the separation, the more insincere will their waiting be.

31

A HOSPITAL IN A SICK WORLD

The Swiss missionaries spare no effort in trying to engage the
sympathy of the blacks, they do not contradict them in the slightest and
they give them liberties that are entirely inappropriate and not
conducive to good manners, such as, for example, holding their hands.
And the blacks in the vicinity of the mission are so used to these
fraternal forms of greeting that on the occasion of my visit, a black
servant boy at this very mission came straight toward me, his hand
held out! It may well be that this is the best way to educate the native
but, from my point of view, I find it unacceptable and cannot tolerate
it. Treating them well, educating them, providing them with good
teaching and making of them able and skillful men, who may one day
be of use to themselves and to society, yes, of course; but to descend so
low as to hold one's hand out to a black savage, certainly not.
—AHM-ACM, SECTION E, BOX 169, DOCUMENT 506, FROM THE ADMINISTRATOR OF
CHAI-CHAI TO THE GOVERNOR OF THE DISTRICT OF LOURENÇO MARQUES,
NOVEMBER 28, 1911

Sitting at the door of her house, Bertha Ryff had fallen asleep with
a photograph album open in her lap. She was waiting for the arrival
of her husband, Georges Liengme. She woke upon hearing our
footsteps, and serenely turned to face us, as if we had been
expected.

When we got close, my father limited himself to a drawn-out, sibilant *Ssskyooze mee*. I took the initiative of explaining the purpose of our visit. I soon realized that the only language in which we could communicate would be Txichangana. Nevertheless, it seemed strange to be conversing with a European woman in an African language. For the first time, I felt pride in the preponderance of an African tongue.

The woman seemed to be made of wax, so spindly and fragile that I found myself speaking in an undertone as if I feared she would fall to pieces if I were to raise my voice in the slightest. She was distant but helpful. Certainly, she said without any hesitation, we could spend the night in one of the rooms in the hospital while her husband was away. She insisted on only one condition: That man, she said pointing to my old father, would be the only man to share my room.

This is my father, I explained.

Mrs. Ryff smiled and glanced sideways at my father, who stood there motionless, his hands clutching his old straw hat next to his chest.

Elizabete will look after you, the Swiss woman concluded. *Sit down and she'll be with you soon.*

We removed ourselves quietly and went to sit on an old tree trunk in the yard that was used as a seat. And we noticed how everything there seemed clean and tidy, in contrast to the disorder at Sana Benene.

The sound of voices and laughter came from one of the huts: It was Elizabete Xifadumela, who taught young black girls sewing and dressmaking. Two months before, when the classes began, the hall was full of young girls eager to learn a new skill. Attendance began to drop, as parents did not look favorably on this diversion from household chores. They feared the girls would forget their traditional roles as future wives and mothers.

At a certain point, the doctor's wife called us over, waving a camera. I thought she wanted some sort of a souvenir of us and my father thought the same, for he quickly tidied his hair. But Bertha just wanted to talk about her husband's hobby. She felt relieved that Georges had forgotten to take his cherished Kodak with him. She never mentioned it to her husband, but his images of naked black women made her feel uncomfortable. And she leafed through the album to illustrate that display of innocent shamelessness. It was one thing to know that Georges passed these women every day. It was another to suspect that her husband lingered in his contemplation of those lascivious bodies. This was why Bertha was rigorous in which rolls of film to select for printing locally and which ones should be printed in Switzerland. At the headquarters of the Presbyterian Church of Vaud, the photographs would be subjected to a second round of censorship. When they were sent back to Mandhlakazi, the images arrived having been screened and changed to conform to evangelical precepts. For example, all the chairs upon which the headmen leaned had been erased. Bertha knew why: chairs were a sign of sinful modernity. Such items originating in Europe distorted the idea of a "pure" people resisting the progress of time by living in its "natural state." These Swiss pastors had been chosen to save a savage, pristine people. They had been given the divine function of naming this people, whom they thus designated as Vatsonga. And the sacred responsibility had been given them to protect this flock from the pernicious influence of the modern age.

My husband won't be long. You'll get to know him, he's a saint!

Suddenly, a noisy group of young girls ran by and disappeared among the houses of the little village. The class had finished and Elizabete Xifadumela came to greet us. Following Bertha's orders, the sewing teacher led us to the hut where we would be accommodated. As we walked along, I contemplated the woman who was leading us and thought that if Georges Liengme had sent photographs of that woman to Europe, then the leaders of the Presbyterian

Mission would surely have been perturbed. Elizabete was a proud mulatto woman who knew she was beautiful. She dressed in a modern way, and wore socks and sandals with a buckle. And she walked like no other woman did in that place: without asking permission to tread on the ground. That mixed-race woman was an aberration in the closed social order. In order to uphold the guarantee of puritan values, divine justice had punished that illegal beauty: Elizabete had inherited syphilis from her father. The dark patches on her hands and feet were like tattoos etched into the skin of the condemned.

Elizabete walked beside me the whole way. She compared my shoes with her sandals. At one stage, she asked me whether I too was a *mulata*. I replied that I wasn't, that I was black and from the VaChopi people. She smiled in disbelief: *That's what you think. You're more of a* mulata *than I am, my girl. You don't know the price to pay for your situation.*

Like her, I was a frontier soul. Those who considered themselves to be of a pure race hated us. Not because of what we were. But for not corresponding to what they expected.

Oblivious to what we were talking about, my father followed Elizabete, fascinated. Katini Nsambe had never seen a woman like that, with such an indistinct skin color and name.

Leave your shoes outside, our hostess ordered.

She stopped at the entrance to the hut and studied my body and face.

Do you know what you should do? Elizabete asked. *You should use a headscarf.*

I should hide my hair, conceal my origins—that was her recommendation. A woman always has another race within her. She gains power by hiding her mysteries. *Become mysterious*, the *mulata* concluded. And then she added:

Then ask the doctor to take a photo of you. He'll like that. He'll like it very much.

The *mulata* withdrew and we still heard her laughter as she walked away. The hut was spacious and airy. My attention was drawn to a sewing basket on the floor in a corner. I rummaged among balls of woolen thread, buttons, and needles. My fingers lingered on a rag doll in the shape of a little black girl. I caressed the soft little figure as if I were returning to what I had missed as a little girl. The wooden closet was full of winter clothes, dangling from the lifeless hangers. In spite of my father's reproachful air, I placed a fur coat over my shoulders. Then I found a piece of paper, rolled up and tied with a ribbon. It was a letter from Bertha to her husband. My father interrupted my incursion, chiding me for tinkering with white folks' things. That was exactly what he said: *white folks' things.*

Maybe Elizabete was right. I should come out of myself more and stop dressing as if there were only one season in the year. I needed no mirror except for Germano's eyes. Until the Portuguese had arrived, all I knew about my body was what a blind woman knows about her own beauty. But now there was a gleam in that man's eyes every time he looked at me. Germano was, after all, like all men, without a homeland. They are given birth to by women forevermore.

From the window we saw the Swiss doctor arrive, along with his delegation. He corresponded to the descriptions people had given of him: short, with an ample brow, and clear, bright eyes.

Georges Liengme did not kiss his wife, who remained seated at the entrance to the backyard. The couple knew that displays of affection should not be made in public. Apart from that, the missionary was exhausted after a journey of several days through the troubled countryside separating Mandhlakazi and Lourenço Marques. Bertha Ryff hurriedly hid the album and put the loose photographs away in the large pockets of her apron. Then she smiled candidly at the silhouette of her tired husband standing in the full glare of the sun. Farther away, one could see a mule and a young guide making up the delegation.

Georges Liengme had returned from an arduous mission. He had been summoned by the Royal Commissioner, António Enes. The Portuguese were expecting the Swiss to convince Ngungunyane to hand over Zixaxa and Mahazul, the leaders of the revolt against Lourenço Marques. Bertha knew her husband and how tenaciously he stuck to his principles; the chances of the meeting being successful were remote. And this was confirmed by her husband:

They hate us, Bertha, the doctor said with a sigh, while loosening his suspenders over his shoulders. *As soon as they can, they'll expel us. They need to find a culprit. A white culprit.*

They can't expel us. Don't we all have the same right to work in Africa, whether Protestant or Catholic? Didn't they sign treaties in Europe about this?

Treaties don't protect us. Portugal will argue that we don't limit ourselves to evangelizing. They accuse us of distributing arms to the blacks and encouraging them to revolt.

Nevertheless, António Enes had shown himself to be a cordial, ethical man. Tall and lanky, with sunken cheeks and deep-set eyes, the Royal Commissioner, much to the astonishment of the Swiss, took pride in his reluctance to respond to the Portuguese government's demands to expel the doctor. Enes put it like this:

I can't stop you from encouraging an act of betrayal. But I hope you don't betray Portugal. The missionary should return to Manjacaze, given that the king of Gaza would certainly listen to him. This way, war might be avoided. As their conversation came to a close, Enes's tone became almost menacing: If there were a military confrontation, the Portuguese would not distinguish between villainous Africans and treacherous Swiss. This, in short, was what had happened in Lourenço Marques.

Is it as serious as that, Georges? his fragile wife asked.

Start getting your things together. You and the children had better get out of here as soon as possible.

Don't show a face like that when you come in, our children need to see a smiling, confident father when they meet you again.

Bertha hadn't understood: The doctor's apprehensiveness had not been stirred by the intimations of the Royal Commissioner. On the way, he had passed hundreds of Portuguese and Angolan troops approaching the State of Gaza.

They're right here, they're not far from Mandhlakaʒi. The war has started, Bertha.

The Swiss woman crossed herself. Then, noticing us at the entrance to the hut, peering across at them and listening to their conversation, she explained our presence to her husband. The doctor shrugged. We would have to wait. He needed to recover from his journey first. Apart from that, there wasn't a day when there weren't dozens of sick people arriving, always accompanied by numerous family members. Illness in Africa isn't a matter for one person alone. The relatives need to be treated too, for there are always many of them living in close proximity to one another.

Are you going to rest, husband? Ngungunyane is here.

Here at the mission?

He's waiting for you at the hospital. He arrived last night, and guess who was with him? Mrs. Fels. Fortunately, she left for the Transvaal today to meet up with her husband. But you already know what I think about the matter, Georges, we cannot tolerate such indecency at our mission.

The king has hundreds of women. What's the difference?

This is different, and you know only too well it is.

So what does Ngungunyane want?

He says he doesn't feel well.

And he's right to feel like that.

It wasn't the emperor who was ill. It was the empire that had come to an end. His soldiers were deserting him en masse. Soldiers were fleeing from hunger, emigrating to the mines, returning to the places from where they had been taken.

The emperor is on his own. And we are even more insecure.

As the doctor was walking off in the direction of the hospital, his wife called after him:

Don't you want me to take your boots off for you, husband?

32

SEVENTH LETTER FROM LIEUTENANT AYRES DE ORNELAS

War waged in Africa against the savages has the painful need to be
thorough in its destruction, in order not to appear weak and cowardly.
The Negroes do not understand clemency and generosity. To cause the
greatest possible damage to the enemy is the only duty of a fighter.
—ANTÓNIO ENES, "THE AFRICAN WAR OF 1895," 1898

Inhambane, November 3, 1895

Dear Sergeant Germano de Melo,

Our resounding military victory at Magul has restored my honor as
a soldier and my pride in being Portuguese. With this action, we
have silenced the backstabbing insinuations on the part of Commissioner António Enes, who vilified one of the heroes of our African
campaign, our good Colonel Eduardo Galhardo. Insistent telegrams repeated the same message over and over again, in the weeks
beforehand, invoking our "duties as patriots," the commissioner
"requesting" that the colonel should proceed to Manjacaze. I was
amused by the refined quality of Galhardo's reply. He said that
there was no need for António Enes to invoke patriotic rhetoric for
him to fulfill his obligations. And he went on to say that in his rela-
tions with his superiors, he was not used to receiving "requests." If
the commissioner were to give him orders, he would obey them
without a moment's hesitation. This dignified outburst proved to be

therapeutic for me. Those who have never ventured from the comfort of their offices can never appreciate what a herculean task it is to transport an arsenal of war over hundreds of kilometers, crossing the rivers, lakes, and swamps of the African hinterland.

The worst defeats we have suffered came about because we lacked the courage to fight a single battle. This explains the intoxicating feeling I received from the news of our engagement at Magul. This euphoria lasted until, some days later, I saw pillars of smoke proliferating across the vast plains of Bilene. Villages were being burnt. I saw hundreds of anxious-looking kaffirs carrying their meager possessions through the countryside. And I confess that the sight caused me sadness. It is not enough for us to have defeated the Vátua army. In a climate of increasing fear, the blood of soldiers is not worth much. The terrible truth is that civilians need to die for a defeat to begin to weigh heavily on a nation's conscience.

During those troubled days, something happened that I shall never forget. You will be aware, my dear sergeant, of the fire which destroyed much of our garrison at Chicomo. It happened on a pitch-black night. As the soldiers were already in bed, the alarm was only raised when the flames had already devoured many of the houses. Amid all the shouting and running about, one dark, stocky soldier of unknown name ran to the hospital building and rescued the patients. After that, the same young man dodged through the flames to reach the munitions store and dragged away the crates of explosives that were nearest to the fire. After that, he went to the corral and cut the ropes tethering the horses. The animals scattered into the darkness, kicking and jumping, knocking over everything in their frenzied flight. But they returned later, safe and sound.

When everything was once again calm, I looked for the soldier in the darkness and the wreckage in order to congratulate him. But I couldn't find him. The following day, now taken up with my usual tasks, my debt of gratitude slipped from my mind. And over the following days, I clean forgot about the matter.

Then one day, during morning training exercises, I ran into him again. There he was, the hero of that fire-filled night. Now, in the light of day, my disillusion could not have been greater. One glance at him was enough to understand: He was not exactly a soldier, he had never fired a gun, and the rifle weighed so heavily on him that his shoulders were all askew. He didn't know how to look through the sight. Indeed, it was as if the opposite were happening: that it was the enemy observing him, targeting his soul. His whole body fell backwards when he fired the first shot next to me. I thought about giving him a word of encouragement, a message that might combine comfort with gratitude. But once again, I put off speaking to this young soldier.

Then, at the height of the Battle of Magul, I was dashing around madly, issuing orders to the soldiers to keep firing, when, blinded by the smoke and dazed by the explosions, I ended up stumbling over our doctor, Rodrigues Braga, who was on his knees tending to an injured soldier. His primary efforts were geared towards keeping the man, who had been shot in the neck, awake. The doctor was shaking the unfortunate man insistently, while begging him: *Speak to me, don't let yourself go to sleep.*

I looked at the dying man in surprise. It was the hero of the firefight. This was the man who had risked his life to save so many of his colleagues, and who was now bleeding to death in Dr. Braga's arms. No amount of heroism could save him, no miracle would be able to bring him back.

For some time, the doctor continued to shake the now-lifeless body. It was I who grabbed the young man from his arms by force, and then laid the unlucky fellow gently onto his last resting place. With a vacant expression, the doctor went on muttering: *Don't let him fall asleep, don't let him fall asleep*. And Braga's arms went on shaking the emptiness, as mothers do when they weep for their children who have left.

It then occurred to me that this was what we should do: Shake the past so that time should remain alive. Perhaps that is why I write so often to my poor mother. Every word is another push against nothingness, a jolt I choose to give myself so as not to fall asleep on the arid road ahead.

And I thought of you, my dear sergeant, when this anonymous young boy fell from my arms. I am sure you have never taken part in a battle. Everyone will tell you that you need it as a lesson for life, but believe me, my friend, there is no lesson that can compensate for what we lose in terms of our humanity. It will not be long now before I am promoted to the position I so richly deserve. At that point, I shall fulfill my promise and you, my young sergeant, will be able to return safe and sound to your old home.

This whole mission is a heavy burden for me, and it is not because of its military dimension. It is for the collateral effects of this, and which I cannot understand. The world could be so much more straightforward, more organized, as we were taught at the military college: Europeans on one side; Africans on the other.

We are far from such a simple scenario. Beginning with who we are, we Portuguese. Among us, in our very midst, there are currents of opinion that are more hostile to each other than those that separate angels and demons. These disagreements are not exclusive to the Portuguese. For in this part of the world there are Europeans at war with each other. For political or religious reasons. Catholics and Protestants fight as if they didn't share one God. There is more rivalry between the English and the Portuguese than between whites and blacks. If there is no unity among whites, there is equally no single entity that we might call "the blacks." They are so scattered and contain such a diversity of tribes that we shall never know which names we should attribute to them. The Changanas and Mabuingelas who predominate here hate us Portuguese, but they hate Gungunhane's folk even more. And there are the Chopes and the Ndaus, who ferociously resist the dominion of the black emperor. And yet a high proportion of the soldiers in the emperor's pay come from the ethnic groups that make up his enemies.

In a nutshell, those who are our allies today will be our enemies tomorrow. How can we begin to wage a war if we are unaware of the frontier that separates us from our enemies?

33

IMPERIAL FEVERS

Once upon a time, there were five brothers who slept on a narrow bed.
Not a night passed without their squabbling over the one meager
blanket. It was cold and they kept pulling the cover from one side to the
other. There was no solution that satisfied any of them: the cold was too
great, the people were too many, and the blanket was too short. Until
they heard the roar of a lion outside their door. In a flash, they huddled
together and the blanket was more than enough to cover the five
brothers. And this is what happens: Fear turns the little into much.
And it reduces the desire for everything to nothing.
—A STORY TOLD BY NGUNGUNYANE

The doctor, Georges Liengme, passed us, and without any form of greeting, bade us follow him to the mud-and-wattle house where they had lodged the emperor. Sitting on their haunches, two VaNguni warriors guarded the door of the improvised infirmary. Between the two sentries, one could see a wide chair, with decorated arms and back and the seat lined with zebra skin. It was the throne the warriors transported to ensure that the king would never have to sit on the ground. The chair was out there in the open, exposed to the flies which covered most of the seat.

Georges Liengme paused for a few moments, contemplating my face as if he recognized me from some distant past. Then he told us to wait for him there. My father took advantage of the opportunity to explain himself:

I don't want to bother you, Dokotela. All I seek is a word with the Nkosi *Ngungunyane. It's about this daughter of mine . . .*

The doctor entered the infirmary before my father had finished speaking. Through a shaft of light, I peeped apprehensively into the hut. I guessed that the figure lying on a litter was Ngungunyane. The sound of heavy, irregular breathing echoed through that little chamber: The emperor was sleeping only a few meters from me. And I prayed that he was lying on his deathbed.

The missionary approached him, wiping his hands on a white towel, and announced in stentorian tones:

Nkosi, *my king, I have just arrived from Lourenço Marques, and I bring bad news.*

The emperor remained silent and motionless, as if he were unaware of the arrival of the man he regarded as his private physician. The Swiss placed his hand on the patient's forehead, which was adorned with the *chilodjo*, the royal crown. In order to better assess the fever, he pushed up the diadem, made of a piece of cloth wrapped in some sort of dark wax. The crown created a river of sweat flowing over the sovereign's cheeks as far as the cracks in his earlobes, which gleamed like dark lakes. Persistent flies perched on the tiny ox bone that he wore stuck in his crown and which the emperor, ignoring his doctor's advice, used for scratching his head and ears.

Holding a box of snuff next to his chest, the king of Gaza raised himself with difficulty, while the Swiss persisted with his somber news:

The Portuguese are in the process of encircling Mandhlakaȥi. And there are thousands of them, Nkosi.

I need you to massage me, Ngungunyane mumbled, changing the subject. *I rule an empire, but my knee joints don't obey me.*

The doctor sighed. He knew his patient only too well. So, arming himself with patience, he sat down in the little space left on the litter.

I told you before, Nkosi: *You need to have your front doorway made taller.*

Certainly not. I would rather have no knees than lose my neck.

The doctor smiled. The thatched roof of the VaNguni houses extended almost as far as the ground. There was no other way of entering them than on all fours. It was a security measure. Some ill-intentioned intruder could be surprised while in a helpless position.

The emperor passed his hands over his legs and then carefully straightened the crown on his head. Only then did he proclaim:

Forget what you saw out there. Concern yourself more with my complaints. No matter how much the Portuguese move around seeking out military posts and fortifications, they'll never find anything. My garrison is my land, my army is my people.

With one gesture, he swatted the flies and wiped away his sweat, which now flowed over his large stomach.

Have I already told you the story about the five brothers?

Several times. This time, there is no story that can ensure your peace of mind. Look what happened at Magul.

They were not my troops at Magul. Do you know what my informers tell me?

How many times have you told me that you don't trust your informers? the missionary asked. And he added solemnly: *This time, it's different.*

What was happening was unprecedented. Three Portuguese columns, consisting of the best armed cavalry and infantry units, were converging on Mandhlakazi. Apart from the hundreds of white soldiers who had arrived from Portugal, the columns included six thousand black warriors, separated into contingents of various origins. Panga and Homoíne had provided two thousand sepoys; the headmen of Massinga and Zavala had also contributed men for the final assault on Ngungunyane's court.

Did you see them all on this journey you made, Dokotela? Well, you can be sure of one thing: Half those people have already turned back, the emperor declared dismissively. *They're already deserting because of hunger.*

And aren't your men deserting? the Swiss asked.

My men, the king of Gaza retorted, *have been immunized by the most powerful witch doctors of the River Save.*

The missionary passed his fingers through his prematurely gray hair. He had no argument against such presumption.

You are very ill, my king. And it isn't to do with the knees.

Forget the war, Dokotela. I have come here as a simple person. And today I am feeling it.

The doctor knew that this was the way we black people complained. We say we are "feeling our body."

Mrs. Fels, that white lady from the Transvaal, had just left the hospital and had massaged the royal knees, according to the monarch. And maybe other parts of the body, Liengme must have felt like saying. But he refrained. With some reluctance, he rolled up his sleeves, and with considerable abashment rubbed some balsam into the patient's opulent organs. His hurried, furtive manner did not go unnoticed.

Do you feel humiliated, Dokotela? Are you ashamed that you are caring for me as if you were one of my wives? You should take pride in treating such a powerful man.

I am proud to have you as a patient.

I don't trust anyone, not even my guards. One day they bring me my chair, next they'll take the floor from under me.

That confession of his own fragility moved the European. And there were other illnesses, the sovereign mentioned. Illnesses with no name that arrive like shadows.

There are dreams that cause me to fly far away.

There was nothing metaphorical about this statement. Liengme knew that in the emperor's language, the same word was used for "to fly" and "to dream."

Bind my legs together, tie me down by my waist, but don't let me fly away like this. You've got your powers. Find out who has called for me to suffer like this.

No one has called for anything. Your condition is called insomnia.

It's Mafemane. It's my brother. It was I who killed him. That's what they say.

They say?

The memory of the murder came back to him through endless versions. That was why he found himself there, confessing his fears to a foreigner. He didn't want to use his witch doctors. He had lost faith in them.

The doctor smiled upon hearing this request. It was a long time since he had been asked something that he found so satisfying in professional terms. His specialty was hypnosis, his reason for studying medicine. And there was an opportunity to put a skill into practice, and that many of his countrymen suspected was closer to witchcraft than to science.

Close your eyes, Nkosi.

For a moment, however, the doctor hesitated. How could one hypnotize someone who not only speaks another language but also uses the same verb for "to fly" and "to dream"?

What do you think is happening to you?

That is the problem, Dokotela. It's that I only think when I am dreaming. And I don't know who I am when I dream.

And what do you dream of, my king?

Of all the dreams, there is one that oppresses me in particular. I am the master of those who sleep and I end up as the slave of that dream.

Tell me this dream that persecutes you so much.

The doctor now spoke in a tone that was so indistinct, so hushed, that I was obliged to lean past the doorpost. The guards were fast asleep. After a long silence, I heard Ngungunyane's muffled speech:

I didn't kill him, the ones who killed him were the elders and the officials. I merely gave the order, and that was my greatest mistake: a brother doesn't die. Mafemane left his life to enter mine.

So what is this dream that disturbs you so much? the doctor pressed him, his eyes closed. *Tell me, Umundungazi, tell me this dream.*

That is where the problem begins. The dream isn't mine. I sleep and my brother dreams inside me.

Umundungazi closed his eyes and spoke, his hands, palms down, resting on the sides of the litter. The doctor listened, his eyelids still lowered. The emperor's voice, by this time dislodged from previous certainties, was a mere whisper in the darkened room.

In Ngungunyane's dream, the brother is alive. Or rather, he is struggling in the liquid frontier between life and death. During his very last moments, Ngungunyane's arms are talons that force him under the waters of the wide lake. Mafemane seems resigned to his end. Gradually, his convulsed jerking turns into a gentle rippling of arms and legs. The death of the inheritor of the throne must be near, and it is not long before he is still, like a tree trunk floating in the waters where the two brothers confronted each other for hours on end.

However, death does not actually occur. Ngungunyane gradually feels his brother's curly hair dissolve between his fingers while the head of the ill-fated man starts to grow, wrapped in a kind of slippery moss. Mafemane's arms and legs shrink visibly and a deformed creature slowly evolves under the warm waters. At first it looks like a mermaid, and soon he has no doubt at all: His brother has turned into a fish. He is alive and remains next to him, alive, now a fish, while yet still his brother. So now, in every lake and river, this ghostly creature lurks, guarding the secret of his guilt.

When he had finished his account, the king of Gaza, breathless and sweating abundantly, began to ramble aimlessly. And he was already in full fever when he murmured:

Throughout my empire, the dead have become so flighty that they are vanishing among the grains of sand in order to later rise into the heavens like will-o'-the-wisps.

In a whisper that was almost inaudible, Ngungunyane begged:

You who are a white king—

I am not a king of any kind, Nkosi.

Whoever is next to me becomes a king. That is why I ask you, Dokotela. Order the dead to be shackled inside their graves.

Before he withdrew, the doctor must have felt a need to comfort his patient. For he leaned over the bed and, with paternal indulgence, spoke in a gentle tone:

I speak to you now in my role as a missionary. You have betrayed, but this was never as a result of a decision taken by yourself alone. Others prevailed upon you to do so. But now you have bravely agreed to protect Zixaxa and remain defiant in your decision against everyone and everything. God is watching you. This proof of your loyalty will remedy all your feelings of guilt.

That is where you are mistaken, Dokotela, Ngungunyane answered. *I am not protecting Zixaxa. Having him here with us is so that I can be his jailer. The Portuguese think I am sheltering him. But I am keeping him shackled.*

The Swiss shook his head, unable to understand. Then the emperor continued:

I cannot allow a possible rival to run free in these southern domains.

The Portuguese saw the fugitive as a symbol of their own humiliation. For Ngungunyane, the man represented something else: the threat of a future adversary.

Under my protection, Zixaxa is condemned. When we deliver him up to the Portuguese, he will no longer be anybody.

As he was leaving the infirmary, the Swiss doctor bumped into me. His eyes narrowed like those of a cat while he examined me from head to foot. Then we crossed a yard together surrounded by ramshackle dwellings. We paused at the entrance to the hut where my father and I had been provisionally accommodated, and the doctor issued precise instructions:

Tomorrow I'm going to Chicomo. I want you to wait for me to return. Bertha will look after you.

He seemed in a hurry to be off, but as he walked away, he changed his mind and came back to look closely at me. One thing was clear: His curiosity was not motivated by any medical interest. He spoke to my father and gave him some brief instructions. He was going to fetch his camera, and by the time he returned I should have removed my shoes and blouse. *I want a portrait of a typical African woman, wearing just a* capulana *around her waist*, he declared.

Fearing what my reaction might be, old Katini whispered in my ear:

They are orders, my daughter. We are here as supplicants.

We? You, Father, are the only supplicant here.

But of one thing I was sure: The biggest beggar was not my father, but the emperor.

34

SERGEANT GERMANO DE MELO'S ELEVENTH LETTER

I dreamed I was an eternal emperor. But I shall have the fate of slaves: They will bury me in some strange land, my body will rot away in the soil of my vanquishers. My bones will dwell beyond the ocean. And no one will have any memory of me. Oblivion is the only way of dying forever. And it will be worse still: Those who remember me at all will be those who never wished me well.

—THE WORDS OF NGUNGUNYANE

Chicomo, November 4, 1895

Dear Lieutenant Ayres de Ornelas,

Shut away here in the infirmary of the garrison at Chicomo, where I have just arrived, I have little news to report. I am surrounded by dozens of patients, but am more isolated here than I was at the outpost of Nkokolani. My boredom is only broken by the repeated summons of Dr. Rodrigues Braga in order to reassess my hands. He has already done this several times. And today, once again, there I was before his desk.

As always happens before an examination, the doctor extended his gaze beyond the confines of the garrison, tired of the somber scene that surrounded him. As if seeking to contemplate the landscape without ever actually seeing it, he removed his glasses. His defenseless, myopic eyes gave him a vulnerable air that was out of keeping with the solid appearance that war expects from those who wage it.

What day of the week is it? he asked wearily.

He knew there would be no answer. I had long lost any notion of time. Braga put his glasses back on and twisted the ends of his mustache upward. *It's Sunday, my young friend.*

Once again, he studied my hands, which lay ignored on the table, as if they were a collection of old odds and ends in a display case. As always, the man examined my fingers, felt my skin, tested the joints.

They are continuing to scar without any problems. Who was it that treated you? He repeated the same question asked a hundred times before.

Once again, sir, I found myself hesitating. What could I say? That it had been a black healer who had come to my aid with concoctions, spells, and ointments? *It was . . . it was a woman*, I stammered. The doctor answered, with a mischievous smile: *A woman? They're the best cure.*

You, sir, are very familiar with the simultaneously abrupt and delicate manner of our physician friend. And this was why he let my wrists drop with blunt disregard, as if he were returning one of my forgotten parts to me. Once again, he fixed his gaze on the horizon. I imitated him in his far-flung contemplation before asking:

Do you think I'll be able to use a weapon again, Doctor?

The doctor shook his head, as if he were disappointed. Between you and me, Lieutenant, I have to admit my question baffled me. At the time when I was first treated, at Sana Benene, I asked a very different question: whether I would be able to make the sign of the cross again. What warlike fervor was now moving me?

I only hope Mouzinho can't hear you, the doctor affirmed. *The captain will recruit you for his punitive expedition, which he is organizing against all advice.*

The sad truth is this, sir: even with my fingers in their present state, I was in better health than most of the soldiers confined to their beds here. Some of them should have long ago been evacuated to Lourenço Marques. Or even to the mother country. But most of these wouldn't survive the journey. Once, Dr. Braga told me confidentially of the doubt that consumed him:

I learned to deal with the sick. What am I going to do with the dying?

The following day, the doctor acted as if he had found the answer. He commandeered two of the carts used for bringing supplies to Chicomo, which returned empty to Inhambane. In them, he placed the most seriously ill of his patients, and to each one he gave two bottles, one with water, the other with liquor. One to allay thirst, the other to guarantee oblivion. He knew that only a miracle would get these wretched folk to their destination. In this way, he fulfilled his role as a doctor. There being no remedy, they would die in the belief that they were going home.

Wouldn't you like to help me in the infirmary?

Then he amended his question. He was my superior, and was giving me orders. He went on to define my responsibilities. I would have the task of ordering and administering the medical supplies. He showed me a pile of papers on his desk. They were requests for matériel: bandages, quinine, purgatives, balsam pills, poultices, and phenic acid for infections. All this matériel had been held up at Inhambane for months.

I'm a soldier, I replied. *I went through military school, it would be a waste for me not to be at the battlefront . . .*

Braga took a deep breath, as if he felt suffocated. Then, all of a sudden, he got up, held out his arm, and said:

Come with me, I'll show you a battlefront.

And he took me to see the wounded. He asked each one to show us his injuries and to relive the circumstances of the battle. *Many of them are mad*, the doctor explained as if he were comforting me. Then he added:

Madness is sometimes the only way to overcome fear.

Within a few minutes, my vision had become blurred. One of the soldiers, who appeared to be in better shape than the others, sat up on his bed and opened his eyes wide while repeating: *The angels, the angels* . . .

This is how he arrived from the Battle of Magul, the doctor said.

The confused soldier launched into a description of the roars and clouds of smoke, imitating the noise of rifle and cannon fire. Then he spoke of the Portuguese and Vátuas all being turned into smoke. And he imitated the guns aimed at clouds and smoke, with such intensity that the heavens were forever torn apart. *Are you my angel?* the delirious soldier asked, digging his fingers into my arm.

I'm not the one who needs you, the doctor declared after the visit was finished. *You're the one who needs me.*

So that is how I came to take up residence in a hut next to the entrance to the infirmary. Now I feel the weight of eternity upon me every time Dr. Rodrigues Braga announces the arrival of yet another Sunday.

I shall leave the account of an incident until the end of this letter, at which point you, sir, will assess its relevance. This morning, we received the visit of the doctor and missionary Georges Liengme. Such an irony of fate: you, sir, prevented me from going to meet the Swiss. And now he has come my way. Dr. Rodrigues Braga is aware of recommendations from on high that he should keep his distance from this missionary. However, possibly because he is also a doctor, he received the visit with graceful good manners.

In defense of our doctor, I should emphasize that, the moment he arrived, he was reminded of the official position of Portugal with regard to the Swiss Mission and its missionaries. His reception was, Braga made clear, an exception to the rule. Georges Liengme, falsely resigned, declared:

The Portuguese dislike me only because I have taken up the cause of the blacks.

You haven't taken up the cause of the blacks, the Portuguese doctor countered. *You have taken up the cause of Gungunhane. And you can be sure, my dear doctor, that the Portuguese are protecting many more blacks than the Swiss and all the other Europeans combined.*

Should we not leave that question to the very people whom you claim to defend? Liengme queried.

Then the Swiss smiled in order to mask his fatigue. He had left Manjacaze three days before on a harnessed mule and leading a cart pulled by two donkeys. He was coming to Chicomo to deliver correspondence for Colonel Eduardo Galhardo. He no longer trusted emissaries. In moments of crisis, loyalty is merely an absence of opportunity.

And they had lunch together. After lunch, our friend Braga invited the Swiss to visit the infirmary. Liengme spent time at each bedside, asking each patient to tell him their story and praying for their recovery. He spent longest by an injured patient who was suffering from hallucinations. The unfortunate fellow was convinced that his body had been pierced by a kaffir spear. And he was writhing and moaning, all doubled up with an endless attack of colic. The Swiss spoke in the softest murmur, the palm of his hand resting on the raving soldier's brow.

What are you doing, colleague? the Portuguese doctor inquired with interest.

I'm not doing anything. What I'd like to try is hypnosis. It's my specialism.

Before long, my dear Liengme, none of us will remember what specialism we studied.

Then, as it was getting late, Braga insisted our Swiss visitor stay the night. So that is what happened. That night, the man who cared for those who would kill us slept inside our fortress.

35

THE VULTURE AND THE SWALLOWS

To have enemies is to become their slave. Peace is not born by defeating an adversary. True peace consists in never making enemies.
—A PROVERB FROM NKOKOLANI

My father looked wrinkled and ancient standing before the emperor, who was occupying the bed in the infirmary as if it were a throne. Old Katini's legs were trembling so much that the flies were unable to land on them. The sentries watched carefully as my old father sat down on the ground, as protocol demanded; visitors should be viewed from a higher position. With his face almost touching his knees, curled up like a bundle of elephant grass, he waited for permission to speak.

Who are you? Ngungunyane asked without looking at him.

Katini Nsambe was slow to speak, moving his lips without articulating a word, as if he were at once gagged and mute. His jaw receded into his face, his gaze drifted through endless space looking for the exact words. Instead of talking, however, Katini burst into an inconsolable fit of weeping. His crying degenerated into uncontrollable sobs.

Ngungunyane showed no concern at all, and stared at the ceiling. I was afraid he would eventually lose his patience altogether. But it wasn't a question of patience. It was disdain. My father didn't exist, and for that reason the emperor was unaffected by the time it took for the crying to cease.

When silence finally returned, the great chief of the VaNguni closed his eyelids and spoke:

The people of your race, the VaChopi, cry as if they were continually being reborn.

According to the emperor, this was how we of the VaChopi nation behaved in order to demonstrate that we were defenseless. The bow and arrow, which had brought us fame as warriors, were, after all, childhood toys. That was how he explained my father's exhibition: solitary and vulnerable, he was asking for a protective embrace. *You are all women*, he concluded, as if spitting at him.

Just as a lumberjack assesses the tree he is going to cut down, the emperor contemplated my old father from top to bottom, while cleaning his nails with his little piece of bone. Eventually, my father seemed able to articulate some words and he mumbled:

My name—

No one is interested in your names. Rather, this: Tell me how many children you have, Muchope.

Katini Nsambe grated his teeth so hard, it was impossible to hear whether he had managed to speak. All one could see were his hunched shoulders. The emperor smiled condescendingly:

You're telling me you don't know. Well, I'm the only one here who has a right not to know.

He didn't know where his domains ended. He didn't know how many wives he had. And there was so much death in his family that he needed to make enough children to lose count of how many there were. Then he returned to his personal hygiene.

As my old father still did not speak or move, I stepped out of the shadows and announced:

My father came here to offer me as your wife.

The emperor did not bother to look up. Instead, he now addressed my father in a harsh tone:

Who said I needed a wife? Who are you to think about what I need?

I took another step forward and my anxiety to become visible distorted my voice so much that I no longer recognized myself:

I know the language of the whites, Nkosi. *I was brought up among them.*

The emperor hesitated. He wasn't struck so much by what I said, but by my irreverent ways. He clicked his tongue against his teeth and nonchalantly pursed his lips:

I have my translators. I don't want any more, they are a risk I can do without.

And he elaborated on his doubts. *The white men's noses are the beaks of vultures,* he said. *Translators also grow the same curved beak. What they didn't know and what they come to know are dangerous. More dangerous still is what they come to know and don't translate.*

You should trust me, Nkosi.

Why?

Because I'm a messenger, I affirmed.

From whom? The Portuguese?

From a woman.

A woman?

From Vuiaze.

Mention of the name struck the emperor like a thunderbolt, his whole body shook, and the bone slipped from his fingers. He stared at me as if seeking a face behind a mask.

The tale of the forbidden love between Ngungunyane and Vuiaze, the most beautiful woman in all the kingdom of Gaza, had become a legend. Her radiant face, her comely body, her light skin, all this had attracted men. When he was still a youth, the pretender to the throne fell passionately in love, and his love was immediately reciprocated. There were anxious murmurings in the court: such an ardent love could distract the future ruler. An unhappy emperor risks the security of the empire. But an emperor in the throes of great happiness is an even greater threat. Rumors soon began to spread that Vuiaze was an easy woman, succumbing to every courtly advance. King Muzila kept her away from Ngungunyane to prevent them from marrying. But he did not have the power to thwart the flame of their romance. From their love, Godido would be born, Gungunhane's favorite son.

One day, Vuiaze was found dead. Mysteriously, the body disappeared within hours. And she was never seen again.

The emperor's revenge was capricious: At the oath of military allegiance, all his subordinates were obliged to pay their respects to the vanished woman.

Vuiaze! they bellowed in unison.

And the emperor asked me to pronounce the woman's name once again. I agreed. *Vuiaze*, I murmured, my eyes closed.

How old are you? he asked.

I have no age, I answered.

He interpreted my answer as a graceful way of confirming that I was a virgin. And he smiled in the way that only victors do.

Then he summoned his aides to ask them if there was still a bottle of port left.

I trust the alcohol given me by my enemies more than the liquor served me by members of my own family.

The Portuguese had been warned to send him only a few supplies at a time, a crate with just four bottles. Otherwise he would be obliged to distribute the gift among his family and officials. Then he turned his attention to me once more.

The indunas, *my counselors, are the ones who will decide the matter of our marriage. I'm tired, tired of myself, tired of all these people.*

He was more bothered by his advisers than he was by his weak knees. This was the king's complaint. He felt like treating his counselors the same way he had treated the swallows. As these swift little birds refused to obey him, he had ordered them to be exterminated. All the travelers told him that not a single swallow was left in the entire country.

Some practical instructions followed. The following day, I would wear the same dress, but would leave my shoes at the hospital.

I cannot appear with a woman wearing shoes. Do you understand?

The advisers would ask me some terrible questions, the women of the court would claim that I would only be doing the tasks of a junior wife, that of collecting and burying the king's stools and urine.

My daughter will do all that is required, my father declared, having suddenly found his voice.

The emperor gestured for us to be silent. *Damned VaChopi, you'll be my next swallows*, the emperor announced. One could see the pain of humiliation in Katini Nsambe's face. Horrified, I saw my father take from his bag the iron crucifix with which he had murdered the Angolan. Raising his cross, he walked resolutely toward Ngungunyane. I waved my arms, I wanted to scream for him to stop. But my furious father was already lurching forward, his improvised weapon on high. Terrified, I closed my eyes, only to open them again when I heard him mutter softly:

We are almost celebrating Kissimusse. I would like to offer you this Christ, Your Majesty.

The sovereign of Gaza was slow to accept the gift from my submissive father's hands. Then he turned his gaze to the skeletal figure of Christ.

Poor man. At the hour of his death, did no one help him?

They couldn't.

Did the son of God die without anyone to comfort and support him?

We all die alone, was Katini's reply.

My father and I withdrew from the makeshift infirmary, leaving the king of Gaza asleep. No less drowsy were the two guards, who were slumped together. From inside our hut, we could hear the imperial snores. My father admitted that, during our audience with the king, he had lacked the courage to fulfill his intentions.

Did you want to kill him, Father?

It wasn't his desire that had flagged, but his courage. The fearlessness that had abounded in him when confronting his son's killers had ebbed away when facing the emperor.

Do you want me to kill Ngungunyane, Father?

I have already arranged everything with him.

With whom?

With the king. Tomorrow you will be subjected to the approval of the court.

Are you punishing me or Ngungunyane?

I'm not sending you to be his wife. You're going there in order to be his widow.

And what about you?

I don't know. For now, I shall return to Sana Benene. Later, I'll go back to Nkokolani.

Nkokolani no longer exists, Father. Who will look after you?

Places are our eternal family. We mustn't let them die alone, my father said. And then he concluded, with a trace of mockery on his lips: *It's a lie, what I told the king. No one dies alone.*

36

SERGEANT GERMANO DE MELO'S TWELFTH LETTER

Fear those who have always felt fear. Beware of those who think themselves insignificant. When they come to power, they will punish us with the same fear they themselves felt and they will avenge themselves with their false grandeur.
—THE WORDS OF KATINI NSAMBE

Chicomo, November 5, 1895

Dear Lieutenant Ayres de Ornelas,

I do not know, sir, whether our Swiss guest got a moment of sleep that night. Throughout the night, he wandered among the sick, taking them their medicines, water, and words of comfort.

I woke up in the morning and there was the Swiss, on his knees, praying. I served him some hot coffee and the man started telling me about himself, his life, and above all about his extraordinary adventures on the African continent.

The passions of Georges Liengme (or just Georges, as he insisted I call him) were many and paradoxical: he was a clock maker, missionary, doctor, hypnotist, photographer, husband, and father of two delightful children. The clock maker observed Life, seeking within it the precision of machines. The missionary was looking for what no photographer could capture. The doctor knew how much the body is made of spirit. And finally, the hypnotist knew the secrets that dwell in the depths of sleep.

Allow me at this point, sir, to record my astonishment: How well this European knows Africa! Forget José Silveira, forget Sanches de Miranda! None of our officers can rival this Swiss in his familiarity with Africa and its people. You and the others will argue that it is because of his command of African languages. But the origin of the problem is much older. Why do we Portuguese suffer from this age-old laziness when it comes to learning these languages? Why is it that we only want to learn the languages of those people we consider superior? I listened to the stories of Georges Liengme, and they weren't tales of lion hunters. They were stories of people, of encounters between people who overcame historical barriers and prejudices. And they confirmed a bitter truth: whether inside or outside the garrison, we Portuguese live surrounded by walls, afraid of everything that we are unable to recognize.

Suddenly, Dr. Rodrigues Braga approached, nervous and hurried. His state of mind was completely different from that of the previous day, and he was gruff in his manner. The missionary should be on his way immediately. He had received instructions that Liengme was to leave. It was only then that the Swiss confessed that he had come in the hope of being able to take away with him any extra medical supplies we might have in our stores.

Extra? There is no such word in Portuguese, my friend. And I'll tell you quite frankly that even if we did have supplies, I couldn't give them to you . . .

Georges Liengme was already heading into the bush when Braga warned him he was going in the wrong direction.

Here, any direction is the wrong one, the Swiss commented with irony. He explained that he wasn't going straight home. He was taking another path in order to visit a patient he had operated upon a week before. It was a brother-in-law of the king of Gaza, who suffered from cataracts and who lived in a village near Chicomo.

He invited us to accompany him, encouraging his colleague with a professional argument: They could provide a joint clinical assessment of Gungunhane's relative.

Come with me. No one will know.

Rodrigues Braga refused. I asked permission to accompany the foreigner. I needed to stretch my legs and a period away from the garrison would do me good. Rodrigues Braga acquiesced. *But make sure it's not for long*, he said. And so off we went into the bush, led by the guide the missionary had brought from Manjacaze. Instead of following the well-trodden tracks, the young man led us through endless detours in the bush.

It was I who asked him to avoid the usual routes, the Swiss explained. *Blacks*, he added, *think foreigners should always stop to visit their chiefs. By avoiding villages, we save a great deal of time.*

All of a sudden we heard footsteps behind us. It was Rodrigues Braga. He was hurrying along furtively, as if he were being followed. And he smiled at us like a teenager flaunting the rules:

No one must know I'm here!

When, at last, we reached our destination, we were surrounded by a crowd of children, leaping and frolicking, and laughing contagiously, while always carefully keeping their distance. A skinny elderly man emerged from his house, a large bandage covering half his face. Once we had been introduced, Braga helped his colleague with the treatment.

My eyes were dead, the old Negro said. *This white man brought me out of my darkness.*

That kaffir's gratitude was so intense that I could not help thinking: Apart from those few serving in the army, what other Portuguese doctors gave the Africans any assistance? As is now evident, you, sir, were correct; I have no aptitude to serve in the military. I ask too many questions, I have too much heart, I have committed too many transgressions.

As we left the village, a new surprise awaited us. Some twenty kaffirs had queued up in a single line:

We want to be seen too, the kaffirs said.

What shall we do? Braga asked.

We'll do what doctors do: We'll get to work, my Portuguese friend!

For over an hour I watched Rodrigues Braga, listening, pummeling, touching, prescribing medicine. And all this he did with a smile that I had never seen before. At the end, the kaffirs and the Swiss laughed together as they bade farewell, with effusive guffaws and handshakes. Dr. Braga gazed, puzzled, at that unusual familiarity between a European and a group of Africans. Then we returned in silence to Chicomo.

When we reached the garrison, Rodrigues Braga touchingly thanked Georges Liengme:

I missed attending to the sick. Now all I see are the wounded.

The doctors were already saying goodbye when Liengme realized he had forgotten his case. He must have left it in the infirmary, and I rushed to fetch it. As I picked it up, a photograph fell from it. My heart almost leaped from my chest while my few fingers touched the portrait. It was Imani posing, her breasts uncovered, a simple *capulana* tied around her waist. There was a strange glow behind her body, as if she were suspended in the light. Doubts gnawed away deep down inside me: Had the girl agreed to exhibit herself like that of her own free will? Had the Swiss attempted to seduce her?

The arrival of the two doctors interrupted that wave of questions. Surprising me with the photograph in my hand, the Swiss commented with a pride verging on the paternal:

Pretty, isn't she?

The three of us stood there, shoulder to shoulder, so as to share the photograph shaking in my trembling hands.

So who is this beauty? Braga asked, unusually enthusiastic.

It's a Chope girl who turned up at our settlement. Her father is going to give her to the king of Gaza.

What a waste! the Portuguese said with a sigh.

I was the one who took this photo, Liengme announced with the pride of a hunter.

And was she alone? I dared to ask.

She was with her father, but he refused to pose. He was scared that his wife and sons would appear in the portrait.

And what would be the problem if they did appear? Braga asked.

It's because they're all dead.

I summoned up courage and asked the Swiss if I could keep the portrait for myself.

It would be better if you didn't, argued the Swiss. *What you do with that photo will only make you haggard and sinful.*

Rodrigues Braga unexpectedly took my side. And he did so with such fervor that after some dithering, the foreigner handed me the brazen picture. The Swiss doctor eventually left, straddled so delicately over his old packsaddle that it seemed as if the mule were more of a traveling companion than a beast of burden.

I was seething with a mixture of rage and jealousy when I returned to my room. You will agree, sir, that there are better ways to conjure up the memory of someone one loves so much. I passed a flock of goats that were chewing sheets of paper, pages from reports, who knows, maybe letters from one soldier to another, or clandestine love messages? Scattered across the earth, the goats were chewing up Time itself. It's what I felt like doing. To lie down on the ground as only animals do.

In the half-light of my room, I looked at the photograph once again and, suddenly, it was no longer Imani posing there. It was a silhouette of light, the contours of which came and went as if they had their own pulse. Who knows, maybe it is impossible to take a photo of the one we love.

37

A BRIDE IN WAITING

*Married women invent stories; virgins hide secrets; widows pretend
not to remember.*
—A PROVERB FROM NKOKOLANI

They've brought me a woman! Do they think I lack women?

At the court of Mandhlakazi, known as the Indaba, the counselors laughed. Without any great enthusiasm, but with considerable display so that the king would see what pleasure he was giving them. None of the *indunas* was absent. They were far more interested in the matter of the king's love life than they were in war. For this reason, dozens of elders, nobles, and military chiefs had gathered together. Seated in a prominent position was Impibekezane, the king's mother. And it was she who ordered that I should step forward slowly and exhibit myself. As I walked barefoot around the chamber, I felt the men's looks shredding my clothes like blades.

The *Nkosi* caressed his belly as if his hands were meandering over the breadth of his empire. As he gazed at my feet, he recalled the words of his predecessor by way of a joke: *Women arrive more quickly because they attract the places they are making for.* The comment was greeted with applause and laughter.

Ngungunyane knew that most of it was forced laughter, each burst a kowtowing of false subjection. Then Ngungunyane vociferated in an atmosphere of growing tension:

What use is it to have millions of subjects if they are not loyal? What use is it to have hundreds of women if none of them are really ours? What use is it to be crowned emperor if those who salute you today will venerate with even greater devotion those who will bring you down?

The nobles of the court cowered in embarrassment. They thought the matter merely involved the selection of a new virgin girl. The emperor raised his voice as he warmed to his subject:

One cannot lift a stone without finding a scorpion hiding under it. There isn't a shadow that doesn't conceal another shadow. There isn't an impediment that is not a trap. How I wish I could sleep, sleep completely, my eyelids shutting me away from top to toe. How I wish I could believe I still had a clear night, without the threat of knives or ambushes.

A chorus of protests rang through the court. His older uncles glanced at each other suspiciously. Was their nephew sober?

I have lost count of the number of times I have got married and I am more alone than ever, the king continued with growing verve. *I need a new wife. And this girl here*—and he gestured to me to approach so that he could touch me with his fingertips—*this girl has not been burned.*

How do you know, dear Nkosi? *How do you know she's still a virgin?*

I know what no one else knows about her. And waving me toward the center of the circle, he uttered a raucous command: *Tell these people your name.*

Vuiaẓe. My name is Vuiaẓe.

A deathly hush descended over the Indaba. The counselors sat staring at the ground. And a suspicion of some conspiracy hovered over the assembly. For a long time now, the Zulu and VaNguni elders complained that Ngungunyane was losing his sense of judgment and justice. One example of his lack of forethought was the way he favored representatives of the tribes he had conquered, including the hated VaChopi and Valengue. Even most of the army of Gaza was composed of men from the so-called weak races. And now was he taking an impure bride from an enemy nation, a woman who brought back memories of the forbidden name of Vuiaze?

The family adviser and relative Queto, who had so much influence over the king, begged him to ponder on his decision. He suggested that I, Imani Nsambe, was not just one more spouse.

This girl knows the language of the Portuguese, the VaChopi, the Mabinguela, and our own. And the door is open for her to enter the territory of our enemies.

Then another adviser, with equal vigor, mounted a counter-argument:

My question, brothers, is how she learned all this. And how can we trust a woman who knows so much?

We know this girl's story, she was educated by a priest, Queto contested. *A brother of hers fought alongside us, against those of his race. I propose the young woman stays with us so that she may be tested, under the control of Impibekezane, far from our king's appetites.*

I'm not sure, I'm not sure, his opponent reasoned. *How can we be sure it wasn't the Portuguese who sent her to spy on us?*

The danger of welcoming me, as they all knew, lay elsewhere. And it was enshrined in the name that I had just announced as being mine. There could be nothing more serious, in the midst of a military crisis, than to repeat what had already happened with Vuiaze: if the emperor were to fall madly in love and distance himself from the affairs of the VaNguni nation.

At this point, they ordered me to withdraw from the chamber so that they could discuss the matter more at their leisure. Outside, the mist had fallen and the night was cold. The light emanating from the grand assembly flickered on the dew. I sat down on the grass and stared at my unshod feet. Where had my sergeant gotten to?

Some time later, Impibekezane came and sat down next to me. The lamps coming from the Indaba bathed us in an intermittent light.

I pity my son, she remarked. *They all obey him, but none of them is loyal. Umundungazi has gone mad and those around him applaud him for his madness.*

So what have they decided with regard to me?

They have accepted you. But not as a wife.

I don't understand.

You are a bride-in-waiting. It is better for you like that, for you will be free of the other wives' envy. Even if you have to carry out other tasks . . .

What tasks?

They want to use you as an informer.

They knew about my relationship with the sergeant. They had found out about the correspondence between Germano and the lieutenant through the messengers. No one better than me to infiltrate the heart of the Portuguese army. And the queen mother continued:

They want me to look after you and to keep you away from my son. Tomorrow we leave here in order to spend a few days at the Swiss doctor's hospital.

The sound of raised voices emerged from the Indaba. There was considerable excitement among the counselors. They were debating military matters and discussing the war, which had reached the gates of Mandhlakazi. Oaths could be heard, death threats, promises of bloodshed. My case had been merely a fleeting moment of diversion.

Nights like these are not for people to be out and about, Ngungunyane's mother commented, as we listened to the hyenas in the distance. Noticing me flinch on hearing the cries of these sinister creatures, the queen affirmed: *Don't worry, there are more hyenas among the counselors at that meeting than there are in the whole of the bush.*

She pulled her seating mat up closer and adopted a more intimate tone. She wanted to give me advice concerning nights I would eventually spend with her son. I thought at first she was going to give me recommendations concerning my sexual conduct. She wasn't. It was a strange warning: On many nights we would be sleeping with others in the same marital bed. Others? And she laughed. The king suffered from terrible repetitive nightmares. On such troubled nights, his murdered brothers would appear.

There was no blood. These brothers died from poisoning. That is why I give you this advice, my dear girl: Take more care in hiring a cook than in choosing a husband.

We don't choose, we are chosen. This was what I felt like saying, but I abandoned the idea when I heard the chants coming from the Indaba. The meeting was coming to an end, and the dignitaries would soon begin to leave. At that point, no woman could be found outside the house. The queen didn't seem worried, and held me warmly by the arm.

You lied to the counselors about your name. Now I want you to lie when you call for me.

I'll do whatever you tell me to do.

Forget my name. Call me Yosio.

Before she had become a widow, that was what she had been called: Yosio. When Muzila died, they changed her name. By whispering the name to her like this, in a confidential tone, she would be transported back to that other time.

In those days, I didn't just have a husband. I had my children. And above all, I had my Ngungunyane.

Don't you have him any longer?

No one keeps a son, she insisted.

It was not, however, just the nightmares that made Ngungunyane unrecognizable. There were other, more deranged moments when no one, not even she, had the courage to divert him from his delirium.

And there were even occasions when the emperor really did journey to the sea. What did he do on such wanderings? Ngungunyane sat on a dune, at a cautious distance from the breaking waves. For the VaNguni, the ocean is a dangerous, nameless territory. The king ordered his bowmen to line up along the wet sand and prepare to launch their arrows. Then he himself led by example: He pulled back the bowstring, and with a vigorous cry fired the first arrow over the ocean. The arrow cut through the air like a demented, featherless bird, before dropping and ripping the water with a hollow sound. A warlike clamor immediately filled the air and hundreds of bowmen shot a rainstorm of arrows that darkened the skies and spattered the surface of the ocean with foam. Then there followed a dense silence until Ngungunyane bellowed:

See the blood! It's bleeding, it is bleeding.

He chose the term *it* to avoid calling it by its name. The sea was prohibited, even as a word. The lips of those who named it would forever be caked with salt. In an undertone, the emperor of Gaza muttered:

It will soon be dead!

And he sat down and waited for the sea to die.

The ocean had been saved. Ngungunyane had survived. But many of her sons had died by poisoning.

I spent so many sleepless nights waiting for them to bring me the news, Impibekezane confessed.

I told her I didn't understand. She explained that she had taken part in the decision to poison them.

Let me speak, she defended herself when she saw my look of utter disgust. *Don't judge me before you have listened to me.*

Those sons of hers were going to die anyway. They would end

up losing their lives in a long, slow process of carnage. They would be riddled with bullets, stabbed, cut to pieces. But it was always a mother's blood that the soil absorbed. She had lived through the bitter experience of the succession wars between her husband Muzila and her brother-in-law Mawewe. They were years of hatred and bloodletting. She wanted anything but those barbaric acts to be repeated endlessly and for no reason. It was hardly her fault. She wished she had played a greater part in it. But the choice had been made long before she came along, and was far beyond her powers. They would always kill those of their own blood. The only prerogative she had was to choose who would survive.

That's why you shouldn't look at me like this, she concluded severely. *Ask your European friends how they chose their kings, ask them how much poison flowed at their royal banquets.*

It was Sanches de Miranda, the Mafambatcheca, who had told her. The history of the whites, according to him, was no more unsullied than that of the Africans.

Early tomorrow morning we'll go to Sana Benene, the queen decreed. *You will go there, my daughter, to bid your folk farewell. And you will fetch your shoes.*

That night I found it hard to get to sleep. They put me in a hut where half a dozen other so-called little wives slept. When they saw me enter, they huddled together in a corner. I could see their venomous eyes even in the dark. I was haunted by sleeplessness until morning broke. By the time the first rays of sunlight burst through, I had already decided to tear my own past up by the roots. I was facing the same cruel decision that had tortured Queen Impibekezane so harshly. I had to choose who would survive within me.

38

EIGHTH LETTER FROM LIEUTENANT AYRES DE ORNELAS

The memory of a distant homeland
Timeless but forgotten and we unsure
Whether foregone in the past or future.

—SOPHIA DE MELLO BREYNER ANDRESEN

Manjacaze, November 9, 1895

Dear Sergeant Germano de Melo,

I have been scribbling this letter for some days now. I began writing it from where I had written to you so many times before: the sad and gloomy Manjacaze. The place was the same. Everything else had changed. I have returned to my military duties, I have returned to myself. I give thanks to the heavens that we have at last broken off the talks that we held right here with the king of the Vátuas. The negotiations were a hoax, an endless delay in implementing decisions. Did the man want war? Well, he was going to get war, and to a degree that he had never imagined. The battles at Marracuene and Magul were just a prelude to an odyssey that would be inscribed in the annals of our history.

My merits were naturally acknowledged at last and, as I have already told you, I was included in the organization of the military offensive that took place at Coolela. It is a pity that you, my dear sergeant, are so far away, at the Chicomo garrison. For you would have experienced the same pride I felt as I watched the parade of our military might. First came a battalion of nine hundred troops of the line recently arrived from Europe. These were followed by other infantry and artillery battalions. They brought with them ten field guns and two machine guns. Munitions for the infantry amounted to two million cartridges. A military parade of these dimensions had never been seen before in our African domains. This unique spectacle was witnessed by thousands of loyal kaffirs (how do we know who is loyal in these remote parts of the world?), and the parade reached its climax with the arrival of the cavalry squadron commanded by the famous Mouzinho de Albuquerque. It is true that the horses are few, badly trained, and scrawny. But the appearance of our dragoons caused a wave of excitement among the rabble. The kaffirs ran alongside the horses with puerile enthusiasm and those who were already adults gained the eyes and laughter of children.

All this accumulation of war matériel was transported two weeks ago to the lagoon at Belele, where we established a provisional base. It is going to be carnage! That is what I thought as I inspected our weaponry.

But weaponry is not enough to initiate a battle. What we lacked was an enemy. Colonel Galhardo followed Caldas Xavier's instructions to the letter. The secret was for us only to take the initiative once the enemy had switched from defense to attack. In the words of Mouzinho de Albuquerque, when Caldas Xavier conceived this tactic, he was inspired by the arts of the seductress. She flutters around the man she has chosen, waiting for him to eventually take the initiative. Ever mordant, ever quick-witted, our dear Mouzinho de Albuquerque!

The fact is that the enemy didn't appear for days. But once again, the wisdom of Colonel Galhardo prevailed. It would be foolish to leave our encampment and march under the intense rain that lashed us every day. It would be even more foolish, indeed it would be a strategic error, to advance through flooded thickets bursting with enemy forces.

Galhardo was right. But it was a bitter decision to have to carry out. Once again, our troops were at a standstill, victims of the weight of our war matériel. As the days passed, I began to feel less enthusiastic about the splendid quality of our artillery. We were equipped with sword and cannon. It would be better if we benefited from the lightness of the spear.

In order to raise the men's spirits, Colonel Galhardo ordered two columns to advance on enemy territory. We were only giving the appearance of ignoring Caldas Xavier's instructions. For our platoons did not engage with military targets. What we did was to attack and destroy villages. Our intention was not to kill civilians but to seize livestock and food supplies. And by doing this, we calmed our spirits and raised our morale. Until one sun-filled morning we decided to move our forces toward the lagoon at Coolela. It would be better to suffer the nightmare of advancing our heavy war matériel than to watch it rot away in the marshes where we had camped. On this sunlit morning, the Portuguese flag fluttered over the shimmering heathland and the bugles sounded in defiance of the African deities.

After a day's march, we camped at the top of a dune looking out over the Maguanhana lagoon. We adopted the usual square formation, protected in its entirety by a barrier of barbed wire.

I was designated to go and carry out some reconnaissance of the area. Guess who was chosen to accompany me? No less than your friend Captain Santiago Mata. We rode out on our horses under a burning sun. Barely fifteen minutes had passed when we caught sight of the village and birthplace of Impibekezane, Gungunhane's mother. Conscious that I was in an area that was too exposed, I ordered us to return immediately to the camp. The captain promptly refused. And he confronted me with an arrogant demeanor: As far as he was concerned, we had not carried out a sufficiently detailed exploration.

What's this, Lieutenant? Are we strolling around the Rossio Square looking at shopwindows?

These were his exact words. No one has ever been so rude to me before. And I made sure the captain knew it. When we returned to the base, Santiago apologized, ashamed that he had been so discourteous.

Early the following morning, we only left behind the baggage that might slow us down. Two prisoners we took along the way confirmed that the headman was in his garrison (which the Vátuas call a kraal), with a large contingent of troops. We were going over the final details of our plan, after having taken our place once more among the body of troops preparing for battle, when some dozen auxiliaries rushed towards us shouting that enemy soldiers were approaching:

Hi fikile Nyimpi ya Ngungunyane! they yelled. *Gungunhane's troops are here.*

Suddenly, as if by magic, the hordes of Vátuas appeared, thousands of them, running with short, rapid steps and venting angry, rhythmic shouts. It was such a vast throng that the glint of their spears blinded us momentarily. These intimidating hordes gathered in a kind of crescent formation extending for more than a kilometer. Suddenly, we lost sight of our auxiliaries. They were rooted to the ground, terrified by the Vátua show of force. And even Xiperenyane's soldiers had been swallowed up by the thick elephant grass. We were all that remained, we Europeans and Angolans, confined in our tiny square. That four-sided human shape was a spider's web about to face a typhoon.

Then that whole devilish multitude of fanatics advanced upon us like some terrifying tidal wave. Although most of the kaffirs were armed with spears and shields, a fair proportion of them held rifles which, luckily for us, they fired chaotically. Arrows rained down on our position and it seemed as if a cloud had darkened the African skies once and for all. A few moments later, our field guns boomed and the assailants retreated. This retreat only lasted a few minutes. Or was it hours? How does one count time when death is the only clock? I know that those terrible squadrons that call themselves Buffalos and Crocodiles turned and advanced upon us once again. They crossed the waterlogged areas that surrounded us, their feet so caked with mud that they seemed to be advancing shod in boots, just as we were. That vision confirmed my own fears: Those men were not warriors, but were issuing from the earth itself.

The gunfire was so intense and the smoke so thick that no marksman could choose his target with any certainty. They fired against shadows and what they thought they saw turned out to be other shadows spinning through the mist before sinking into the ground. And so, for a moment, our soldiers perhaps thought of themselves as floating patches of fog, smoke amid the general smoke. And what we call courage may have been no more than a fiction of this temporary delirium.

The battle lasted little more than half an hour. Just as had happened at Magul, it was the machine guns that dictated the outcome of the confrontation. With the same wonder I feel when I hear my heart beat, I can still remember the efficiency of the machine gun, this formidable instrument of modern warfare which cuts the enemy troops down at a rate of five hundred rounds a minute. The VaNguni hosts, who totaled some twelve thousand troops, fled in disarray.

We did not celebrate immediately. After a moment of disbelief, the sound of cheering resounded and hats were thrown into the air. It had been such an unlikely victory that we thought it had resolved the entire war. And we rejoiced so vigorously that at first we forgot to mourn our losses.

In the center of our square, Mouzinho de Albuquerque could be seen. There he was, as rigid as a statue. He remained as he had been throughout the combat: stock-still, on foot, in the thick of it, bullets whistling past him. At his feet lay his horse, covered in blood.

Once the euphoria of victory had died down, it was time to take stock: Some ten white soldiers had died, and there were about thirty wounded. And when everyone had joined together in military formation to honor the fallen for the last time, I have to confess to a moment of weakness. I walked away to stand next to a cart so as not to see or be seen. But I could not get away from the sounds of the improvised funeral ceremony.

In the absence of a chaplain, it was Colonel Galhardo in person who called for a prayer. And it was then, as I looked around, listening to my comrades in the distance honoring the dead, that I saw Captain Santiago Mata hiding under a cart. Perhaps he was hiding there for the same reasons as before, when he had soiled his uniform, who knows?

I lingered on the description of this episode because at that moment I asked myself how sure we can be of the loyalty of our own comrades in arms. But there was no time for further misgivings.

As always, there was much urgency in organizing our withdrawal from those wastelands, and Colonel Galhardo issued speedy instructions for us to march back to Chicomo.

Turn back? What we should do is advance on Manjacaze, protested Captain Mouzinho.

In the face of such opposition, all the colonel could do was to explain himself. There was no point in besmirching our brilliant triumph with a mistake, no matter how insignificant that might be. Did we know who had been in command of Gungunhane's forces? His own son Godido, and his uncle Queto. Our action at Coolela was not only a military victory. It was a slap in the face for the king of Gaza himself.

All this is not enough, Colonel. Wars are not won with slaps in the face.

That is my final word on the matter. We return to the garrison. I don't want to take risks.

Mouzinho muttered between his teeth. Maybe Galhardo heard his final comment: *I don't know how one can command without taking risks.*

39

A ROOF COLLAPSING UPON THE WORLD

Only when you learn to love fear will you be a good wife.
—THE WORDS OF QUEEN IMPIBEKEZANE

We arrived at Sana Benene as evening was falling, and we headed for the church. There we found Father Rudolfo praying in front of the altar. Father Rudolfo felt a cloud of dust falling upon his shoulders. He peered up into the church's beams and saw luminous flakes dancing through the air as if there had been a silent explosion high up there. Termites had been corroding the timber for ages, without him noticing. Placing his trust in the roof's overall appearance, Rudolfo believed himself to be protected by eternity. To all who visited the church, the priest proudly showed off the robustness of the roof, in contrast to the decrepit walls and furnishings. It is the ceiling that makes a temple sacred.

Now, however, the roof had begun to cave in. The beams were so hollow that they fell without warning, noiselessly, weightlessly. The timbers turned to dust in the air so that by the time they hit the floor, they had no substance at all. This was what enabled Father Rudolfo to survive. The doves escaped, flying out into the open air. But the bedazzled owls, blinded by the light that suddenly flooded through the large holes at the top of the building, flapped around the priest, who made a dash for the yard outside, hurriedly closing the doors behind him in the vain hope that the birds would not abandon the building. Having lost their habitual perches, the birds would have to find new places to land. It was too late. The birds of prey were already hovering over other roofs in search of new shelter.

People are going to die, Rudolfo said with a sigh.

But there was no one left at Sana Benene. Recovering from his fright, Rudolfo sat down and looked at the decapitated church. Then he got up and went down to the river carrying a bucket. It had rained intensely for two weeks, and the River Inharrime had almost burst its banks. Out of precaution, the priest avoided passing the landing stage. The timber might be as rotten as the roof beams. Kneeling on a rock and busy collecting water, Rudolfo Fernandes didn't notice me, the queen, and a small retinue of people approaching along the path that he had just trodden.

Curiously, the priest burst into tears when he recognized me. And it was in tears that he accompanied me to the dwellings. I imagined the worst. The queen indicated that she would wait for me down by the river. In the meantime, her bodyguard would buy fresh fish from any fisherman who might chance to pass that way.

Where is Bibliana? I asked apprehensively, the moment we reached the church.

Bibliana has gone. They've all gone. There's no longer anyone left at Sana Benene, and he pointed at what was left of the church roof. *Everything has collapsed, Imani.*

Where has Bibliana gone?

She's gone to the north. She went to the mouth of the River Save, to the place where they buried her brother. And there's no point in your waiting for her. She won't come back. Then he asked: *Why did you want to speak to her?*

I want to be a black woman, Father.

Are you crazy?

I raised my hand to indicate gently but firmly that it was my turn to speak. I wanted to be initiated into my traditions. I wanted to be reborn into my language, my beliefs. I wanted to be protected by my ancestors, to speak to my dead, my mother and my brothers. I was tired of being different and of being viewed with a mixture of envy and disdain. I was sick of hearing people say that I spoke Portuguese "without an accent." What tired me most, however, was having no one with whom to laugh or cry.

But what about the sergeant? Rudolfo wanted to know.

I don't know, Father. I'm scared of a love that asks so much of me. And apart from that, I don't know where he is, I don't know whether I shall see him again.

I imagined the priest's infinite sadness. He too might never meet Bibliana again. When I tried to console him, his reaction surprised me:

Sadness? The fact is that I'm relieved, my daughter.

I did not understand, it was impossible to understand. All that devoted love, all that self-denial, all that had suddenly disappeared? That was what I wanted to know. Rudolfo pointed at the church and said:

It wasn't time that destroyed the roof. It was the war.

Did they attack the church?

It was another war. It was the termites. Those cursed creatures have their own soldiers. And do you know why these soldiers are so efficient? Because they're blind. Pray that your sweetheart never becomes a real soldier.

I haven't heard from Germano for a long time, Father. I was told he was at the garrison at Chicomo.

Do you want to write to him? I can get you a messenger by tomorrow.

I did not know what to answer. I confessed that I had come to see Bibliana. The priest replied:

Even if she were here, she would be unable to see you, my daughter.

The sorceress had fallen ill from a particular form of

blindness. She saw through the eyes of the gods. And she was so sure of what she saw that the priest began to fear her. In her last days there, hundreds of wounded and refugees from the war had arrived at Sana Benene. And there were so many that the sorceress had taken it upon herself to put the world together again. Blacks, whites, men and women, slaves and the powerful, all were at fault. And she was the justice maker chosen by the God of the whites and the African gods. This is what Bibliana proclaimed before a terrified priest, who was unable to imagine an army commanded by the woman with whom he had shared his bed for years.

Inspired by her mission, the sorceress had abandoned Sana Benene. The waters of the Inharrime were no longer enough to wash away so many sins. A much bigger river was needed. On the banks of that river, her husband and brother-in-law lay buried. Along the shores of the legendary River Save dwelt fortune-tellers and prophets whose powers were well known beyond our borders. This was Bibliana's fate. That river would be her church.

So you've discovered you want to be African? Rudolfo asked, changing the subject, but this time failing to conceal an ironic tone. *I'm curious, my daughter. What is it to be African?*

I shrugged. Maybe I was just sad, maybe I just felt insecure. It felt good to have one simple certainty at hand, some indelible symbol of one's background, a roof that was more eternal than the sky itself. And the shadow of a smile flickered on the priest's face. He too had so often dreamed of being white and European. Now, for example, all he desired was to cut his locks, shave his beard, and wash his cassock before presenting himself at the Chicomo garrison. Who knows, maybe they would take him on as a chaplain? And he would celebrate mass in the camp, he would pray for the sick, absolve them of their sins, and administer last rites. And he would fully be what they had always denied him: a Portuguese priest.

Anyway, that's enough talk for now, he said. *Before I forget, I've got something to give you.*

From deep in the pocket of his cassock, he took a sheet of folded paper.

Your father left this for you, he announced.

My father was here? Tell me, how was he, and where has he gone?

Father Rudolfo then recalled that, in the previous week, my father had been found unconscious, sprawled across the landing stage. Katini Nsambe had disappeared some time before, and everyone feared that he had been eaten by wild animals. But there he was, weakened, skinny, and reeking. He had come from Nkokolani, his home village. He had been taken and brought back by the madman Libete on his old raft. Once in the church and washed, Katini opened a sack from which fell two dozen flat little pieces of wood all cut to the same size. They were the keys for a marimba that he was now intending to make.

I took this wood from the same tree my wife took to, he explained.

It would be his last marimba, the most perfect one he had ever made. He himself had climbed the fig tree, had captured a few bats, torn off their wings for the membrane with which to line the resonators. Day and night, the man had taken the utmost care to make the keys, the gourds, and the mallets.

This mbila *isn't to be played by people*, he declared.

So who is going to play it?

The music is going to play all by itself.

He finished making the instrument on the same day Bibliana announced she was leaving for the great northern river. It was no coincidence. The two had planned it between them. And they had left together but separated, like husband and wife. When they reached their destination, they would share their duties as old couples do. Bibliana would talk to the spirits; Katini would play for the gods. The two of them together would heal the world.

This was the news of Katini Nsambe. The priest had delivered his recollection while still holding out the piece of paper that my father had left with him.

On the sheet, stolen from Germano's notebook, there it was, my old father's labored, imperfect handwriting. I had to decipher his mysterious message word by word: "I began it, you complete it. There are still two to crucify."

The priest didn't ask any questions. He gave me a canteen of water for the journey.

And what are you going to do, Father Rudolfo? I asked.

He smiled and replied:

For now, I'm going to cut my hair and shave. After that, I'll see.

At that moment, Impibekezane joined us. She asked Rudolfo whether we could sleep there that night. And when I asked the reason for the delay in our return, she pointed to the sky that would have begun to darken, were it not for a sea of fire that was devouring the whole horizon.

40

SERGEANT GERMANO DE MELO'S THIRTEENTH LETTER

It is not just because of tiredness that I am in this state of depression,
which has neither color nor weight. What is happening to me is suicide.
A suicide with neither person nor death.
—EXCERPT FROM A LETTER FROM BERTHA RYFF TO HER HUSBAND, GEORGES LIENGME

Chicomo, November 10, 1895

Dear Lieutenant Ayres de Ornelas,

I spent the day clearing the infirmary of soot, which had cast a black
sheet over everything. For the sick confined to bed, these obstinate
clouds of ash were a sinister sign. And the suffocating heat they felt
was proof that the inferno had settled over Chicomo. But I knew
that good news was written in that soot: our troops had been victo-
rious at Coolela. After their victories, they had set the neighboring
villages on fire. That is what we do, and that is what the others do
as well. It was you, sir, who explained it to me as a way of writing
one's signature as a victor over a much wider area than the field of
battle. Those who live far from rivers only know of their existence
when their waters bursts their banks.

At the time of this writing, our troops will be returning. It will
be a slow, tiring march back along higher ground, away from the
fires that have spread out of control. I do not know whether you, sir,
are returning directly to Lourenço Marques or whether you will be

coming with the column that will stop at the garrison here. I hope it will be the latter, and that we shall finally meet in person.

I thought of the Swiss doctor who left this outpost two days before. Knowing the stops he intended to make along the way, it was more than likely that he would now be encircled by that sea of flames. There would only be one route left for him to take: He would have to follow the riverbanks which, in that region, create an intricate web of waterways. Georges Liengme would have to repeat the prowess of Christ, walking on the waters of so many rivers and streams that he would lose count of them all.

I waited anxiously all morning for the arrival of a messenger bringing news from Coolela. This is the usual procedure: an advance guard reaches the garrison so that preparations can be made in good time for the arrival of our glorious combatants. I prayed that this time the carts would not be loaded down with the injured. With my help, Dr. Rodrigues Braga prepared the beds with clean linen. Then our doctor spread mosquito nets around to prevent ashes from getting into areas where he might have to carry out surgical interventions.

At midday, messengers did indeed arrive. But they were enemy emissaries. It was half a dozen Vátua soldiers bringing with them, his hands bound, a tall, proud-looking man. One of the emissaries from Gungunhane stepped forward and declared:

Our king ordered us to bring you this man. We know him as Uamat-ibjana, but you call him Zixaxa. Here he is.

Here was the trophy we had been after for months. More than Gungunhane himself, this Negro was the Portuguese crown's most sought-after target. The headman, Zixaxa had had the audacity to lead a rebellion in the south and to organize an attack on our most important city. Portuguese had died, Africans had died. And Portuguese national pride and prestige had been damaged in the comity of civilized nations. And there was the famous rebel, hands bound behind his back, exhausted and disheveled. In spite of it all, I have to admit that the man held himself with the dignity of a prince. His haughtiness left me feeling uncomfortable, but was much more of an irritant to his escorts. For, the moment they had introduced him, they pushed him toward me as if he were a sack. Stumbling forward, the prisoner ended up crashing against my body, and I had to embrace him to prevent us both from falling over. It was only then that I noticed that the Vátuas had two women with them. They were Zixaxa's wives.

So why have you brought them?

So that they should see their man die. Then they will go back to their homelands to tell people what they have seen.

The women were pushed forward so violently that nothing could stop them from sprawling on the ground. The Vátua who had led the committee spoke once more:

We have fulfilled our part of the agreement, the emissary said, *now you fulfill yours. Stop the war immediately.*

It is too late now, I thought. The war had already consumed itself, leaving specks of soot floating across the savanna. The messengers had been late in coming, and Gungunhane's obstinacy had lasted too long. But I kept quiet in front of those emissaries, thinking that it would be extremely useful to hold the captive we had been seeking for so long. The surrender of Zixaxa was a sign of the despair of our old enemies. And Gungunhane had ordered his handover at the place he judged the most secure: our garrison. The choice of the location and timing of the handover erased the humiliation of surrender. It was he who issued the order, even when all he was doing was obeying.

Gungunhane's envoys asked us to untie Zixaxa. They wanted their ropes back. Forgetting my handicap, I tried to undo those tight knots. It was the guard who completed the task. Before he left, the king's emissary watched the captured headman being led away, escorted by our soldiers. After a while, the prisoner turned and addressed the Vátuas who had brought him there:

Tell your king that the skies over Gaza are full of swallows after all.

The prisoner and his two wives were tied to the pole in the middle of the garrison where we usually tethered the mules. For some time I sat there just staring at the prisoner, without exchanging a word with him. Nor could it have been otherwise; the man's Portuguese was less than rudimentary. And I was a mere amateur when it came to the language of the Landins. But there was something in Zixaxa's face that spoke of nostalgia for some distant realm, of a time long gone of lightness and joy. And I had already seen this yearning in our own people's eyes.

Late in the afternoon, the guards alerted me to the arrival of another messenger. He was on his own, worn out, and looked as if he could no longer see. He was so covered in ash that one could not tell what race he belonged to. He wanted to deliver a letter to the doctor. *I've brought this for the white* dokotela, he managed to articulate. When we gave him water, he merely wet his lips. The rest of the mug he used to wash his face and neck. Then he turned and disappeared into the bush.

Not long afterward, Rodrigues Braga came into my room and tossed an envelope into my lap.

This letter isn't for me, it's for Georges Liengme.

He turned and left as quickly as he had come.

It was now obvious that the white doctor to whom the messenger had referred was the Swiss missionary. But this was a minor slipup compared to what was subsequently revealed: This letter had been written by Bertha Ryff, Liengme's wife. The envelope lay untouched in my lap while I could not rid myself of a doubt that assailed me. Why had that woman used a letter in order to communicate with someone with whom she lived? And why had she chosen to have it delivered so far away? I acknowledge my lack of scruples, sir, but I was overcome by curiosity. Maybe my intention to involve you in this little peccadillo is to allay the guilt that weighs so heavily on me. But you, sir, may be no more master of your decision than I was of mine. If you do not wish to be party to the secrets of Bertha Ryff, then stop reading these lines of mine. Whatever the case, I am transcribing her letter, translated by myself into Portuguese with the help of Rodrigues Braga.

My Dearest Georges,

Once again you have invited me to accompany you on one of your frequent, lengthy digressions. I would go if I were a bird. If I could fly over marshlands, lakes, and exhaustion. But I no longer have the strength or the health to even be a person. I am not happy enough to be a wife. Nor do I have sufficient hope to be a mother.

I shall proceed now as I have throughout my many periods of waiting: I shall pray that you do not return as distant from me as when you left. You always tell me that it is I who have become remote. The continual sporadic bouts of fever have left me withdrawn. But I am not losing my sense of feeling because of illness. It is out of sadness.

I am ill, Georges. But it is the malady of emptiness from which I suffer. That is why it is not a doctor I need. It is a lover. For this reason, I beseech you: Look at me with the same distraction that you possess when you photograph naked black women. Look at me, Georges. And you'll see that it is not a missionary I am waiting for. I yearn for a husband who is not afraid of the volcano burning within me.

You are recognized back in Switzerland for your valuable work as a missionary among the people of Africa, combating witchcraft and witch doctors. Well, my dearest Georges, now I want you to bewitch me. They are proud of the doctor who has saved so many lives. But I have died in your hands. I died every time that you failed to love me. I died even more when you thought you were saving me. And I returned to my everyday existence devoid of light or hope. It is not greater belief that I need. It is life. It is not your cruelty that has harmed me. It is because you have done nothing. It is because you left me feeling small, unfocused, nonexistent. This is what I am: a mere image seen against the light. A photograph that was never developed.

41

FOUR WOMEN FACING THE END OF THE WORLD

The last one to join the line of sick patients was a man with thick,
tangled hair carrying gold sovereigns wedged into his orbits. My eyes
have turned into money, he explained. My brother-in-law had dead
eyes, the native added. And the dokotela *treated him. But I don't want*
him to cure me. Far from it: I want to be left like this forever.
Do you know something, Doctor? I've never been looked at
with such respect. Do you think it doesn't pain me to be blind?
It pains me far more not to be anyone.
—EXTRACT FROM THE DIARY OF SERGEANT GERMANO DE MELO

Impibekezane and I returned from Sana Benene, encountering on
our way whole expanses of forest hemmed in by the belt of fire. When
we arrived, we circled the village of Mandhlakazi from a distance. All
that remained of the capital of the kingdom were ashes. We hurried
toward the hospital of the Swiss Mission.

Here in the hospital we are safe, the queen of the VaNguni said.
Whites don't attack other whites.

The white woman, Bertha, the mixed-race Elizabete, and the
queen and I sat on the top of the dune where the hospital was situated. We were four women watching the grasslands burning. Four
such different women sitting there overlooking the abyss of the end
of the world. At that point, I thought that there is no such thing as

an external landscape. It was we who were burning. The whites told us that the inferno was a fire lit by demons in the depths of the earth. These infernos were now rising to the surface.

Where is your son, Your Majesty? asked Bertha. *Where is Ngungunyane hiding?*

He has gone to Txaimiti, answered Impibekezane. *But he is not hiding there. He has gone to ask for the protection of his late grandfather, Sochangane.*

Ngungunyane's mother then corrected my way of sitting. As my dead mother had done so many times, she encouraged me to fold my legs under me on the sitting mat. Then, once I had assumed the correct pose, she smiled at me and said:

And you, Imani, are going with me to Txaimiti, for I no longer want any dealings with counselors. I shall make you queen forthwith.

A queen crowned on the day the kingdom died? This was the question it occurred to me to ask. But I contained myself as I contemplated the aged monarch with her long bead necklaces, her endless metal rings around her ankles and arms. And I thought: The fewer the dreams, the more the adornments. Father Rudolfo was right: Bibliana was far more of a queen, with her band of loyal followers. And I had a vision of myself, already elderly, rotting on a sleeping mat in *Nkosi's* kraal. And then I thought Impibekezane merited my complete and utter candor.

Your Majesty, I have something to confess: I am not here of my own free will. It was a demon within me that propelled me here.

I know what that demon is. Do you want to kill my son?

Who told you that?

They all do. They all want to kill him.

But then she revealed that she had a plan. And she had already attempted to tell it to Sergeant Germano de Melo at Sana Benene. But the boy had fainted, bleeding profusely. Something to do with bewitchment, no doubt. So she had withdrawn without revealing her secrets. This is what she had envisaged happening: The Portuguese would withdraw without disturbing the VaNguni crown:

After this battle at Coolela, they had already agreed they would withdraw without mistreating Ngungunyane. They wouldn't kill him or take him prisoner. For this son of mine, according to the promise I made the whites, would cross the border to the Transvaal. And over there, beyond the mountains, they have my assurance that he will no longer bother the Portuguese.

The plan seemed muddled to me. But as far as the queen was concerned, it made sense: she would save her son from the hands of the whites, and especially from those of the blacks. Her son had survived thus far. But he would not escape from the next confrontation. And it would not be necessary for the Portuguese to defeat him. For his own troops, dying of hunger and frustration, would enact justice with their own hands. What Impibekezane needed was to convince the king of Gaza that, following the Battle of Coolela, the Portuguese would fall back voluntarily to Inhambane and Lourenço Marques. Free of the Portuguese threat, Ngungunyane could quietly dispense with his troops. Having been ordered to disperse by the king, the VaNguni army would be relieved of the burden of humiliation. And the Portuguese would have no reason to prolong the conflict. The queen had already begun the task of convincing her son. The problem was the generals who surrounded him. War might be risky, but it was the source of their wealth. Above all else, Impibekezane was confident. What she could not achieve by force of argument, she could obtain with poison.

I don't know, Your Majesty. How can you be sure the whites will accept your plan?

Because they already have, Impibekezane insisted. *I've spoken with them.*

And do you know why they accepted it? I argued. *Because it probably had been their plan all along, to withdraw straight after the Battle of Coolela.*

All the better. It means this is the last fire, the last inferno.

Bertha Ryff listened in silence to Impibekezane's invitation to me to become her daughter-in-law. And she took advantage of the queen's presence to make herself heard.

Think carefully. You'll give her a throne, but take her life away from her.

It was not only the war Ngungunyane needed to free himself from. There were other challenges. Bertha recalled that two weeks before, one of Ngungunyane's newest wives had turned up at the hospital. The king had gone to get her from the mountains of Swaziland. She had been tormented by constant fevers ever since she had arrived at Mandhlakazi.

It's the mandikwé, *the demons*, declared the young virgin.

She received treatment and the following week she returned to offer them a basket of eggs as a token of her gratitude. Then she addressed the doctor in the following terms:

Ah, mulungu*! Don't you have a cure that will stop our king from drinking so much?*

If it were true that the king had stopped appearing drunk at his official functions, then in his private life it should also be acknowledged that he was so intoxicated that he was deviating from his conjugal duties.

If you cannot cure my husband, the young wife said, *I would rather you gave me back my old demons. Sometimes being ill is a way of suffering less.*

Georges was categorical in his diagnosis: Drink was depriving the king of his virility, Bertha suggested.

Don't pay any attention to people who talk like that, his mother begged me.

If I was destined to be the king's wife, Impibekezane argued, I should combine the wisdom of water and fire: to be able to work my way around obstacles, and embrace enemies in order to burn them with the fierceness of a kiss.

Then the queen spoke in Txizulu: I shouldn't listen to a white. After all, wasn't I dreaming of regaining my black, African soul?

Aware of the growing pressure upon me, Bertha called me aside and shook me as she murmured:

They make a queen of you. But will you ever become a wife? Or will you never be more than a slave?

All of a sudden Georges Liengme arrived, breathless. A week after having left for Chicomo, he returned without his mule or his traveling companion. He yelled instructions for us to gather our things together and get away from there.

They set fire to Mandhlakazi. And now they're on their way here to burn the mission.

Without panicking, as if she had been expecting this outcome all along, Bertha went into the house to collect her children. Beside himself, her husband hurried to get his cameras and photographic plates while commanding operations at the top of his voice. He told the queen that at the foot of the hill a group of VaNguni soldiers was waiting to accompany her to Txaimiti. The *mulata*, Elizabete, was ordered to collect the medicines together and to hide the patients in the surrounding bush. The girl shrugged and, in contrast to the commotion that we were going through, smiled at me and muttered:

It wasn't me he was talking to, Georges doesn't speak to me in that way.

In an instant, as if this were a scene that had been rehearsed, half a dozen servants transferred the contents of the residence to the back of the house, where two carts drawn by mules were waiting. One of the carts was full of effects. The driver commented laconically, "They are the king's things." All the belongings of the Swiss family were therefore going to have to fit in the remaining cart. The doctor hurried backward and forward, urging us to abandon the place as quickly as possible. As he passed me, he issued a hurried invitation:

Come with us, Imani.

And he held out his arm to stop me. He held me back for a moment as if he knew this would be our last encounter. I pushed him out of the way gently but firmly.

I'm going to help your wife, I justified myself.

Without any ceremony, I entered the residence of the Swiss and surprised Elizabete emerging from the couple's bedroom. She was wearing a fur coat belonging to Bertha Ryff.

Everyone's leaving except me. And Georges is going to stay with me, she said. *I'm this white man's true wife. Bertha's a vanquished woman. She's got no spark. She's damp timber. She can't catch fire.*

Flaunting those absurd clothes, the mestizo woman went out into the yard and showed herself off, spinning around and around as if she were doing a dance, until the coat slipped off her, leaving her breasts exposed. But she did not retreat from her carelessness. On the contrary, she exposed her whole body, and stepped back into the house naked. The queen was amused and applauded her performance. Only I noticed Bertha Ryff making for the cart and, taking her husband's photographic plates from her bag, she flung them into the long grass. And I shall never forget her fury as she cursed Elizabete and her race:

Damned mulattoes! Let them burn in Hell!

Her curse pained me. It was a physical pain, a ripping through my body, a stab with a dagger sharpened by demons. I never thought words could hurt so much. And I crossed my arms over my belly as if, by so doing, I could shut out the white woman's malediction.

42

SERGEANT GERMANO DE MELO'S FOURTEENTH LETTER

*The whites don't know that stones are planted. And that they die when
they are torn up without the gods' permission. The whites take them
away in order to build great cities. They build them with stones that
have died, and in this way they cause the soil all around to fester.
That is why the cities stink.*
—BIBLIANA TALKING ABOUT PROSPECTORS

Chicomo, December 24, 1895

Dear Lieutenant Ayres de Ornelas,

I fear this letter will never reach you. I am sending it without any
great hopes to Lourenço Marques. It is more than likely, however,
that you, sir, will have left Mozambique. Be that as it may, I am
using the cook, who is leaving Chicomo today, as the bearer of this
message. And I am doing all this because the news I bring you bears
no relation to that which I have sent you up until now. Let me begin
by saying how sorry I am that you were not in the officers' mess at
Chicomo when Mouzinho de Albuquerque summoned Captain
Sanches de Miranda. I haven't the words to describe the burning
passion in Mouzinho de Albuquerque's eyes, and which contrasted
with his military composure and calmness. When Miranda appeared, Mouzinho spoke sparingly:

I'm going ahead with my plan!

Right now, in the middle of Christmas, Governor?

The sooner the better. And don't call me that. I'm a captain and nothing more.

Mouzinho had just been appointed governor of the military district of Gaza. And as for the attack on Gungunhane's new headquarters, he had thought of everything: As far as the kaffirs were concerned, the Portuguese military offensive had stalled. Even Lisbon considered the matter closed. Orders had come from the mother country to withdraw our forces.

Do you want a better opportunity than this one? asked Albuquerque.

Sanches de Miranda responded with caution to these audacious instructions. He wanted to know what we would do with Gungunhane, whether we would kill him or take him captive. We'd decide that later, Mouzinho answered. Miranda had another opinion, as a result of news just received from the military post at Languene, on the northern bank of the Limpopo. He knew that the goodwill of the population in the vicinity of Chaimite could not be guaranteed. However, Mouzinho was now much more than a mere captain. And he had received very different information: Fifty-three village headmen had sought the protection of the Portuguese flag. After Coolela, most of the local chieftains had sworn loyalty. *Don't confuse loyalty with fear*, Captain Miranda argued. The kaffirs were living between two terrors. On the one hand, there was their fear of Gungunhane's cruelty; on the other, their panic that in the wake of our victory we would punish anyone who wasn't on our side.

It was on these terms, sir, that the conversation between the two officers took place. What made Mouzinho so enthusiastic was precisely what terrified me the most: Imani was in Gungunhane's final refuge. I found this out from one of the soldiers who set fire to Liengme's hospital. According to this witness, the queen mother had forced Imani to go with her. The final assault on the king of the

Vátuas might, in some form of crossfire, kill the woman who had stolen my heart.

Can I go with you? I asked timidly.

And who are you? asked Mouzinho.

Sanches de Miranda offered the information. He knew who I was and the tasks I had been performing in the infirmary over the last month. Given Dr. Braga's absence, it would be better if I stayed at the garrison until the expedition's return. Rodrigues Braga would return the following day and assume the command of the post.

Then the two captains returned again to debating their views, by now in a more solemn tone. For Miranda, the intervention would merely be an act of temerity that ran the most serious risks. But nothing could shake Albuquerque's conviction. Gungunhane wouldn't be expecting them. He had just surrendered up Zixaxa to us, and for this reason he believed he was in our good books. At the end of their discussion, Miranda asked whether the High Command in Lourenço Marques had been informed of the operation. And here, sir, it is worth quoting Mouzinho's reply word for word:

High Command? Lourenço Marques? I've never heard of either.

When Mouzinho had moved away, Captain Miranda commented:

This fellow's mad. Fifty foot soldiers under these rains are going to get bogged down in Hell. It's going to be mass suicide.

I'll go instead of you, I offered when I saw him organizing his haversack.

Sanches de Miranda sighed and smiled.

I have to go, he replied. *And my main reason is a sad one. I have to go because I shall be taken for someone else.*

The natives thought that he was Mafambatcheca. They took him for the late Diocleciano das Neves, the Portuguese hunter who had gained so much sympathy among the kaffirs. And because of this mistake, the Negroes welcomed our troops with a great show of hospitality every time they were led by Miranda.

The advance platoon had already passed the entrance to the garrison's gunnery when Captain Miranda, as if assailed by some urgent thought, turned back to tell me in an almost desperate tone:

Do you really want to make yourself useful? Well, send a message immediately to Lourenço Marques. Alert them to the tragedy that is about to happen.

Then he rejoined the group, which was moving out into the bush. Still puzzled by that strange order, I watched the troops depart from the garrison's palisade. It was three days before Christmas and it was raining so hard that it was as if those Portuguese were ships crossing an ocean. From the quayside, I watched the sails braving the waves. The scene had the quality of an epic. But it was worrying: The men could scarcely keep to their feet, the skinny mules lacked the strength to pull the carts. It was not an advance guard. It was a procession of sick men on their way to their final resting place. In contrast to this tragic scene was Mouzinho de Albuquerque's fanatical gaze and godly demeanor as he led the march.

After that, I returned to my own tasks. In fact, there was only one, and this left my conscience in torment: Sanches de Miranda's fateful order. How I wish you were here, my dear lieutenant. Because at that moment I had a double-edged blade in my hands. By obeying the captain, I disobeyed the governor. By sending the message, I might prevent a major disaster from affecting the whole nation. By not sending it, I might render the capture of our most powerful enemy even harder. And then there was the practical question: How was I to get a message to Lourenço Marques with sufficient speed? Then I remembered that among the sick in the infirmary there was a telegraph operator. It was he who sent the message, while I supported him in my arms. He was so weak that I had to hold his fingers on the keyboard. The unfortunate soldier occasionally forgot the Morse code. Then, with a flickering glint in his eye, the man began to type again and that annoying clatter of the keys was music to my ears.

Once back in my room, I thought again about António Enes as the recipient of my telegram. I was aware that by then the Royal Commissioner might have already returned to Lisbon. But then I thought someone in command in Lourenço Marques would have re-transmitted the message to Lisbon. That was my belief. That was what I bet my life on. But my hopes crashed against the barrier of reality. And you, my dear lieutenant, know what I mean here. In the hierarchy of our military command, the idea prevails that as a result of the Battle of Coolela, Gungunhane has been decisively beaten, his headquarters destroyed and his army scattered.

Who knows, sir, maybe you yourself, along with all the other chiefs of staff, have returned to Lisbon? Maybe the war is over for you as well. Gungunhane may well be able to roam around his lands without having to give himself up. With the exception of Mouzinho, no one seems in a hurry to capture him.

The following day, an incoming message shook our telegraph. The same patient, now even weaker, gradually transcribed, letter by letter, what an unknown sender had dictated on the other side of the world. Eventually, the message was written out. The messenger hesitated, and then awkwardly handed me the manuscript. He said it was essentially a summary of a much longer text. There were few lines, but the effect they had on me was schismatic. Here is what was written:

Captain Mouzinho,
    Abort your mission and return immediately with your troops to Chicomo!
    Signed, Acting Governor-General

In a flash, I had decided what to do. I packed a bag and asked the garrison's cook to immediately accompany me southward. We had to stop Mouzinho in his tracks. The cook resisted. I might be in charge of the garrison, but he didn't take orders from me. I promised him more money than I had at my disposal. And along he came.

The Negro, who was short and tubby, carried a haversack with food and water. Before we had even left the garrison, he announced:

Langa.

I don't understand.

That's my name. Don't call me cook anymore.

And the newly born Langa, the cook, led me along at a quick pace. He showed himself there and then to be an indispensable traveling companion. For, knowing that I was the bearer of an important piece of paper, he suggested that I take it from my pocket. *Sweat envies ink*, he said good-humoredly. He was from Lourenço Marques and had served in the army for some ten years. In spite of his bulk, Langa was able to keep up a steady pace, and without slowing he suggested that I should never look down on cooks. The great general of Gungunhane's army, Maguiguana, was a former cook at the court of Muzila.

At one stage, we passed a group of women. They confirmed that they had passed some Portuguese soldiers. At that very place, the column had been stopped by a group of Vátuas wearing headdresses. They told us that upon seeing Mouzinho, they had dropped to their knees and saluted him:

Bayete, Nkosi!

They spoke with the help of a black Portuguese interpreter. They claimed they had come to join the Portuguese forces.

We want to see Umundungaɀi, that blind vulture, defeated, the kaffirs said.

The Portuguese were unsure whether to accept their help.

They can come with us, but without any firearms, Mouzinho allegedly declared.

Then kaffirs and whites set off again toward the south. There must have been about two thousand auxiliaries marching across the Maguanhana plain.

An hour later, we arrived at the liquor store of some Indian traders who were sitting at the door, sprawled on the shop's wooden steps, enjoying the morning sun. The drinks trade was in the hands of these Indians.

The Indians confirmed that Mouzinho's troops had stopped at the shop to replenish their supplies. On that same veranda, they had received two envoys from Gungunhane, who had offered two large ivory tusks and six gold sovereigns as a gift for the wife of Mafambatcheca, the name by which the natives knew Captain Sanches de Miranda. I could not prevent myself from smiling, sir, when I thought about how the mistake would have amused Miranda. The Indians know the local language well, and followed all the negotiations. And they told us that through his messengers, Gungunhane asked Mouzinho de Albuquerque to meet him by the river. There they would discuss the peace that the south of Mozambique needed so much. According to them, Mouzinho declined the proposal.

We decided to spend the night in the establishment. The traders put the shop at our disposal after spreading cloths over the floor to make it more comfortable for us to lie down. The smell of spices might put off the mosquitoes, but it was so strong that it deprived us of sleep. Outside, the night was as heavy as a liquid sheet, such was the intensity of the rain. I thanked God for the downpour because it would delay the progress of those we were chasing.

We set off before the first light of dawn. That day, the clouds were covering the sun. I was heartened by Langa's relaxed manner in that unreadable terrain, for the forest through which we were walking was so dark that our arms reached farther than our eyes. As soon as we moved out into open country, we caught sight of two Portuguese soldiers who were walking with difficulty. They were accompanied by half a dozen blacks. The whites recognized me. They belonged to Mouzinho's troops but had fallen so gravely ill that they were returning to the garrison at Chicomo. When I told them my intention, they laughed: *Stop Mouzinho? It would be easier to stop the wind!* The troops we were pursuing were some six miles ahead of us. The sick soldiers remembered that the last place they had reached was a lake, the name of which was Motacane. The Portuguese were dying of thirst and the lake was wide and deep. But the moment they saw that sheet of water, the black auxiliaries dashed forward in their hundreds to bathe. They washed themselves and drank at the same time, churning up the mud and turning the water into a viscous, foul-smelling liquid. The thirsty Portuguese cursed the blacks for their lack of consideration. Concerned about the health of Captain Sanches de Miranda, it occurred to Mouzinho de Albuquerque that his companion in arms should also be evacuated back to Chicomo. Ever since they had left the garrison, Miranda had been suffering from high fevers and vomiting so profusely that his eyes were drying up like two dark stones. But the sick captain refused to turn back. Even in adversity, he would pursue their mad odyssey until the end. Not for what he might be able to do, but for what he might prevent.

The news was not so bad. That was what I thought. Any delay in Mouzinho's march was a comfort as far as I was concerned. Maybe I am by nature a pessimist, but every minute that passed, I could imagine Imani's bullet-ridden body. Sometimes they were stray bullets. Other times, the slaughter was deliberate and targeted at the whole royal family. My beloved fell, assumed to be one of the emperor's wives.

43

ALL THAT FITS INSIDE A BELLY

Here are my instructions. Go to the young, at the point when they are
just leaving childhood. Steal their names, take them away from their
homelands and their families, and desiccate their souls: Your
soldiers will conquer empires.
—NGUNGUNYANE, QUOTED BY BERTHA RYFF

Portuguese called it Chaimite. The preciseness of its name is not important: Txaimiti was not the type of place one would expect to find a king. Perhaps that was Ngungunyane's intention—no one would guess his whereabouts. He who flees does not just want to leave a place. He wants there to be no such thing as places. And the king of the VaNguni wanted to be together with those who had already died. This was where Manicusse was buried. It was sacred land. He could not have chosen better protection.

It was to Txaimiti that the queen and I were heading after having crossed the plain of Mandhlakazi in flames. Far away, behind the curtain of smoke, lay the hospital of the Swiss Mission. In order to reach the dwellings where the emperor was, it was necessary to get through a circular fence made of wooden planks and thorny branches. The only way of doing so was through an entrance that was less than a meter high and another meter in width. It was by crawling like animals that the queen mother and I entered a spacious yard surrounded by some ten hovels built of slate and thatch.

These VaNguni villages are known as *xigodjo*. We had just arrived from our troubled journey and presented ourselves immediately without taking a bath or having time to rest. In the middle of the enclosure were seated the queens the king had chosen to accompany him on his pilgrimage. All seven queens, endlessly seated, the queens without a throne. Suddenly, from the shadows on one side, there emerged another woman whom I immediately recognized, although I was so astonished that I distorted her name as I cried:

Bibliana!

I hurried forward to fall into her embrace, but with a simple gesture the soothsayer of Sana Benene indicated that I should control myself and keep my distance.

It was I who called her, Impibekezane asserted. And she explained: Bibliana was of the Ndau nation. The queen herself belonged to those folk. The two kings who had preceded Ngungunyane had established their capital in that other nation's domains. They needed someone who could speak to the powerful spirits from the other side of the river. This was why Bibliana was there. Txaimiti was a sacred place. And a place like that could only be enlivened with the blessing of powerful priests.

Darkness fell quickly. We slept in the open, for there was not enough room in the houses. And even if there had been, I felt better protected far from their walls. I sought out a spot far from everyone. It was out in the open air that most people from Gaza had been sleeping for months. The houses came alive only during the day. At night, they were as faint as a new moon.

In the middle of the night, Bibliana emerged, wrapped in a black overcoat. She resembled a creature emanating from the night itself. She lay down next to me and told me to keep my voice down.

My father? I asked anxiously.

He stayed there, I came on my own. But he's well.

Does he talk about me?

He sent you a message. He just asked you not to forget your promise.

I should have gone with the Swiss.

You'll go with the Portuguese.

I don't believe in your predictions.

It's not a prediction. It's a negotiation. And it wasn't I who did it. It was the queen. She negotiated with the Portuguese. So you will go with them.

I don't believe it.

Well, you had better believe it. Impibekezane sent a messenger to meet Mafambatcheca tonight.

That man died long ago.

That man you say died will enter this enclosure tomorrow in uniform.

A finger on her lips was her way of telling me to keep quiet. I should listen to her important advice in silence. The following morning, I should sit near her, but not too close. There would be a war of spirits in the place. There was no point in invoking those who might be envious. That was why I should keep away from the queens. At the appointed time, Impibekezane would summon me. I would present myself barefoot, so barefoot that it would seem as though I had lost my feet.

This is how things have been arranged, Bibliana concluded. And we remained silent, engulfed in the darkness. When I assumed she was already asleep, the sorceress spoke again.

It will be a boy, and she paused. *The baby you are bearing is a boy.*

Then Bibliana placed her hands over my stomach. I was petrified, all of me turned to stone except for the water moistening my face. I was pregnant. I already loved this creature nestled within my body. I loved it more than Germano, who was unaware that he was soon to become a father. I loved the baby more than I loved myself.

I was riven by conflicting emotions. Part of me wanted to conceal my pregnancy. Another part prayed that my growing belly would be noticed. And more than noticed, celebrated. On the eve of becoming a mother, I needed more than ever to be a daughter. And I sensed a maternal presence comforting me. A mother that was mine on loan, who lulled me by simply putting her arm around my shoulder.

That night, I was once again visited by the dream about giving birth to weapons. This time, Sergeant Germano was standing next to the midwife. He was waiting in military posture for the arrival of his child. After my final spasm, a spear emerged from my belly. It was a beautiful spear, its handle adorned with black and red beads. Disappointed, the sergeant took a step back and complained:

I asked for a sword. A sword, Imani. Now what am I going to tell my superiors? What am I going to say to my mother?

The distress at not having fulfilled Germano's expectations reinforced my birth pains.

I'm sorry, Germano, I lamented, *but this is your daughter, the spear, hold it in your arms.*

The Portuguese looked uneasily at the newborn, his hesitation dancing in his eyes, and eventually he admitted:

I can't. Forgive me, Imani. But that is not my daughter.

I awoke at first light, soaked in water in the middle of the dew. Bibliana was already up. In her place sat the queen mother, who greeted me in a low voice. Then, in a level tone, she eased my concerns over what was going to happen that morning. I should remain calm, for she knew the commander of the Portuguese forces. That man had two names and two lives. The Portuguese called him Diocleciano das Neves. The blacks called him Mafambatcheca. Diocleciano had died twelve years before. But Mafambatcheca still roamed happily through the savanna. And he was still a good white, an old friend of the family. The moment he entered the *xigodjo* and saw her, the Portuguese would greet her in a friendly manner, embrace her son, and play with her grandson, Godido.

We've been away these last few days, how do you know it's this man who is commanding the soldiers? I asked fearfully.

Someone told me they had seen him marching along the shore of the lake.

But, Your Majesty, twelve years have passed. Might it not be his son? Impibekezane was in no doubt.

It's him, the old lady assured me. *In every race, there are those who die and come back. The whites have them as well. It began with Christ.*

Come with me, I'm going to tend to Ngungunyane, Bibliana told me. It was dark, and without waiting for me to react, she walked off, while, even with her back turned, she pointed to a little fire that was flickering in a corner of the porch. I sat down sleepily, thinking about the soothsayer's words. She said she was going to tend to Ngungunyane. She didn't say she was going to be tender to Ngungunyane.

Before long, Bibliana reappeared, bringing with her the emperor, maddened by his anticipated yearnings for his own empire. Wrapped in a blanket, the king trod the open space of the yard with the steps of a prisoner, as if he feared falling into some hidden abyss in the darkness. Ngungunyane came to a halt in front of the flames, his bare feet perilously near the fire. The woman pushed him a little farther back, whispering in his ear:

Look out for the flames.

Where others see flames, all I see are shadows.

I know what makes you afraid, the woman said. *Whoever looks at the fire sees the ocean.*

Tonight I dreamed of the sea. Do you know what that means? That my end is near.

At that point, Bibliana poured water from a bowl over the emperor's feet.

The sea may be a prison, the soothsayer affirmed. *But it can be your fortress, a fortress that may protect you far better than any* xigodjo. *Those who want to kill you are no longer the others. They are your people*, Nkosi. *Protect yourself from your own.*

Then she threw the last few drops over Umundungazi's legs, while she said:

This water comes from the sea. Now I'm going back home, Bibliana declared at last. She spoke more loudly so that I could hear her. I tried to get near her, but she held out her arm. *There are no farewells, I shall always dwell within you.*

The sun had just risen and I had taken my place, as instructed, in a discreet position in the sandy yard in front of the house where Ngungunyane was hiding. I sat with my back to Bibliana. And I copied what the other women were doing: silent, gazing at the ground, I waited for time to pass. Around the edges of this open space were seated the dignitaries of the court. They sat in ornate chairs and used the traditional oxtails to lazily swat the flies buzzing dolefully around them. All this was happening under the protection of huge sunshades held aloft by young men for hours on end.

They were awaiting the arrival of the *indunas* Zaba and Sukanaka, who had been dispatched by Ngungunyane to try to halt the Portuguese advance. They took with them six hundred pounds and ivory tusks. With these gifts they would try to buy the cessation of hostilities.

It wouldn't be long before these emissaries returned to Txaimiti. They entered the redoubt and shook their heads. Manhune, the chief counselor of the court, then sent out another delegation. This consisted of the same *indunas*, led by Godido, the king's favorite son. There was further waiting, the same heat, the same sideways glances from the queens. One of them got to her feet to distribute water to those present. I was the only one excluded from such favor. It was Impibekezane who, with a simple wave of the hand, corrected this omission.

An hour later, Godido returned. He had taken the Portuguese a new offer: the same amount of money and ivory, supplemented by sixty-three oxen and ten of Zixaxa's wives. Once again, the offer was declined. It was the last throw of the dice. Now all they could do was to await the invasion.

Impibekezane's powerful voice resounded against an ominous silence. She spoke as if the next day would see the end of the world:

No one is to fire, no one is to protest. There will be no bloodshed. It was Muzila who spoke to me last night.

Then they heard the first signs of the arrival of the Portuguese. They had reached the entrance to the *xigodjo*. I turned my face, reluctant to face reality. And what I saw was the astonishment on the queen mother's face. The man who had broken through the palisade was not the expected Mafambatcheca. Neither he nor Diocleciano, his twin who had been stubborn enough to die. The man who now broke into the sacred redoubt was another Portuguese soldier, who was shouting furiously. Other whites came in, and there was no sign of Mafambatcheca. We found out later that the captain had been spared from the final assault because he was so ill. He was resting some hundred meters from the village.

The queen mother felt at an utter loss. All her certainties had crumbled away. And the expression on the white man's face as he yelled, "*Gungunhane! Gungunhane!*" suggested he had no wish for a friendly chat. It was the end.

At this point, the great lady threw herself at the feet of the Portuguese in tears. She begged him to spare her son's life and that of her grandson, Godido. I, on the contrary, secretly beseeched him to bring his sword down on the emperor and for those white hands to avenge my black brothers. A mother's tears, however, were more powerful than my appeal to God.

44

SERGEANT GERMANO DE MELO'S FIFTEENTH LETTER

*... I called Gungunhane at the top of my voice in the midst of absolute
silence, preparing to set fire to the hut if he delayed, when I saw the
Vátua chief emerge, the lieutenants Miranda and Couto recognizing
him straightaway, given that they had seen him more than once at
Manjacaze. You cannot imagine the arrogance with which he answered
the first questions I put to him. I ordered one of the black soldiers to tie
his hands behind his back and told him to sit down. He asked me
where, and as I pointed to the ground, he replied proudly that it was
dirty. I then forced him to sit on the ground (something he never did),
telling him he was no longer chief of the Mangunis but a* matonga *like
any other black. I asked the chief to point out Queto, Manhune,
Molungo, and Maguiguana. He pointed to Queto and Manhune who
were next to him, and said the others were not there. I upbraided
Manhune (who was Gungunhane's demonic soul) for being an enemy
to the Portuguese, to which he replied that he knew he should die. I
then ordered for him to be tied to one of the posts of the palisade and he
was shot by three whites. He couldn't have died with greater* sang-
froid, *with haughtiness and true courage; he merely pointed out with a
smile that it would be better to untie him so that he would fall when
shot. After him, it was Queto's turn ... He was the only one of
Muzila's brothers who had wanted to wage war against us and the only
one present at the battle of "Coolela." ... I ordered him to be tied
up and shot.*
**—JOAQUIM MOUZINHO DE ALBUQUERQUE, EXTRACT FROM THE REPORT PRESENTED TO THE
COUNSELOR CORREIA E LANÇA, ACTING GOVERNOR OF THE PROVINCE OF MOZAMBIQUE,
BY THE MILITARY GOVERNOR OF GAZA, 1896**

Chaimite, December 31, 1895

Dear Lieutenant Ayres de Ornelas,

A brief foreword:

This time, it is not you to whom I write. Merely to myself, in order to keep up the practice of writing. These papers will never be letters. Nevertheless, I shall carry on writing as if you, sir, were going to read these scrawled lines tomorrow. I see them as if they were a diary of my most troubled days in Africa. I see them as forming part of me.

I reached Chaimite but was stopped from going where I wanted: a crowd of over two thousand people surrounded Gungunhane's new *xigodjo*. You are doubtless aware, sir, that *xigodjo* is the name given by the natives to royal citadels. Although there were so many, the crowds maintained an almost religious silence. Upon seeing so many people, Langa, the cook, declared hurriedly: *You go, I'll stay here.* And he sought the shade of an African fig tree some fifty meters from the crowd. I went with him, attempting to dissuade him. I still needed his help, no longer as a guide but as a translator. All of a sudden, I noticed Captain Sanches de Miranda in the same patch of shade. He was lying, deathly pale, on a mat. Two soldiers were keeping him company and they explained that the captain was so weak and dehydrated that he frequently passed out. At that precise moment he seemed to be awake, and I, without even greeting him, took the paper from my haversack with the governor general's instructions. *Read, Captain, read*, and I waved the paper in front of him. But Sanches could see neither letters, nor paper, nor people.

I heard the crowd explode into feverish uproar, the warriors beating their shields on the ground. A group of women passed by us shouting:

Gungunhane has sat on the ground! The Portuguese have tied him up.

And groups of people passed, all singing in chorus:

Vulture, vulture, be off with you, vulture. Never again will you swoop on our chickens.

I looked for the cook, but he had disappeared. I reached a decision and got to my feet. I would open a path through the crowd of blacks, no matter how many of them there were and no matter how long it took. Between oaths and the use of my elbows, I managed to create some space, but after a few desperate minutes the palisade around the *xigodjo* was still not visible. Then I suddenly heard shots. An old man sitting on the shoulders of a herculean young man told me that they had just shot one of Gungunhane's most important men. He offered to vacate his position for me so that I could climb up onto the shoulders of his gigantic friend. It took me a few moments to mount the shoulders of this brute, whose back was sweating copiously. From high up, I could see a man being tied up. Next to me, someone muttered: *That's Manhune, the greatest of the* indunas. Then, strangely, the counselor was untied. Was he going to be freed? That was what it looked like, judging by the confident smile lighting up his face. But then there was a salvo of gunfire and Manhune slumped to the ground. A deathly hush followed. Fearing that the shooting might become more widespread, the crowd began to retreat. A small clearing opened up in front of me, and I jumped off the Negro's back, shouting urgently:

Abort the operation! Abort the operation!

I was in such a state of excitement that I did not at first realize the absurdity of my intentions and, above all, the clumsy use of the verb *abort*.

I stopped yelling but continued to break through among the multitude of blacks. Leaning on the palisade, I managed to peer through the wooden branches and caught sight of Mouzinho, his back to me, and an elderly woman kneeling at his feet, begging:

Mulungu, *I am the queen. Don't kill my son or my grandson Godido.*

In despair, I looked around for Imani. But I could not see her among the women in the yard. A young man who had climbed up into a tree told me what was going on inside the redoubt: Gungunhane was handing over gold and diamonds and was promising cattle and ivory that he had hidden away. At that point, a group of soldiers widened the point of entry by tearing down part of the palisade. At long last, I overcame the remaining obstacle, and began to call for Imani. In my haste, I bumped into Lieutenant Costa, who was Mouzinho's second in command for the operation. He greeted me and told me that one of the soldiers who was helping Miranda had mentioned the strange purpose behind my arrival.

Don't you believe me, Lieutenant? It was António Enes himself who wrote this order, and I waved the piece of paper that my few fingers were still holding.

The lieutenant pushed me in the direction of a group of soldiers and prisoners who were just forming into a line. While he guided me through the hustle and bustle of the crowd, he explained himself. The problem, if there was indeed a problem, did not lie in who had written the message. The problem lay in who was going to read it. And that would never happen. For a bombastic Mouzinho de Albuquerque, his sword held aloft, only had eyes for demonstrating his triumph and rubbing it in the faces of those who had doubted him.

Forget the message. You can't cancel something that's already finished. And now come with us, we can return together.

So I set off following the procession, while still searching the mass of people gathered around us. Fortunately, the soldiers requested a rest to regain their strength before the return. Mouzinho reluctantly agreed. Their pause would have to be brief. He feared that after the initial shock, the Vátuas might reorganize themselves and seize back their emperor by force.

Supported by two soldiers, Captain Sanches de Miranda then emerged. The unlikely success of the mission seemed to have given him a new lease on life. Mouzinho got down from his horse to embrace his debilitated comrade. But before responding to his greetings, Sanches de Miranda asked in an enfeebled voice:

Why did we have to shoot them?

If we hadn't, we would have been seen as weak, Mouzinho replied.

They were already calling us women and chickens. We needed to stamp our authority with blood. And Mouzinho remounted his horse. From high up on his steed, he saw his men looking for a dry patch among the grass saturated with water. Suddenly, a smile lit up his face. Through his personal interpreter, he ordered the Vátua warriors to lay their shields on the ground. These shields would serve as cushions for the whites to sit on. A murmur of protest rang through the ranks of Gungunhane's soldiers. They were beaten but they had not lost their pride. If they dropped their shields, this would be the ultimate humiliation, according to their code of honor. In the face of this incipient display of disobedience, Mouzinho raised his rifle and rode his horse in a wide arc in full view of all. The vanquished soldiers immediately began to place their weapons on the ground. Then the captain returned to Sanches de Miranda wearing an almost imperceptible smile:

Do you see how it's done?

45

THE LAST RIVER

*It has never been possible to ascertain the true feelings of the Nguni in
relation to Gungunhane. There is no doubt that they looked upon him
as a military and political chief, but they feared him more than they
loved him. It is said that when Gungunhane was finally taken away by
the troops of Mouzinho de Albuquerque, the multitude shouted:
"Hamba kolwanyana kadiuqueda inkuku zetu," a Zulu expression that
means: "Be off with you, you vulture, who destroys our chickens."*
—RAÚL BERNARDO HONWANA, "MEMOIRS," 2010

I could have sworn I saw Germano among the crowd. A white
among a multitude of blacks is always exposed. Not so much because
of the color of his skin but in the awkwardness he shows for being
part of such a crowd. I ran to meet him, my heart leaping in my
breast. I wanted to hug him, I wanted to tell him I was pregnant, I
wanted to feel an embrace that might extinguish my longing. But the
silhouette disappeared. I too became invisible in the middle of that
chaos. Once again, I caught sight of a white soldier and I called Germano's name. But it was an astonished Santiago Mata who turned to
face me. It took him a few seconds to recognize me. He looked red,
his complexion ruddy, and he was doubled over as he walked. He
hurriedly asked me:

Keep an eye on my rifle while I take advantage of those clumps of grass over there. Careful, hold on hard to that little treasure, there are a lot of niggers on the loose around here.

He left me holding the weapon. One could see that he was in an urgent hurry by the shortness of his steps and the speed with which he took them. Then he started unbuttoning his trousers as he crouched down among the foliage. And there he remained amid contortions and groans.

A whirlwind of thoughts swept through my head. I saw those wives of the emperor pass by, whose main task was to be invisible. And in the opposite direction marched women in shoes, with dignified steps, carrying books and notebooks in their hands. Others were dressed as nurses and walked with their shoulders high and a steady look. The one question that presented itself to me at that particular moment, succinct but terrible, was this: What was it that no black woman had ever dared do? And the answer came to me clearly: Shoot a white man dead with a rifle.

Then, suddenly, as if I had been taken over by another soul, I picked Santiago's rifle up by the breech and walked straight around the bushes where he was hidden. I found the captain crouching on his haunches, in that devoted surrender that provides relief from an intestinal infection. I pressed the barrel against his wrinkled forehead and fired. And I watched the man fall with the same expression Francelino had on his face as he died, his eyes full of the astonishment of a newly born baby. The soldier was bleeding and twitching so vigorously that I shot him again without hesitation. That other soul now occupying me used my mouth to affirm:

Yes, you're right, Santiago Mata, there are a lot of niggers on the loose around here.

For a moment, a new sentiment gripped me: I was the mistress of the world, the avenger of injustices, queen of the black people and the whites. I was Bibliana's partner in the divine work of putting the world right.

Then, coming to my senses, I looked around, afraid that the shots might have attracted attention. But in the midst of so much celebration, no one had noticed what had happened. Holding the gun, I opened a way through the hysterical crowd. In front of me the line of VaNguni prisoners passed by, flanked by Portuguese soldiers. Seven of the king's wives headed the line. Farther back came Godido and Mulungo, respectively Ngungunyane's son and uncle.

I concealed the gun under one of the *capulanas* that covered me. My left hand, hidden under the cloth, nervously brushed against the barrel of the rifle. I waited for the king of Gaza to appear so as to carry out my final act of revenge as promised. The group of Portuguese officers passed by in front of me. This was when Mouzinho de Albuquerque appeared on parade. He looked like a god on his white horse. As our eyes met, Mouzinho seemed to give me a slight nod. What seemed at first to me a transparent butterfly detached itself from his face. And a kind of wing of light, a fragment of sun, fell. I stepped forward and opened my right hand to catch it. The moment I did so, I saw that it was a tiny round piece of glass. I returned the transparent object and Mouzinho smiled and thanked me. *I shouldn't have come to the bush with my monocle on*, he said. And there was a deep sadness in his smile.

All of a sudden, someone shouted in a familiar voice: *It's her!* And the cry was repeated. It was Impibekezane who was pointing to me and yelling, causing the captain on his horse to stop.

It's her, it's the woman I told you about earlier, she said breathlessly. And she added, sighing deeply as if uttering her last words: *This is my son's last wife*.

Bring her along with the other women, Mouzinho ordered laconically, pointing at me.

But we've already got seven, Captain, Lieutenant Couto protested timidly.

Well, we've got eight now.

I realized I had no time to lose. For at that very moment the despised figure of the emperor emerged behind Impibekezane. With great care, I pulled the gun out and prepared to fire. But it was as I did this that I felt the gun being pulled away from me. Someone was snatching the gun silently but firmly. It was Germano, my Germano! Next to me, by my side, my sergeant was forcing me to give him the rifle. Then he whispered:

Are you crazy? Do you want to get killed? And then, incredulously: *And what about Santiago? Was that you?*

Our hands secretly touched, my fingers feeling the ones that still remained of his. And my whole life migrated in that single gesture. It was no more than a few seconds but they lasted an eternity until a soldier forced me away. Mouzinho was in a hurry to leave, there were a lot of armed men around there and peopled still wondered why the operation had gone off without any widespread violence.

The group quickened their steps and the soldier leading me grabbed a rope with which to start binding my arms. Germano, who had been left behind, didn't understand what was happening. When he saw me being bound, he thought I was being charged with Santiago's murder. That was when he waved the rifle and started shouting:

That woman is innocent. It was I who killed Santiago! It was I who killed him.

And the last thing I saw was two soldiers seizing Germano de Melo. And I heard his unmistakable voice begging:

Careful with my hands, don't bind my wrists.

I was on the point of rushing back to come to my beloved's aid, when the queen wrapped her arms around me in what seemed like a farewell embrace. As she hugged me to her, she whispered:

Leave him, now you're my son's wife.

The sergeant was now out of sight, out of earshot. He was swallowed up in the pandemonium of the cortege. And I, with my wrists tied, and still more firmly bound by Impibekezane's embrace, sighed in resignation. Only then did the queen mother loosen her grip.

For a king's wife, you are not wearing enough, she said.

And she placed a string of beads around my neck with a pendant in the shape of an ornate copper spear. She told me this amulet would protect me from everything in the same way that she hoped I would protect her son.

And the queen mother turned around and began her journey back to her village. Or rather the ashes of what had once been her village. Bibliana had predicted that Impibekezane would be murdered by her own troops. But the old lady seemed already to be deprived of life as she silently bade her son and grandson farewell.

Then I advanced as if I were alone in that long train of people. We headed south, across the Languene plain. We walked for two days under intense rain until we arrived at Zimakaze, on the banks of the great river which the Portuguese call the Limpopo and that the locals know as "the pregnant river." There, Mouzinho ordered me to be untied. I would have preferred to feel the ropes digging into my flesh rather than the treacherous looks the seven queens directed at me. Then I plunged into the river, a body within a body. Only then did I realize both banks were crowded with people.

A column of Portuguese soldiers was approaching the port from the direction of Chicomo. They were bringing with them Zixaxa and two women who were imprisoned there. These women had been joined along the way by his eight other wives. I must confess that I was struck by Zixaxa's dignified serenity. Sitting by the landing stage, his hands tied behind his back, he contemplated the opposite bank of the river as if he were the world's only inhabitant. Over there on the other side lay his domains, to which he doubted he would ever return. His aristocratic bearing disturbed the king of Gaza, who pretended to ignore the man he had protected for months. And it must also have disturbed Mouzinho de Albuquerque, for he interrupted the ceremony distributing rewards to the local chiefs who had helped him in the assault on Txaimiti. The Portuguese addressed the prisoner:

Choose three.

The two men knew what was being talked about. With a simple flick of his head, Zixaxa indicated the women who would accompany him. The remaining wives were given by Mouzinho to his allied chiefs.

At this point, they began the process of boarding the *Capelo*, a three-masted ship that the Portuguese called a corvette. Panic immediately spread among the king of Gaza and his court. They knew the river was only a route for us to reach the sea. That journey was therefore the most deadly of transgressions. For those people, the ocean was a forbidden place, without name or destination. They embarked weeping, as if they had been condemned to death.

On deck, now at ease as if the ship were their homeland, the Portuguese drew their swords and burst out with cheers to their king. On the riverbank, the vast ranks of warriors raised their spears and responded as one: *Bayete!* And it was impossible to make out which king they were saluting.

Mouzinho contemplated the disconsolate Ngungunyane in a corner. And he asked them not to start the engines immediately. He marched up to the ship's prow and exhibited himself as if he were posing on his horse. Impressed by this sight, the thousands of warriors launched into a vibrant military anthem. At the end of this song of praise, a storm of insults was directed against Ngungunyane, the same king they had idolized for years. Mouzinho de Albuquerque was enjoying the luster of his victory. And he was making it clear to all those warriors that the kingdom of Gaza had come to an end.

The ship set off downstream, the crew intent on the shoals that might halt a journey they wanted to complete smoothly and as speedily as possible. Mouzinho came and stood next to me, and after a moment asked if I spoke Portuguese.

I'm learning, I replied.

He smiled, as if my confession were another sign of my race's submission. The ship's captain came up to us, saluted, and handed the Portuguese a sheet of paper. Then he announced:

This telegram from the governor general in Lourenço Marques arrived three days ago.

Mouzinho de Albuquerque smiled at me while he took his monocle from his pocket.

Let's see whether you saved my eyesight for a piece of good or bad news.

He read it in an undertone, shook his head, and sighed: It wasn't even a piece of news. And he gave the telegram to the commander, ordering his officers to assemble before him. When they were all present, the captain announced that he was going to read a message that had come from Lourenço Marques. They all thought it would be a message of congratulations for the success at Txaimiti. *Has there already been a reaction?* one asked impatiently. Mouzinho's leisurely reading of the message came as a surprise:

Captain Mouzinho de Albuquerque,

We do not wish to expose our forces to the risk of a catastrophic defeat that would annul the moral and political effects of our victories achieved so far, and for this reason, you should immediately abstain from any intervention against the Kraal of the king of Gaza. Signed by the Acting Governor General of Mozambique, Counselor Correia Lança.

After a few moments of silence, the officers burst out into a collective fit of laughter, and the uproar was such that Ngungunyane himself, unaware of what it was all about, smiled timidly in a spirit of good humor.

I walked away from those people and their joy that I felt no part of, and went and sat by the ship's rail. It would be natural for my soul to be torn asunder by my great doubts over the future that awaited me. But at that moment all I was made of was the past. I allowed the river's current to flood my gaze. And my relatives passed me by, both the living and the dead; the places where I had lived and the people I had loved also passed by. And more than all, I recalled Germano de Melo. And I thought: Even if I never meet him again, that man is now alive within me. And I stroked my belly as if I were touching the being that lived within. In touching my soon-to-be child, I was comforting the mother I had lost. My hands were stitching together the threads of Time.

There were not just different people traveling on that ship, but worlds in collision. Ngungunyane's women divided their somber looks between me and Zixaxa's wives.

The two monarchs didn't look at each other. Zixaxa and Ngungunyane cut two very different figures. The first sat on a coil of rope, his trunk stiffly erect as if that improvised seat were a throne. Wrapped in a blanket and doubled up, the king of Gaza was a picture of decline. At a certain point, Zixaxa pointed to the clouds and said to Ngungunyane:

Don't look at the waters that cause you nausea. Look at the skies instead, Umundungazi.

The king pretended not to hear. But Zixaxa insisted that the other should gaze up at the firmament, and his hand swept in an arc over his head. I was the only one to note a vengeful shadow in his smile as he declared:

And look at all the swallows still crisscrossing the skies!

The swallows helped Zixaxa humiliate the one who had betrayed him. But I had no scores to settle with the world. That was why I sat vacantly, feeling the spray from the waves that broke as they encountered the prow. The river was now wider and the waters more turbulent. Here and there islands formed by weeds floated past, upon which dwelt elegant, acrobatic snipes. Maybe I was one of those white birds, maybe our vessel was an island of weeds taking me to an unknown destination. The ship passed close by these long-legged creatures that remained unperturbed as they busily sought to keep their balance on their unstable perches.

Suddenly, one of the Portuguese soldiers leaned overboard and, with a swipe of his sword, decapitated the nearest snipe. The bird's head and neck spun in the air and fell onto the deck, writhing before our very eyes like some dying serpent. A spatter of blood splashed my breast. I wiped it with a corner of my *capulana*. And it was Zix-axa who brought my attention to something:

A drop of blood fell from your spear.

It took me a few moments to realize that he was referring to the amulet that hung from my necklace. But it was as if I myself were bleeding. Then a wave swept over the deck and left me soaked from head to foot. It was the river cleansing me. A sailor tossed me a piece of cloth to dry myself. I wiped myself slowly as if my body were as wide as the land I was leaving behind. But I left my belly soaked with water. A river was being born within me. Outside me, the last of the rivers was draining away. The two streams of water didn't touch, and didn't bid each other farewell.

Everything always begins with a farewell.

GLOSSARY

Terms from local vernaculars, place names and ethnic groups, and characters based on known historical figures.

CALDAS XAVIER (1852–1896): Portuguese military officer who participated in the campaigns against Ngungunyane.

CAPULANA: A dress worn mainly by women, akin to a sarong.

CHAIMITE: The Portuguese name for Txaimiti, the capital of the State of Gaza.

CHAPUNGU: A bird of good fortune.

CHICOMO: A small town between Inhambane and Manjacaze, in southern Mozambique.

CHILODJO: A royal crown made from animal skin, and worn by the Gaza rulers.

COUNSELOR JOSÉ D'ALMEIDA (1858–1922): Portuguese diplomat and colonial administrator, who held various posts in Mozambique in the 1880s and 1890s. He was married to a woman of the Goan Portuguese nobility.

DIOCLECIANO DAS NEVES (1829–1883): Portuguese customs inspector and game hunter, who traveled widely in southern Mozambique and Transvaal. He knew Muzila, Ngungunyane's father.

DOKOTELA: A local adaptation of the European word "doctor."

EDUARDO GALHARDO (1845–1908): Portuguese military officer, colonial administrator, and diplomat.

GEORGES LIENGME (1859–1936): A Swiss doctor and missionary who lived for four years at the court of Ngungunyane.

GODIDO (1876–1911): A son of Ngungunyane, who accompanied his father into exile. Sometimes known as Godide or António da Silva Pratas Godide.

INDUNA: A local African administrator and tax collector.

GLOSSARY

LANDINS: The generic Portuguese term for native peoples living in southern Mozambique, some of whom were recruited into the colonial army.

LIEUTENANT AYRES DE ORNELAS (1866–1930): Soldier and politician during the final decades of the Portuguese monarchy. Took part in the campaigns against Ngungunyane headed by António Enes, and was later a protégé of Mouzinho de Albuquerque.

LOURENÇO MARQUES: The colonial name for Mozambique's capital city, now known as Maputo.

MAFEMANE: Ngungunyane's half brother and heir to the throne of Gaza, because his mother was King Mazila's principal wife. Reputedly murdered by Ngungunyane, who then became king.

MANDHLAKAZI: Manjacaze in Portuguese, a town and important center of operations for the VaNguni.

MANGOLÉ: Term used to describe Angolans by the VaNguni.

MANICUSSE: The founder of the State of Gaza in the early nineteenth century.

MATONGA: Someone of low status or a slave.

MOUZINHO DE ALBUQUERQUE (1855–1902): Portuguese cavalry officer and leader of the expedition responsible for capturing Ngungunyane.

MUZILA: Father of Ngungunyane and son of Soshangane, the founder of Gaza. Muzila ruled the kingdom of Gaza from 1861 to 1885.

NDAU, VANDAU: An ethnic group in southern central Mozambique.

NGUNGUNYANE: The VaNguni ruler of the State of Gaza, eventually defeated by the Portuguese in 1895. Known in Portuguese as Gungunhane.

NKOSI, NKOSICAZE: Terms of address directed at people of high social status among the VaNguni. In Portuguese orthography, usually spelled *Nkossi*.

NSALA: The fruit of the spiny or kaffir orange tree.

NSOPE: A type of alcoholic drink.

NTXUVA: A board game played widely in sub-Saharan Africa, probably originating in Egypt.

NWAMULAMBU: A snake-like monster, blamed in local lore for cyclones.

SANCHES DE MIRANDA (1865–1931): Portuguese artillery officer, and later colonial administrator.

TERREIRO: An open area for dancing or performing religious ceremonies.

TIMBISSI: A Zulu word for hyena, but used to describe an elite VaNguni military squad.

GLOSSARY

TXICHANGANA: The language spoken by the Shangaan, an ethnic group inhabiting southern Mozambique and adjacent areas in South Africa.

TXITXOPE: The language spoken by the VaChopi.

ULTIMATUM: The Ultimatum of 1890, in which Great Britain demanded that Portugal drop its claims to Central Southern Africa, areas now corresponding to Zimbabwe, Malawi, and Zambia.

VACHOPI: Known in Portuguese as Chope, an ethnic group in southeastern Mozambique, here in uneasy alliance with the Portuguese.

VANGUNI: An ethnic group originating in South Africa, which migrated up into southern and central Mozambique in the first half of the nineteenth century, bringing many other ethnicities under its political control.

VÁTUA: Portuguese term for the VaNguni.

XIGODJO: A fortified VaNguni village.

XINDAU: The language spoken by the Ndau or VaNdau.

XIPERENYANE: A VaChopi military leader, who rebelled against Ngungunyane's rule. Sometimes known as Xipenenyana.

A Note About the Author

Mia Couto, born in Beira, Mozambique, in 1955, is one of the most prominent writers in Portuguese-speaking Africa. After studying medicine and biology in Maputo, he worked as a journalist and headed several Mozambican national newspapers and magazines. The author of *Woman of the Ashes*, *Confession of the Lioness*, *The Tuner of Silences*, and *Sleepwalking Land*, among other books, Couto has been awarded the Camões Prize for Literature and the prestigious Neustadt International Prize for Literature, among other awards. He was also short-listed for the 2017 International DUBLIN Literary Award and was a finalist for the Man Booker International Prize in 2015. He lives in Maputo, where he works as a biologist.

A Note About the Translator

David Brookshaw is an emeritus professor at the School of Modern Languages at the University of Bristol. He has translated several other books by Mia Couto, including *Woman of the Ashes*, *Confession of the Lioness*, *The Tuner of Silences*, *A River Called Time*, and *Sleepwalking Land*.